On the Ninth Day

A Novel

R.J. DeFilippo

PublishAmerica
Baltimore

First printing

ISBN: 1-4137-8862-9
PUBLISHED BY PUBLISHAMERICA, LLLP
www.publishamerica.com
Baltimore

Printed in the United States of America

To my Cynthia…you are more than a soul mate to me…you are flesh of my flesh and bone of my bone…the mother of my children.

To all families everywhere…you are not only the inspiration for this book; you are the very fabric of our culture.

And in memory of Joseph and Ursula…my first teachers…I will see you at the banquet table where we will drink a toast to your excellent parenting, with Bettina and Dominico.

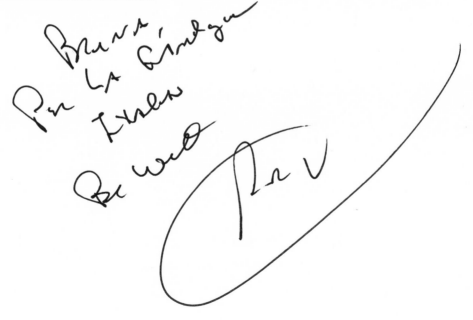

Acknowledgements

I wish to thank all of those who read my work-in-progress and provided much-needed input. Margaret Ryan, you are a true professional, whose mind I admire and respect. Sister Barbara-Ann...where would I be without your influence?

To the sisters of Divine Providence and to the Christian Brothers who have dedicated their lives to education in the Christian tradition.

Such dedication comes only with intense resolve and calling.

I adore in all things the God whose hand has led me all my life!
~St. John Baptiste de la Salle

Chapter 1

Dr. Sean Patrick Dempsey pulled his Silver Lexus SC 430 convertible into the underground parking garage at Four Gateway Center. He waited impatiently for the automatic gate to provide him with the required ticket for entrance, pressing the button several times with increased pressure and frequency, and punctuated with vulgarity unbecoming a doctor. Once the gate finally lifted to provide access, the sleek sports car accelerated into the garage with screeching tire noises that caused the attendant at the exit booth to turn, annoyed, in his direction. Dr. Dempsey circled down to one of the lower levels in the bowels of the garage, where there were fewer cars; he detested the careless dings created by adjacent car doors. When he found a suitably isolated spot, he pulled in and glanced at his Rolex. He was late for his meeting with Dr. Antonio Cipullo. Tony and he had been friends since medical school. Their friendship had grown over the years, tempered by shared passions and non-medical interests required by doctors to help them achieve balance in their lives.

As he clicked on the key's alarm button and walked toward the escalator, his beeper vibrated against his left hip. He hated his beeper interfering with his life as it always does, but accepted it as all doctors must. Pagers are a necessary nuisance doctors learn to live with. He glanced at the digitized phone number and recognized it as the nurses' station at Western Psychiatric Hospital, where he was on staff.

"Damn! I'm not even on call tonight!"

He reached into his pocket, hit the appropriate programmed button on his cell phone and waited next to the escalator for an answer. In the early years of his practice there was a mild rush of excitement when he was paged—a feeling of importance, a sense of being needed. To be in a position to assist his fellow man with a word of advice or a regimen of medication stimulated him—then. Now, being paged was an annoyance that he deplored.

"Dr. Dempsey returning a page at this number."

His voice was stern, his cadence abrupt, as if to telegraph his annoyance to the person at the other end of the line.

"Good evening, Dr. Dempsey. This is Dr. Todorovich."

"Yes?"

"Dr. Dempsey, I'm the third-year resident on call tonight."

"I know who you are, Frank. What do you need?"

"A patient of yours, a Mildred Frankton, presented in a state of agitation and on the qui vive."

"Is she delusional?"

"I don't believe so, sir."

"Well, *is* she or *isn't* she, Frank?"

"No, sir, she's not."

The resident's voice wavered, as it does when speaking to a stern superior. He understood the pecking order principle in medicine.

"I have treated her for anxiety and coping disturbances in the past. She suffered from mild paranoia, but I never found her to be a threat to herself or others."

Sean's voice was matter-of-fact and bordered on insensitivity.

"Was there a recent acute event, or do you observe any behavior that would have contributed to a change in my original assessment?"

"No, sir, she fits the clinical picture that you describe."

"Then are we in agreement that this is not a patient that requires admission at this time, Dr. Todorovich?"

Dr. Dempsey's tone was patronizing.

He continued, "She probably needs some words of reassurance, and a short course of a mild psycho-sedative. Tell her you spoke with me, and that she'll be fine, and to come see me at my office in the morning. I'll fit her in. Is there anything else?"

"No, sir, I'll take care of it."

"Fine. Thank you. Have a good evening"

Sean clicked his cell phone's disconnect button and looked at his watch again.

"Damn!"

He was already fifteen minutes late for his meeting with Dr. Cipullo. He stepped onto the escalator that led to the restaurant's foyer. In the past, he would have handled the patient incident differently. He would have been less abrupt with the resident, and perhaps even gone to the hospital to see the patient. He would have held her hand and reassured her that, yes, life can be hard at times, and difficulty in coping is nothing to be ashamed of. He would have exercised his gifts of compassion and empathy that he developed in all the years of his training. In the end, he would have left as satisfied as the patient—a satisfaction that can only come from helping another human being by some self-sacrifice—a satisfaction that he now all too often either failed to pursue or had forgotten how to.

Sean opened the large etched glass door that led into the restaurant proper. He was upset that he was late. He had been looking forward to meeting with his friend since last night, when Tony had called. The last time they were together was several months ago, just prior to Tony and Cathy's separation. Tony called late last night and asked to meet him at the *fish bowl*. There was a sense of urgency and need in Tony's voice.

Very unlike Tony to be agitated so, Sean thought as he entered the restaurant.

The *fish bowl* was Sean's name for *Palomino's,* one of their favorite Italian restaurants. The restaurant was on the ground floor of a large office building. The entire front wall was floor-to-ceiling glass. People walking by could look in at the trendy types dining and drinking at the bar. Hence the *fish bowl* nickname.

Sean reflected on how his life had changed because of his association with Tony. Tony was his antithesis in many ways. Tony was tall and dark—perpetually tan and as Italian as they come. Sean was of moderate height, with the proverbial ruddy Irish complexion. Tony was gregarious…a people person, almost to a fault. Sean was withholding, to be kind…shy if the truth be known. Tony could start a conversation with any person on any subject and almost immediately endear them to himself—his attractive personality was that strong. Sean admired that in Tony and informed him on many occasions that he possessed a gift. If opposites attract, then Tony and Sean were proof-in-fact. They became the best of friends, and Tony often told him that he loved him like a brother. Sean, having issues that only a psychiatrist could decipher, would never admit to having such feelings for Tony, but he held them in his heart nonetheless, embracing them in solitude, and feeling all the more lonely for his inability to share what was in his spirit.

He and Tony shared many passions. It was amazing how the energy that surrounded them overlapped and, as if a catalyst was present, increased the intensity of their shared pursuits. They both loved college football and basketball as only college sports enthusiasts could appreciate—talking about it every chance they could, and on every imaginable level of intensity. They embraced gourmet cooking as if they were chefs, exchanging recipes and trying to perform in the kitchen as if in some sophomoric attempt to outdo one another. In their travels they would visit various stylish restaurants, sampling their fares and expounding on how they could improve on the presented dishes. Travel was a primary pleasure. To visit exotic lands and partake of unusual cuisine was their real passion. Each tried to outdo the other with tales of their travels to intriguing places on the globe, hoping to trump the other's last best story.

Tony had brought Sean to a point of being in touch with his feelings and brought him face to face with emotions that he could not on his own fully appreciate. He realized the importance of this relationship—the importance to his well-being and to his psychological health. More importantly, Tony had helped him understand that the facade that Sean built around himself was masking his true self, and what was truly important was being hidden underneath this facade. He understood all of this, intellectually. He just could not explain his suppressed posture. How could he when he didn't understand it fully himself?

Sean walked past the greeter's station, turned right and into the bar area of the restaurant. There were beautiful people sitting at the wine-taster tables across from the bar, eating and enjoying themselves. There were even more beautiful people—young ladies—at the bar, drinking and pretending to be joyous, yet if the truth be told, they were waiting to be connected to well-to-do others. They were so transparent, Sean thought. A few glanced at him as he walked by.

Tony was sitting at the very end of the bar on the next-to-last stool. Sean took one look at him and sucked in air—with a surprised gasp. He walked toward him, his gaze fixed on his friend.

Tony rose from his seat, took a step forward and embraced him with a firm grasp.

Sean reflected back on their first meeting some twenty-five years before, as well as every encounter since. Tony was Italian, and therefore was one who would greet you with a hug. When they would meet, instead of a handshake, Tony would embrace his friend. A quick hug and a tap on the back—a greeting as foreign to Sean as if Tony had grabbed his wallet and begun counting his money—yet it felt comfortable and natural with Tony doing it.

Tonight's encounter was different. Tony embraced Sean and held him close to him. Instead of a quick tap on the back, Tony held him close against his breast. Sean was both touched and confused. He pushed away from his friend.

"Tony…you look like shit!"

"Thanks, Sean. I love you too!"

Sean smiled briefly, and then his face formed a serious, concerned expression.

"No really, you look like shit! How much weight have you lost? Your color is bad and what's with those bags under your eyes?" He held Tony at arm's length and looked long and hard at his friend. He placed his hand alongside Tony's cheek and, elevating his left eyelid with his thumb, tilted Tony's head back and examined the white of his eye above the pupil. This was not an encounter of friends at a bar, but more like a clinical evaluation between physician and patient.

Tony pulled back away.

"Sean, you're a psychiatrist. If I had wanted a clinical assessment, I would have met with Tim Stein."

"I'm a physician first. It doesn't take an internist to see how bad you look!"

"Sean, get a drink. I'm already three Jacks ahead of you."

Tony motioned for the bartender, holding up two fingers.

"Two more Jack Daniels, rocks."

Sean turned toward the bar, resting his left elbow on its edge. He lifted the glass and downed the drink in two swallows. He motioned for another.

"Tony, I know you were going through some shit. Why didn't we get together sooner? You know that I've always been there for you."

Tony turned toward his friend and shook his head in a slow and somber sway. Just then, an attractive young lady in her apparent early thirties approached them. She was tall and slender, with short blond hair that fell just to the level of and parallel with her lower jaw line. It was a cosmopolitan cut that framed her face well. She wore a black business suit, with a very short skirt that drew attention to her shapely legs. She addressed Tony.

"Excuse me, Dr. Cipullo? I thought that was you."

She extended her delicate hand toward Tony and rested it on his shoulder.

"I'm Gina Evans. Do you remember me?"

Tony rose and faced her, now shaking the hand that slid off his shoulder.

"Of course, I do. Gina, this is my friend, Sean Dempsey. Sean, Gina."

Gina smiled and nodded at Dr. Dempsey, then turned again towards Tony.

"I just wanted to tell you how grateful I am for the wonderful job that you did with my surgery last January. You know how concerned I was about scarring. Well, I made it through swimsuit season, and no one even noticed."

"Gina, I'm sure that when you wear a swimsuit, no one would ever notice a small scar on your shoulder."

Tony smiled at her, and for the first time that evening Sean saw Tony's charm come through.

"Now remember, with your fair complexion, I want you using nothing less than a 35 sunscreen. Even so, limit your exposure. Better yet, use a self-tanner."

"I'll remember, Dr. Cipullo. Thanks again and enjoy your evening."

As she walked away, she looked back over her shoulder and smiled. Tony sighed and looked down at his drink.

"Microsurgery on a blue nevus cluster on her right shoulder. Piece of cake. Even you could have done it, Sean."

Sean was glad to see some glimpse of his friend's humor return.

"Gentlemen, your table's ready. Please come this way"

The two friends walked to their table, with Tony mocking the waiter's contrived highbrow demeanor.

"It's really good to see you again, Tony. I've been looking forward to this evening."

"Me too, Sean. I really needed to talk to you."

Tony waved off the offered menu when their waiter extended it to him.

"My turn to order, Sean."

Tony turned toward the waiter, looking at his nametag and, smiling, said, "Good evening, Tom. We'll start with two more Jack rocks. Ask Giorgio to grill two orders of his garlic calamari cassuola to start with, then one order of the mixed seafood grill, and one order of the frutta de mare. Don't bother with a breadbasket; we'll have some of Giorgio's rosemary crostini instead. Skip the vegetables, we'll have an antipasti insalata, and please bring two extra dishes, because we share entrees. Also, bring a bottle of the Pinot Grigio #57 to be served with the calamari."

"Very good, sir. Excellent choices!"

When the waiter left, Sean smiled at Tony.

"You read my mind."

"I always do, Sean—been doing it for years. Almost scary, isn't it?"

The buzz from the bourbon was relaxing Tony now, and he had almost forgotten how comfortable he felt when he was with his old friend.

"So, Tony. Have you heard from Cathy or the kids?"

Tony just shook his head. A doleful sway, as he looked down at his drink.

"Not since just before the separation. Cathy's alienated the kids from me. They want nothing to do with me. I'm some kind of beast in their eyes."

Tony rubbed his eyes, maintaining the somber sway.

"I should have listened to you, Sean. I was so fucking stupid."

"Look, that's not what's important now. You can't second-guess past choices. You had justified them in your mind at the time. Decisions have to be made, all within the framework of human frailty."

"Within the framework of human frailty? And exactly who is this talking...Sean, my friend, or Dr. Dempsey, the psychiatrist?"

"Both. I'm your friend and I'm a psychiatrist. It's a buy one, get one free scenario. I can't separate the two."

12

"Well, I can. I know you better than you know yourself, so don't give me any bullshit! Don't talk to me about human frailty. I'm a physician too! I deal with human frailty each and every day. You know what, Sean? I've discovered a truth; the frailty lies not in those who are being treated—not in all of those patients who for whatever reason have fallen victim to some disease state—but in those who do the treating. It rests within the decision makers…those who are forced to make quality decisions for others, when we can't make the simplest quality decisions in our own damn lives, Sean Patrick Dempsey! Don't you dare talk to me about human fuck'n frailty! I've got a Ph.D. in human frailty knowledge!"

Tony addressed him by his full name. Sean knew that he only did this when he wanted to make a point. When he used all three names, it was during the rare times that Tony meant business, being only one of a small handful of people who knew Sean well enough to know his middle name. It also was a reflection on Sean's Irish heritage, and he saw it as a negative statement. However, he also saw the pain and heard the anguish in his friend's voice. He backpedaled quickly.

"Look, Tony, calm down! You are right. We all have frailties. It comes to light when we are called upon to make decisions for others. It is a tremendous responsibility and a burden that we in healthcare must bear, but bear it we must, and bear this I must. Tony, I only want to help you, and I know that you are hurting. It pains me to see you so."

"Human frailty," Tony repeated. "More like human fuck'n stupidity. I can't believe I made such ridiculous choices—choices that involved the lives of people that I cared so much about." Tony reached across the table, placed his hand on Sean's, and made eye contact. "My family, Sean!"

Tony looked away and took another swallow from his drink. Sean looked on and nodded in agreement. He was playing the part of the concerned listener now. This was what he did for a living, and he had perfected his technique over the years. All psychiatrists must.

"Go on, Tony."

"That's just it, Sean. I don't know if I can. I don't know if I want to. I don't know if I know how to…"

Sean knew that it was now the Jack Daniels talking. He had listened to enough pained stories over the years, from enough hurting people. Many were numbed with alcohol or medication.

Tony reached into his inside jacket pocket and pulled out a business-sized envelope. He slid it across the table to his friend.

"Get a load of this!" Tony said. "It just keeps getting better. It's almost like Mardi Gras, only without the beads and booze"

Sean took the envelope from the table. It was addressed to his friend—registered mail from Med Shield, the managed care provider.

"You had a third-party audit?"

Tony nodded. Sean took the reading glasses from his jacket pocket, opened the envelope, and leaned forward toward the candle burning in the center of the table. In the glow of the candlelight, he read the letter.

> *Dear Dr. Cipullo:*
>
> *The result of our recent audit revealed billing irregularities consistent with fraudulent behavior on the part of your practice. Our legal department has advised us to freeze all account activity, holding same in escrow until this issue is resolved. In the meantime, we have referred this issue to the State Department of Professional Licensure for investigation. We encourage you to cooperate with us for a quick resolution of this problem, and...*

Sean looked up at his friend.

"Insurance fraud? Is this true?"

"It's a long story, Sean."

"Damn it, Tony. You could lose your license to practice medicine."

"So now you're an attorney, Sean?"

"It doesn't take a lawyer to see that you are in some deep doo-doo, friend. How did this happen? This isn't you, Tony. You don't even cheat at cards."

"I said it was a long story."

"I have the time, Tony."

Just then the waiter brought the grilled calamari, brushed with olive oil and laced with garlic. He opened the Pinot Grigio, poured a small amount into Tony's glass and handed him the cork. Tony took in the bouquet and nodded his approval.

"Enjoy your meal, gentlemen."

Chapter 2

One year earlier

Tony walked into the closet in the dressing area of his bedroom and selected a tie. He didn't usually wear a coat and tie to the office, since he preferred to work in scrubs. Today, however, he had to interview three applicants for the soon-to-be vacant position of office manager at his satellite practice. Specialty practices in medicine frequently have more than one office location, relying as they do on primary-care physicians for patient referrals. Tony's dermatology practice was no different. Having two office locations —a primary and a satellite—placed him in the proximity of twice as many referring doctors.

His primary practice location was in the Fox Chapel area close to his home. It took him all of ten minutes to drive there in the morning and this suited him just fine, detesting city traffic jams as he did. His satellite practice was in the Oakland section of the city close to the university, where he also held a faculty position as assistant clinical professor of dermatology.

Between his lecturing and research responsibilities, his two offices, his community and charitable involvement and his wife and six children, he managed to keep quite busy. He preferred it that way. He had a high energy level, and keeping busy not only suited him—it brought him joy and a sense of fulfillment

He stepped in front of the mirror in his dressing area and finished tying his tie, slipping it tight against his adam's apple and remembering how much he detested the damn things.

"Useless rags. What purpose do they serve, anyway?" he mumbled under his breath.

He looked into the mirror and combed his salt-and-pepper wavy hair back with his open fingers. He tapped his stomach with an open palm and thought he looked pretty good for forty-eight. He worked out three days a week at his club at anaerobic training and ran on the odd days; completing three or four

15

5K races a year for charity. "Forty-eight going on thirty-nine," the trainer at the club would often say with a degree of sincerity.

His eight-year-old daughter, Angela, walked in slowly, carrying a cup of coffee filled to the brim. Her eyes were fixed on the cup. She was trying hard not to spill any—and failing miserably. A trail of coffee spills marked her path as well as the front of her pajamas, hitting Winnie the Poo several times, but thankfully missing Tigger.

"Here's your coffee, Daddy. I might have spilled a couple of drops," she said as she handed him the cup, proud of her dutiful service.

"That's all right, sweetheart. That's why Daddy wanted a brown carpet in here," he said, smiling. "Look at the bright side. I can easily find my way to the kitchen now, by just following the drips!"

"Just like Hansel and Gretel, Daddy," she said with a smile.

"That's right, pumpkin! Some people think that they laid a trail of bread crumbs, but you and I know it was really coffee drips!"

He placed his cup on the counter and picked her up, giving her a long hug and swinging her back and forth until she giggled. In the process, he transferred some of Winnie's coffee stain onto his white shirt.

"Who's Daddy's little angel?" he whispered in her ear.

Angela was his favorite—not that he would ever let on that he had a favorite. She was not only his youngest and final child before his vasectomy, but was the one who was most like him in personality and demeanor. She was named after his paternal grandmother, Angelina Cipullo. Cathy, his wife, preferred to shorten it to Angela, justifying it because "little angel" would be an inappropriate name when Angela reached adulthood.

"Angela will be tall, like you and I. It was all right for your ninety-year-old grandmother to be a 'little angel,' because she was only four feet nine," Cathy said with authority.

He couldn't argue with Cathy's logic. He never could, and stopped trying years ago.

"She'll be Angela on paper, but always 'Daddy's little angel' in my heart," he always would say—*his* logic based in emotion and not intellect, at least where multi-factorial issues as this one were concerned.

He picked Angela up and carried her over his shoulder downstairs like a sack of potatoes. Cathy, his wife of twenty-two years, was in the kitchen preparing breakfast for "the boys." His four sons were sandwiched chronologically between his two daughters. Kathleen, nineteen, was away at college, and Cathy missed her terribly. She was a sophomore at Tony and Cathy's alma mater, Bucknell. Rob was sixteen, Troy was thirteen, and Joseph and Dominick, the twins, were eleven.

16

When Tony walked into the kitchen, Joseph and Dominick were fighting over a box of cereal for the premium pictured on the back of the box. Tug… push…tug…spill.

"I saw it first!" screamed Dominick.

"Dad, tell him it belongs to me!" countered Joseph.

"Dad! I don't believe these two," added Troy.

"Tell them that they have to send away for it. No way there's going to be a 1/24-scale NASCAR race car inside that box!" he continued.

Dominick looked at Troy and in a mocking voice asked, "How do YOU know? Did you look?"

"No, I didn't look! It's called common sense, numb nuts!"

"Hey! Watch your language, young man!" Tony corrected.

"Sorry, Dad. Tell them that if there *was* a 1/24-scale car in there, there wouldn't be any room for the cereal."

"So what!" added Joseph.

"We don't even like that cereal!"

Rob broke his silence. He looked up from the book that he was reading.

"You two are the reason that Madison Avenue continues to take advantage of the uneducated mass consumer public. You justify their actions and help perpetuate their greedy existence!"

Rob was not only his oldest son, but by far the most gifted intellectually. He was an honor student at Tony's alma mater—a private all boys Catholic prep school in Oakland. Tony was so very proud of him.

"Here, justify *this*!" Dominick said as he flicked his middle finger toward Rob.

Tony grabbed Dominick by the back of his neck and squeezed hard.

"Where did you learn such behavior, young man?"

Dominick broke away and ran crying up the staircase toward his bedroom.

"Nice going. You're a regular Henry Kissinger!" Cathy added as she shook her head back and forth.

"Cathy, where do these boys learn such behavior? If I would have done that in my father's presence when I was eleven years old, I would have been wearing a cast on that hand!"

"They learn it from me, Tony. I taught him that gesture," Cathy added sarcastically.

Tony smiled, put his arm around her waist and kissed the back of her neck as he reached over her shoulder and grabbed the waffle as it popped out of the toaster.

"Hey! Leggo of my Eggo!" teased Troy.

"And, hey, you two, get a room!"

"I'll give you a room!" Tony said as he turned toward Troy, extending both hands in an implied choking threat.

Troy got up and ran around to the other side of the kitchen table as if frightened and trying to get away from his father.

Tony chased him around the table, slowing in an obvious attempt not to catch him.

"I've got FIVE boys!" Cathy said, rolling her eyes back.

"You're too fast for me, Troy!" Tony said as he returned to Cathy and the waffles.

Tony repositioned his arm around Cathy's waist, and this time whispered into her ear, "So, what time do you expect your husband back, beautiful?"

"Tony, grow up!"

"I refuse!" Tony emphasized.

Tony then looked over Cathy's shoulder at Angela.

"By the way, dear, I spilled some coffee on the way down to the kitchen."

He winked at Angela, and she placed her tiny hand over her mouth as if to hide her giggle.

"That's OK, dear. I'll call Kauffman's carpet cleaning service. You can afford it!" She then turned, and *she* winked at Angela.

"Tony, look at your shirt!" Cathy proclaimed, pointing to the coffee stain just to the right of his tie and next to the third button above his belt.

"Now how on earth did THAT get there?" Tony asked in mock surprise. "Don't worry. My sports jacket will cover it."

"Hey, Dad. Why are you all dressed up today? It's Saturday," remarked Troy.

"Dad's got to go the office to interview some people, Troy."

"Bummer!" Troy shrugged as he got up and left the kitchen just behind Angela, Joseph and Rob.

Tony turned around and found the kitchen empty, except for Cathy, who was now seated at the table, clutching her coffee cup with both hands.

"Was it my imagination, or was this room a bundle of activity just a few seconds ago?" Tony asked.

"It's a metaphor for life, Tony. Enjoy it while you can, because before you know it the children will be gone, and all that will remain will be you and I," Cathy said as she stared blankly at the kitchen wall.

The truth of Cathy's statement hit Tony like a brick. He could not imagine life without the energy and activity of the children in the house. The very thought of it saddened him as he stared blankly in Cathy's direction.

"Speaking of the children, Claudia from LaLathe Studios called. Our family portrait is ready. Tony, I'm so excited!"

18

Every year Cathy would have a photographer come to the house to do a family portrait. Each new portrait took its place above the family room sofa, the prior year's portrait coming down and being placed up in the attic as if for posterity. Cathy would create the family's Christmas cards from the current year's portrait. This tradition was important to her, and Tony, knowing this, faked a shared excitement. If the truth be known, he was saddened to see the children growing up with such apparent quickness—this march towards adulthood chronicled in these framed captures of moments in time. Every so often, he would go up to the attic and review past years and relive memories of missing front teeth, cowlicks and white baby shoes. Sometimes he laughed. Sometimes he wept. Always he left the attic with the feeling of how important his family was to him. How his life had no meaning, save the meaning that his family brought to it.

This year, instead of doing a photographic portrait, Cathy commissioned a portrait artist to do the family in oil. Since Tony's time was a premium, and he could not sit for Claudia, she sent her portrait photographer to capture the sitting on film. She could work in her studio from that. Tony thought the process redundant and wondered if Claudia was such a gifted artist, why couldn't she work from last year's photograph and just make everyone look a year older. He kept these thoughts to himself, of course, not wishing to upset Cathy.

When the oil portrait was nearly finished, Cathy and the children *did* sit for her, so that Claudia could reproduce their color, shading and facial character—this being difficult to do from a photograph. Tony was away at a conference on collagen enhancement and lip augmentation and could not make the sitting.

"Claudia will just have to make a best guess regarding my facial character from the photograph," Tony joked at the time.

"Claudia told me on the phone that it was her best work to date, Tony. She felt that she captured the true essence of the children, and that Kathleen's inner beauty really shines," Cathy added with excitement.

"For what she's charging, I hope that she captured some of her outer beauty as well," Tony quipped.

Cathy continued, tuning Tony out as she so often did. "She'll deliver the portrait early this afternoon, so I'll need a check for the final payment."

"Shouldn't we have a coupon book, like they give you when you buy a car or a boat?" Tony joked.

"What time do you expect to be getting home, Tony?" Cathy asked.

"Shouldn't it be 'Tony dear' or perhaps 'Tony darling,' when you need a check with that many zeroes?" Tony smiled, and continued, "I should be home around three p.m. After the interviews, I have to run over to my office at the med school and pick up some slides I need for my lecture to the Rotary Club, then I'm meeting Sean for a late lunch over at Western Psych's cafeteria after he makes rounds."

"Great! Oh, by the way, speaking of zeroes, there was a minor cost overrun on the portrait."

"Cost overrun? This isn't construction here. We're talking about a frig'n painting, for cry'n out loud!"

"It's a *portrait*, Tony! The overrun is only twenty percent over her quoted fee. Relax!"

"Well, as long as she captured our 'inner beauty'…I guess that twenty percent is reasonable," Tony said sarcastically. "Really, Cath…this is extortion! How would it look if I did that to my patients?"

Tony began an imaginary conversation with a patient:

"Mrs. Smith, I've just completed your lip enhancement injections on the right side, and I must say that when I hold my hand over your left, untreated side—you look just like Julia Roberts. Now, before I finish the other side, let's talk about cost overruns!"

"Very funny, Tony!" Cathy glanced down at her watch. "Shoot! I've gotta run. I'm late! I've got to get to the office and finish my presentation for the McTigh account before Monday! I'll drop the kids off at Barbara's. She's taking them to the club. Love ya!"

Cathy kissed Tony on the cheek and hurried off.

Cathy took extreme pride in her work. She was an advertising major at Bucknell with an emphasis in public relations and graphic design. She was an account executive for a large PR firm in the City. She often teased Tony that her office had windows, with a view of downtown, a reference to the sterile, viewless treatment rooms in Tony's office.

"Love ya too, dear. I'll leave the check on your desk."

Now he was totally alone in the kitchen, and he wondered what *this* was a metaphor for. Tony sat down at the table and finished his coffee. In between sips, he reflected on his and Cathy's days at Bucknell. He was a senior and she was a sophomore when they met at a protest rally against the war in Vietnam. He was certain that she was the most beautiful woman that he had ever seen! She was tall—five feet and ten inches—and slender. She was wearing hip hugger jeans, with a wide bellbottom cuff. Her midriff was exposed, revealing her navel and a narrow waist above her slim hips. She wore a tie-dyed T-shirt, her braless nipples pressing against the cotton fabric of her shirt, her firm breasts swaying back and forth as she walked toward the grandstand. She had straight and long light brown hair that fell to the small of her back. A headband around her forehead held her hair back and added a highlight accentuation to her eyes—almost as punctuation. Tony was mesmerized as she walked past him. She turned and smiled at him, and he thought that he would surely drop on the spot.

He looked to his fraternity brother Dan, standing next to him, and said, "Did you see her, Danny? I'm going to marry that girl! You are looking at the next Mrs. Cipullo, my friend!" Dan just laughed.

Tony and his friend moved closer to the grandstand. Tony's motivation was not so much to better hear the speakers as to position himself closer to his vision. Tony maneuvered himself just behind and to the left of his future bride. His eyes were fixed on her, and although there were protestors shouting into microphones on the grandstand, he didn't hear a spoken word.

Antiwar rallies were intended to incite the crowd, like throwing bloody chum into shark-infested waters. A speaker on the grandstand stepped up to the microphone. He was of apparent Hispanic descent , with an afro/teased hairstyle that, from Tony's perspective, looked like a football helmet.

He began, "Are we going to let this administration tell us that our young men are supposed to die for what IT, not WE believe in?"

"Hell no!" chanted the crowd in unison.

"Are our youth—the very future of America—supposed to die to support the military-industrial complex, just to place money into the coffers of those in control?"

"No way!" the frenzied crowd proclaimed.

"I say, let us stand up tall and let us stand up NOW against these travesties!"

"Right on! Right on!"

The energy of the crowd could now be felt by all those in attendance. It was catalytic and Tony had never experienced anything like it. This power was far greater than the sum total of all the parts. Tony thought for a moment that he could almost smell the adrenaline rush of the crowd. It frightened him, momentarily, as if a power was unleashed, and Tony feared the crowd, inexperienced as it was with such power, it could misdirect this incredible force. This realization was enough to even divert Tony's attention away from his vision—it was that strong!

Evidently, those in authority sensed this as well, for at about this time, the campus and local police arrived on the scene, presumably for crowd control. Tony could see this dangerous combination unfold—unbridled energy and absolute authority and force colliding.

Reflecting, as Tony often did, on what happened next, he had trouble then and still had to this day justifying the actions of those security persons. They entered into the crowd wearing helmets and acrylic visors; apparently ordered by people with more authority than discretion. They began shoving students to the ground—their faces pressed into the grass by storm troopers with laced combat boots. Reflex shoving by the students in retaliation led to more force exerted by security. The situation quickly spiraled out of control, now sliding down the slippery slope of confrontational chaos.

What Tony witnessed next would remain with him forever. One of the rent-a-cops—a young man not much older than the students he confronted— took his nightstick and hit a student from behind across the back of his head. There was a resounding *CRACK* that seemed loud enough to be heard all the way back to the administration building. Tony stood and watched in horror, this apparent act of unsolicited violence that occurred not more than ten feet in front of him. The student dropped immediately to his knees and then collapsed flat on his face. He lay motionless on the ground, save for a quivering of his left hand. Blood streamed from the wound on the back of his scalp, quickly forming a halo around the young man's head. The future physician ran instinctively to the fallen student. Tony removed his shirt and, using it as a compress, placed firm palm pressure against the wound in an attempt to slow the bleeding. With his other hand, Tony cradled the student's forehead and gently turned the boy's head to the side to allow for easier breathing, taking care not to exacerbate any possible injury to the boy's neck. Tony looked up to another security person, who had now come onto the scene.

"YOU—call for an ambulance! NOW!"

Tony spoke not as a student, but with the authority of one in charge of the situation. Before the injured student could regain full consciousness, a quiet moan preceded a gurgling sound, and vomit gushed from his mouth and nostrils. Tony quickly swiped the victim's mouth clear with two fingers, as the student coughed in an attempt to clear his airway. Tony positioned him to allow the remaining vomit to flow from the student's mouth, thus allowing him to suck in air and reflex-cough repeatedly.

When the ambulance crew arrived, Tony backed away. Adrenaline caused his heart to continue to race and he felt it pound against his sternum with such force that he pressed against his chest with his bloodied hand, as if to contain it.

"That sadistic bastard!" he repeated to himself as he shook his head.

Tony returned to his apartment and showered off the blood and vomit, then crashed onto his bed and slept until late afternoon.

Early in the evening, Tony went to the Kappa Sigma fraternity house, where his fraternity brothers were sitting around, shooting pool and drinking beer. Dan was telling them about the event, when Tony walked into the poolroom.

"Here comes the medic now!" shouted Dan. "Tony, let me buy you a beer!"

Dan walked over and pulled back hard on the lever and filled a plastic cup with draught beer from the keg, then handed it to Tony, slapping him on the back.

"Nice job today, Doc. You saved that kid's life!" Dan said as he raised his cup to Tony.

"I hardly saved his life; just slowed the bleeding until help arrived, is all...."

"Bullshit! I saw the whole thing! He would have choked to death on his own vomit if it wasn't for you, man!" Dan continued, "You are an ace-boone-doone hero, man!"

"How many beers have you had, Danny?" Tony kidded.

"I wasn't the only one who was impressed, big guy! That babe you were eyeing was watching you like a TV set, man."

"Really?" Dan had Tony's attention.

"Really, man. I kid you not! But for crying out loud, Tony, there are easier ways to meet women! I mean, staging an anti-war rally, arranging for speakers to be there, slipping a pig a few bucks to crack open that kid's head, just to impress some chick..."

Tony pushed Dan gently against the pool table in mock anger.

"Seriously, Dan—she was hot! Who *was* that girl? I've never seen her on campus before!"

"Let's see if she's a Greek," another brother said, taking last year's yearbook off the bookshelf. He flipped through the sorority composite pictures, with Tony looking over his shoulder in excited anticipation.

"Greg, you are a frick'n genius! Why didn't I think of this?"

"I guess you can be either a genius or a hero, but not both!"

Tony smiled as he said, "Not so fast, man! This isn't speed-reading!"

"Hey, remember her, Tony?" Greg asked, pointing to a girl's picture on the Tri Sigs' page.

"Did she put out for you, like she did for the basketball team?" Greg teased.

When they reached the Kappa Kappa Gamma's page, Tony shouted, "Hold it, Greg! There she is!"

Tony ripped the yearbook from Greg's hands.

"*Cathy Mathias, first year. Pledge,*" Tony read aloud.

"Hey, I know her!" an underclass brother joined in. "She's in my ancient-Chinese poetry class!"

"Who the hell takes ancient-Chinese poetry?" another brother teased.

"Cathy Mathias Cipullo, ancient-Chinese poet. I like the way that sounds," joked Tony.

"Now that's your problem, Tony. Your priorities are all wrong! You are wasting your time in those boring pre-med courses like biochemistry, microbiology, cell biology, organic chemistry, and theoretical physics, where, I might add, the only girls taking them are *built* like theoretical physicists. Then there are babes like *this* in ancient-Chinese poetry class with nerds like Thomas," added Dan, pointing to Cathy's picture.

"Fuck you! I'm not nerdy, just well rounded!" Thomas objected.

"You certainly are!" Dan added, tapping Tom's stomach.

Tony walked over to the telephone. Next to the phone, hanging from a small brass chain attached to the wall, was a university directory. Tony thumbed through the directory, then picked up the phone and dialed the Kappa Kappa Gamma house. As the phone rang, he quickly looked up the name of last year's vice-president in the yearbook composite picture—assuming, correctly, that she would be president this year.

"Hello, Kappa house. Jennifer speaking."

"Hello, Jennifer. May I speak to Amy Collins, please?"

"May I tell her who's calling?"

"This is Tony Cipullo, Rush chairman over at Kappa Sigma, calling."

"One moment, please."

During the silent moments that followed, Tony handed Dan the yearbook and tapped nervously on the wall with his fingers, figuring how to play this thing out.

Dan stared down at Cathy's composite picture in the yearbook. "She's gorgeous! They're both gorgeous!" He looked over to Tony. "She's a frick'n twin, man! There are two of 'em.... One for you and one for me, man!"

"You've got beer vision, Danny. You'd better go sit down."

Dan staggered toward the couch, still looking at the composite. "Hey, wait a minute. They're ALL frick'n twins, man! What are the odds of that happening?"

"Hello, this is Amy Collins. May I help you?"

"Amy, so nice to talk to you. I'm Tony Cipullo and I've been meaning to call you for some time now. I've heard so many nice things about you and of course your outstanding sorority. Listen, as you know, Rush is coming up, and as Rush chairman, it has occurred to me that we have never had a mixer with you people over at Kappa. What's wrong with *that* picture?

"You did say Kappa Sigma, didn't you?"

"That's right Amy, Kappa Sigma."

"Aren't you the *sports* fraternity?"

"Well, Amy, we try to downplay that aspect of our well-rounded selves. We here at Kappa Sigma like to look at ourselves as *total* students. It is true, we have won the All Sports Trophy the last three years, but a little-known fact is that we are also the only fraternity in university history to win the class-B All Sports *and* All Academic Trophy two years in a row."

"You won the All Academic Trophy? You mean for highest Q.P.A.?"

"Two years in a row—for class-B fraternities."

Class B referred to size. Any fraternity under sixty members was in the B class. Kappa Sigma tried to challenge the class-A fraternity champion to a football match to determine "all campus" champion, but the A fraternity declined—having everything to lose and nothing really to win, having the A title already.

"That's impressive, Tony!"

"I think so. We stress excellence! I think that it is important to always strive for excellence. That way you can always sleep well at night."

Amy was impressed. Tony was charming, even on the phone. She thought that she would like to meet with him. What did she have to lose?

"Well, you know, Tony, we usually don't do mixers with fraternities during Rush. You see, we here at Kappa feel that there are many opportunities for the girls to do the frat party scene. We concentrate on the girl-to-girl encounters, relating to feminine needs and wants, especially as they relate to girls being away from family, friends and home—sometimes for the first time."

Tony turned towards Dan, who now was trying his level best to eavesdrop, his ear poised next to the receiver. Tony pretended to push his index finger down his throat , indicating his desire to throw up. Dan laughed, taking another sip of his beer.

"I see what you mean, Amy. I agree that there is a real need for what you suggest. I just wish that we Greeks on the fraternity side of the fence could be as innovative as you. Listen, perhaps I can drop on over there and we can discuss this. I feel that there is a real need for interaction along these lines. There is so much untapped knowledge that we need to avail ourselves of," Tony said with apparent sincerity.

"Fine. Why don't you come over to our house and we can talk about this?" Amy suggested.

"Excellent idea, Amy! I can come over in, say, twenty minutes."

"Fine. I'll be looking forward to seeing you then, Tony."

"Great. By the way, what is the name of your housemother?"

"Mrs. Smyth."

"Smyth, as in Smith with an English attitude?"

"Exactly!" said Amy, laughing.

"Excellent! See you then, Amy."

Tony hung up the phone, and Dan looked at him with a degree of amazement.

"You are incredible, man! Amy fuck'n Collins, the librarian, man? You are going to try and endear her to *this* party house?"

"Not exactly…but exactly, my good man!" Tony said with a smirk.

Tony held out his hand, and Dan slapped it hard, turning his over for Tony to return the favor, which he did.

"So I take it that you know this Amy Collins then?"

Dan looked down at the composite. "I know both of them. The one on the left is nerdier than the one on the right. They are nerdy to the core, man. You'll never get past her—not in a thousand years!"

Dan belched, then pointed his index finger at Tony.

"You are good, man, but not THIS good!" Dan said in reference to both Tony's power of persuasion and his own perception of the Herculean task ahead of him.

"We'll see," answered Tony. "We'll just see about that. A thousand years for a chance to meet a face that could launch a thousand ships. Small price to pay!"

"Tony, did I mention that this Cathy has a boyfriend?" Thomas added. "Some dude from Notre Dame."

"No problemo, compadre!" Tony said with a confident smile. "He's in South Bend with the golden dome. I'm here at Bucknell with her! Besides, 'out of sight, out of mind.'"

"Yes, but 'absence makes the heart grow fonder.'" rebutted Thomas.

"Tippecanoe and Tyler, too!" Dan joined in, raising his beer in a mock toast.

Tony ran back to his apartment and took a three-minute shower. He put on a clean shirt and pants and ran out the door, combing his wavy black hair with an open hand as he went. On the way to the Kappa house he stopped by the Student Union to buy two single red roses at the tuck shop and asked that they be wrapped individually in green tissue paper. He arrived at the Kappa house, glanced at his watch, took a deep breath and rang the bell.

The housemother answered the door with a stern, protective look.

"Good evening, Mrs. Smyth." Tony smiled as he handed her one of the roses, catching her slightly off guard.

"I'm Tony Cipullo, from the Panhellenic Council, to see Ms. Amy Collins." Tony smiled once again as he continued.

"Amy tells me what a wonderful housemother you are, and it is indeed a pleasure to finally meet you!"

"Why, thank you, young man," Mrs. Smyth cooed. She was unaccustomed to such polite conversation, let alone roses! "Please do come in."

Tony walked into the entrance hall and was immediately struck with the difference between a sorority and fraternity house. This place was neat and clean. There were paintings on the wall, and the furniture looked like it was to be seen and not sat on. The rose-colored carpet was freshly vacuumed, and there was a subtle, pleasant aroma like lilac throughout the place.

"If you'll wait in here, I'll ring for Amy," Mrs. Smyth said as she showed Tony into the living room. There were two coeds talking with another male student whom Tony recognized, having seen him around campus, but he didn't know his name. Tony nodded politely and perused the books in the bookcase that framed the fireplace.

"Tony?"

Tony turned around to see Amy Collins walking toward him with her hand extended.

"Amy, I presume," Tony said, smiling. Tony had an infectious smile that he used frequently. It was part of his charm. It endeared people to him, and he knew it.

"This is for you." He handed Amy the second rose.

Amy *looked* like a library science major. She was cute, with attractive features, but she made no attempt to draw attention to them. She wore no makeup and her medium-length dishwater-blond hair was pulled back tightly in a ponytail. She wore glasses whose frames were much too large for her petite face, almost as if a cartoonist had painted them there. It was difficult to assess her figure—it being hidden under an oversized sweatshirt that displayed her sorority's Greek letters across the front.

She smiled warmly back at Tony as they shook hands.

"Thank you. How thoughtful!" Amy said as she tore back the tissue paper and smelled the rose. "Would you like a cup of coffee, Tony?"

"Why yes, I'd love a cup of coffee, thank you," Tony lied.

Tony was not especially fond of coffee. He drank it, as most college students did, to stay alert during late-night study sessions and "all-nighters." It served that purpose. However, he needed a social prop, a crutch—something to hold in his hands. He sincerely doubted that Amy was going to offer him a beer, so a cup of coffee would have to do.

They went into the common room—a large open room next to the kitchen

27

whose only furniture was cafeteria-styled tables and chairs. On the walls were composite group photographs of the sorority's members, certificates of achievement and award plaques.

Four coeds were sitting at one of the tables playing hearts. At another table a girl was writing in a notebook and sipping tea as her boyfriend read the current issue of *Newsweek*. Tony took a seat at one of the empty tables as Amy excused herself to retrieve the coffee and to look for a bud vase.

As soon as he sat down, in walked Cathy Mathias with another sorority sister.

"Kismet," Tony whispered to himself.

They sat down two tables away from Tony, with Cathy facing in his direction. Tony stared at her, and again he couldn't believe how beautiful she was, even in the unforgiving fluorescent light. She brushed back her long, silky hair with her hand, revealing her face to him fully, and he memorized her features. If the unthinkable were to happen and he was never to see her again, he could take this image of true beauty with him through eternity, he thought. This magic moment seemed to bend nature's laws of time and movement. She almost seemed to move in slow motion and he could almost hear music playing. He had a sense that she touched his whole self at a level heretofore uncharted and virginal. The experience was cosmic in proportion—like he was encountering his destiny, and the proposition caused him to burn with unimagined desire for her. He didn't want this moment to ever end.

He had to speak with her—to hear her voice, to take more of her in—to involve more of his senses. He wanted to now hear her, touch her, smell her, and taste her. He wanted to experience her spirit and her mind—to encounter her metaphysically.

As he got up and walked toward their table, he felt weak in the knees. How could another person have these effects on him? He knew that this was more than just attraction and lust, which had initiated all prior relationships. Exactly what it was, he wasn't sure.

He approached her. She was talking about someone named Charlie and something about Georgetown Law School to her friend, when he interrupted them.

"Pardon me, but aren't you Cathy Mathias?" His tone was friendly and self-assured.

"Why, yes, I am," Cathy answered, somewhat surprised that he knew who she was. "Say, I know you!" She had a gleam of recognition in her eye as she waved her index finger in his direction. "You were at the rally this morning!"

"Yeah, me and about a thousand other people!" Tony said, laughing.

"You were there also?" Tony asked, suppressing the tug of guilt that he felt, rationalizing that he had an entire lifetime to be open, honest and truthful with her.

"Yes, I was! I saw how you helped that boy." She turned to her friend. "Barb, this is the guy I told you about." Looking back to Tony, she added, "You were fantastic! How did you know what to do?"

"I didn't. I just reacted with instincts and common sense. The empathy comes natural."

Tony turned toward Barb in an effort to change the subject, being embarrassed talking about the incident.

"Hello, Barb, I'm Tony Cipullo." Tony extended his right hand. The irony struck him. Here he was touching Barb, when he wanted to—*had* to touch Cathy.

Barb was attractive, with a turned-up nose, shoulder-length blond hair and intensely blue eyes. She was wearing a Notre Dame T-shirt.

"I see that you are a fighting Irish fan," Tony remarked, pointing to her shirt.

"To a fault!" Barb said, looking down at her shirt, and brushing something from her left breast, almost as if to draw attention to it. She looked back up at Tony. "Very nice to meet you." Her tone was sincere.

Time would reveal that Barb's boyfriend went to Notre Dame. He introduced Cathy to his roommate; a guy named Charlie Vantare, who was pursuing Cathy big-time. He was applying to Georgetown Law School and was pretty hot on himself. To say that Tony would come to dislike him was an understatement of major proportions.

Tony now turned to Cathy, extending his hand and swallowing hard.

"Thank you for your kind words."

Her touch was soft, her handshake mildly firm. Tony looked into her eyes and saw his future soul mate.

There are events that occur in life that one never forgets—locked in one's reverie as if by necessity. Tony would never forget the first time that he ever touched her flesh and looked into her eyes. He swore that the earth moved. His life would never be the same again.

Chapter 3

Later that morning

Tony entered his satellite office through his private entrance and set his briefcase down beside his walnut desk. He glanced through the mail that Joan, his current office manager, had placed on his desk's polished surface. Joan had been with him since Cathy was pregnant with Angela—almost nine years now—and Tony hated to see her go. She was dependable and efficient in her job, managed the other staff members well, and his patients loved her. She knew the third-party insurance procedure codes, as well as the computer software that the office used, having been there as long as the software had been in use.

Joan heard Tony come in and came back from the reception area, knocked twice, and entered his private office. She handed him the three résumés for him to peruse before the first interview at 10:00 a.m. She was eight months pregnant with her first child and looked bloated and uncomfortable.

"Just look what Frank did to you, Joan!" Tony kidded as he pointed to her stomach. "And look what he did to ME!" he added, pointing to the résumés.

Joan smiled and rubbed her belly.

"Doctor, I know how much you love parenthood," Joan said as she pointed to the various family photographs displayed in his office.

"Now don't you want me to experience some of that joy as well?"

"So you're serious then. You really are pregnant, and you really are going to leave me?" Tony teased. "Listen, Joan, this kid thing is *really* overrated! They can be a royal pain in the ass!" Tony continued, tongue-in-cheek. "When they are little, they cry often, and when they get older, they complain all of the time. Unspeakable substances and fluids come out of every imaginable orifice. They keep you up at night and wake you up way too early in the morning. When they are not driving you crazy, they are breaking your heart. They crawl into your bed, between you and your spouse, when you want to make love, or knock loudly on your bedroom door once you've started—which is why Cathy and I have not made love in over eight years!"

Joan laughed out loud, throwing her head back to exaggerate her amusement.

"What's more, they are expensive as hell! They eat twenty-four-seven, and leave every light on in every room, as well as at least four unwatched television sets. They play loud, impossible to listen to music when you are trying to read. They bang on drums or pots and pans when you are on the phone, and they wreck your cars—repeatedly—so that your insurance premiums look like the defense budget of some small nations. They throw up all over the table when you take them out to dinner. They say the most embarrassing things about your most private lives in front of your friends, and what's more, they fart loudly in church."

He stood up, gently rubbed her belly and said, "And I wouldn't trade one minute of it for all of the tea in China, Joan. You know how happy I am for you and Frank. Welcome to the parenthood club!" He smiled warmly at her.

"It's just that I hate to see you go. I'll miss you so, Joan!"

"And I'll miss it here, Doctor. You were wonderful to work for! I'll especially miss your sense of humor," Joan added.

Joan heard the reception room door open and looked at her watch.

"You're on, big guy! Heck, you will probably forget about me five minutes after you hire this chick!"

"Fat chance!" Tony said.

Joan went out and introduced herself to the first applicant. She brought her back into Tony's office, where he was seated at his desk, hands folded on her résumé, trying to look professional.

"Dr. Cipullo, this is Mrs. Campbell."

Tony got up and shook hands with her. She was short and very thin— sixty-two years old according to her résumé, but she looked older. Her short gray hair was neatly combed and pulled back tightly. She wore a simple blue dress, perhaps better suited for a church social than a job interview, and appeared outwardly nervous.

"Please relax, Mrs. Campbell. I don't bite," Tony said, trying to place her more at ease. "At least not until it's closer to lunch time."

She looked at him deadpan, not even cracking a smile.

"Yes—well, let's see—your résumé indicates that you worked for Dr. Sichi, a podiatrist, for two years. That's fine. The insurance procedure codes will be different, of course, but claims processing will be similar, I'm sure. Did Dr. Sichi utilize e-claims?"

"E-claims?"

"Yes, electronic submission of insurance claims."

31

Mrs. Campbell stared blankly at him.

"Via computer modem."

Again, she said nothing.

"Perhaps your front office software didn't support e-claims."

She fidgeted in her seat.

"Mrs. Campbell, can you hear me?

Tony raised his voice slightly—enough to arouse, but not alarm—thinking that she may be having a petite mal seizure or perhaps a hearing aid malfunction.

"Yes, Doctor, I can hear you, I just don't know what you mean."

"Dr. Sichi submitted all of his claims by hard copy and snail mail, then?"

"I don't know."

"Mrs. Campbell, what exactly were your responsibilities at Dr. Sichi's?"

"I was his cleaning lady."

Tony had been looking at her résumé but now looked up at her in amazed disbelief.

"Mrs. Campbell, I'm sorry, but there seems to have been some miscommunication. This job was posted as business office manager."

"I know, Doctor. I stretched the truth on my résumé."

"But why?"

"Because you wouldn't have given me an interview, otherwise."

Tony couldn't argue with logic like that. He didn't try.

"I'm tired of cleaning. I think that I can do this office job," she said matter-of-factly.

"But, Mrs. Campbell, this is a busy practice. Do you have ANY computer skills?"

"No, but I'm a fast learner."

"A VERY busy practice, Mrs. Campbell!" Tony leaned forward. "Mrs. Campbell, I'd like to help you out, but I have a responsibility to my other staff members, and to the practice. We are really looking for someone with experience." Tony tried to be kind. "Perhaps you can find something in a slower-paced situation, where you would have time to grow into the position."

Tony stood up.

"Thank you for coming, and I really do wish you well."

After Mrs. Campbell left, Joan came into Tony's office.

"So how'd it go?"

"I'll give you $5,000 to stay, Joan!"

"That bad?"

"That bad!"

"Well, the good news is, your next interview is here. She's early."

"Hey, that's a good sign! Show her in, Joan."

"You mean show *them* in, Doctor."

"Them?"

"You'd better sit down."

Tony braced himself for the worst. He did not brace himself well enough.

"Doctor, this is Miss Eve Costa and her daughter, Satana," Joan said with a straight face.

"Satana. What a—uh—unusual name," Tony said. *Who would name such a beautiful child after Satan?* Tony thought.

"Her father named her that. I told him that it was stupid, but, you know— it fits his image and stuff like dat dere."

"His image?" Tony asked, almost afraid to ask.

"He's a drummer in a heavy-metal rock band."

"Whew! I mean, your husband's a musician, then."

"He's not my husband."

"Sorry."

"Yeah, me too!" Eve said, cracking her chewing gum loudly. "Now you just sit right there, and don't you move!" Eve said to her daughter, pointing to the third chair.

Her daughter was about three, maybe four years old. Tony noticed that she had two different-colored socks on, but her shoes *did* match. She wore a pair of pink pedal pushers with a grass stain just below her left knee that extended down onto her shin. The pants were too short for her—even for pedal pushers—revealing the un-matched socks. She had on a white short-sleeved jersey with a small tear in the shoulder area.

Eve was twenty-three, according to her résumé. She wore a sleeveless dress that had a mesh fabric at the waist that revealed her midriff and pierced navel. The hem was extremely short, and when she sat down, it came to a rest high on her thigh, almost revealing the bottom of her panties. There was a tattoo of a crescent moon high on the inside of her left thigh. It came into full view as she crossed her legs. *This outfit must be very popular with the boys in the band,* Tony thought, as he shook his head in disbelief.

Her face was almost boyish in appearance. This impression was reinforced by her short haircut, combed back on each side, with a wet look reminiscent of the "duck's ass" hairstyle of the 1950s, popularized by cinematic juvenile delinquent types.

Why me? Tony thought as he rubbed his forehead just above his eyes. He continued to read her résumé.

She had worked for Bob Tunney, an internist that Tony knew quite well.

"I see that you worked for Dr. Tunney. Did you manage his front office?"

"Yeah, for about eight months, or so." She looked down at her nails, almost as if she were having a casual conversation at a bus stop, and not at an interview, the outcome of which would determine needed employment. She cracked her chewing gum as if to punctuate her statement.

"And why did you leave his employ?"

"My old man and I was having some problems an' stuff."

"And quitting your job helped?"

"Kinda."

"Mommy, I'm thirsty!"

"No, you're not! I told you to sit there and be quiet, while Mommy talks to this man."

Her daughter began to moan and fidget in her chair, as one would expect a bored three-year-old to act.

"But, Mommy, when are we going to leave?"

Eve turned to her and, grabbing her tiny shoulders with both hands, repeated her prior orders to sit still and be quiet.

Tony pushed the intercom button on his desk.

"Joan, could you please bring back a cup of water for...this little cutie pie?"

He couldn't bring himself to refer to such a beautiful child by using such a dark name, he thought, as he smiled at her.

"I think that you are being a very good girl! Mommy's almost finished, sweetie." Tony remarked as Joan entered the room and handed her a paper cup filled with cold water from the polar cooler.

She took the offered water without saying thank you and without being corrected by her mother.

"Now sit still, Satana!" Eve said with a firm voice.

Tony clenched his teeth.

"Would you mind if I called Dr. Tunney for a reference?" Tony was being polite, already deciding on her employment potential, feeling that she would fit into his practice about as well as her daughter's name fit beautiful and innocent little girls.

"Well, OK, but you should know that no one ever had any proof that I had anything to do with that missing money from the petty cash drawer," Eve said as she continued to crack her chewing gum.

"I understand. Thank you for coming in for the interview. Someone will get back to you within the week with our decision," Tony said as he got up to shake her hand. He turned and winked in her daughter's direction as she threw the empty cup onto the carpet. She hopped out of the chair and left with her mother.

"How did it go, Doctor?" Joan asked with a raised eyebrow, as Tony walked around his desk and picked up the paper cup from the carpet.

"I'll give you $10,000 if you stay, Joan!" Tony said, folding his hands as if in prayer.

Joan laughed.

"It was THAT bad?"

"Well, I suppose it could have been worse. She could have showed me her pierced labium, or exchanged body fluids with me," Tony said with a crooked smile.

Tony sat back down at his desk and started to go over some pathology reports until the next interview at 11:00 a.m.

"There's a Sergeant Brinker from the Fox Chapel Police Department for you on line one, Doctor," Joan's voice said over the intercom. "He said that it was important, but not urgent," she continued.

"Donation solicitation?"

"I don't think so, Doctor."

"It's not about Eve, is it?" he said, laughing, as he picked up the receiver and punched the button for line one.

"This is Dr. Cipullo. Yes, Sergeant, Troy is my son. What has he done?" Tony sat up in his chair "Uh-huh. Yes. Uh-huh. The Brunswick house? Yes, they are our neighbors. Yes, their backyard approximates our backyard. Uh-huh. A what? What on earth is a spud launcher? It does WHAT? You must be kidding! Of course I didn't know that he had one. I wouldn't know one if I saw one. No, of course I know what a potato looks like, Sergeant, I meant the launcher! Yes, I suppose Troy has access to potatoes. Doesn't everyone? How much damage? Uh-huh. Mr. Brunswick's mother-in-law? Uh-huh. On the second floor? The large bay window? Uh-huh. Is she all right? Thank goodness! Yes. Yes! Yes, Sergeant, I'll take care of it! I will go over to the Brunswicks' this afternoon and smooth things over and make restitution. Yes, I'll handle that as well, Sergeant. You have my word. Yes. Thank you. Please accept my apologies to the police department. I'm sorry that you were inconvenienced with this. Yes, Sergeant, I guess boys WILL be boys. Yes, I understand that this is the second time that the Brunswicks had to call you regarding an incident with our family. Yes, Sergeant, it was OUR dog who ate his daughter's pet rabbit last month. The two incidents were completely unrelated, I assure you! No, sir, I'm sure that Troy has nothing against the Brunswicks, nor do we. You have my word as a doctor on that. I did buy her another rabbit. Yes, I'm aware that she didn't think that the new rabbit was as friendly as the first one—but maybe that's not such a good trait for rabbits to have—I mean maybe that's what attracted our dog to the first rabbit to begin with. Thank you. I'm just trying to break some of the tension here, Sergeant. Accept my apologies once again. You have a nice day as well, Sergeant."

Tony hung up the phone and buzzed for Joan.

"What was *that* all about, doctor?" Joan asked as she re-entered his private office.

"It seems that my son Troy went on maneuvers yesterday. My son the munitions expert! He has somehow acquired a bazooka-like device that shoots potatoes—like a mortar shell—up to six hundred feet. It's called a 'spud launcher.' The Afghan rebels held off the entire Soviet Military in all its glory with less artillery and firepower than this baby has! He launched a spud from our front yard, over our three-story house, through a bay window on the second floor of our neighbors' house, knocking over the neighbor's seventy-five-year-old mother-in-law."

"Is she all right, Doctor?"

"Thankfully, yes. It hit her in the leg, startling her more than anything else. Could you just hear the *First alert* call? 'Help! I've been hit by a flying potato, and I can't get up!'"

Tony shook his head, as Joan laughed.

"You know, I wanted to name him Rambo. Rambo Cipullo. It has a nice military/Italian ring to it, don't you think, Joan? But no…Cathy had to tap into her Irish heritage and name him Troy. Perhaps we can send him over to Northern Ireland with his spud launcher to straighten things out over there! One thing's for sure; he'll have no shortage of ammunition in Spud Country!"

Joan laughed hard. She loved Tony's sense of humor, and often told him so. She would miss it so very much. She would miss much about the job, especially her coworkers and the patients. But ever since she was a small child, all she ever really wanted was to be a mother. This need overshadowed all other needs and wants.

She had been abandoned by her own mother at the age of three—about the same age as the little girl who was in the office earlier, abandonment coming in many forms. She was raised in various foster homes, as a ward of the court, until she was eighteen, at which time she came to work for Tony as a filing clerk. She worked her way up to office manager at his satellite site with dedication, loyalty and an enviable work ethic.

She loved Tony as a surrogate father figure, having been taught so much by him, and growing so much under his caring guidance. She would do anything for him. But now was the time for her to fulfill her destiny as the mother she had always desired to be. Tony knew this, of course, and, despite his kidding, wanted it for her as much as she did.

She married Frank last year, asking Tony to walk her down the aisle and give her away, which Tony did with pleasure and pride. When she became pregnant, she fell to her knees, thanking God for her gift, and wept. She wept the tears of fulfillment and happiness that one feels when realizing a lifelong dream. When she told Tony the news, he wept as well—knowing from where she came and the measure of importance the event held in her life.

"Joan, please look up the Brunswicks' address and call the florist to send something nice over to the house with my apologies."

"Didn't we just send a basket of fruit to them last month?"

Tony nodded.

"I believe that according to the Book of Etiquette, rabbit restitution calls for fruit—mother-in-law restitution demands flowers," Tony joked.

The telephone rang, and Joan went to the front office to answer it.

"That was your 11:00 a.m. interview, Doctor," Joan said as she returned to his private office. "She just took a job as the financial councilor at the dental school. It was the interview just before yours. She thanked you for the interview opportunity and wished you well in your process."

"She thanked me for the interview opportunity, and wished me well in my process. What, no an' stuff like dat der?" Tony said, mocking Eve's butchering of the English language and use of *Pittsburghese*. "Now isn't that a kick in the head, Joan? Here I am, interviewing the woman from *American Gothic* and a pierced rock groupie as interview one and interview two, while interview three—probably a candidate for distinguished front office staff member of the decade—takes a job at the dental school! And so, as it is true in life, Joan, so it is true in the interviewing process. Timing is EVERYTHING!" Tony said, philosophically. "OK, Joan. $12,500. I'm talking about a tax-free bonus here! That's my final offer!" Tony said, smiling.

Joan smiled back. She looked at him, not as a staff member to an employer—but as a child to a surrogate father figure, with love and true regard.

"I'm not too concerned, Joan. I'm sure that things will work out. They always have in the past!" He thanked her for coming in on a Saturday and told her to please go home and get off her feet. "I'll call you from the Fox Chapel office on Monday. Don't forget to take your prenatal vitamins."

Tony left his office and walked the three short blocks over to the medical school. He climbed the stairs to the third floor, rather than wait for the elevator. He waved to some maintenance people changing fluorescent bulbs in the hallway.

"Hi ya, Doc. Work'n on Saturday?"

"No rest for the wicked, I guess."

Tony unlocked his office door and turned on the light. The department secretary had left some correspondence on his desk. He glanced at it quickly, tossing the junk mail into the waste can. He jotted some notes on a few of the others and placed them in the "out" bin on his desk.

Flipping through the telephone directory on his desk, Tony found and dialed Barbara's cell phone number as he booted his computer to check his e-mail.

"Hello, Barbara? Tony here. How are the kids doing? Super! Listen, that was very nice of you to take them swimming at the club. I know…but still. We owe you one! Please don't let them eat too much junk, and don't let Troy give you a hard time about putting on his sunscreen. I know, Barb. I know. Thank you anyway. And please put everything on my chit. I insist. Thanks again, for everything. I have my cell phone if you need me. Bye!"

Tony turned to his computer monitor, which now displayed his e-mail messages. He skipped through them.

"There's more e-junk than snail junk! Soon we'll revert back to smoke signals to avoid this shit!" Tony said under his breath, as he shut down the computer.

He picked up an 8x10 picture of Cathy and the children from his desktop. They were sitting in the woods of western Pennsylvania. Cathy was seated on a rustic bench with Kathleen, Rob, Troy, Dominick and Joseph surrounding her. Angela sat in her lap, the privileged position of the youngest child. Cathy was stroking Angela's hair as the photo was taken. There was a babbling brook in the background. The leaves were in brilliant autumn splendor. Their colors of red and gold provided a tinctured background that not only provided a seasonal mood, they added contrast to the white cotton shirts that the children wore. Cathy had given Tony the photograph as a birthday present last November. He treasured it, looked upon it, and reflected on his family every time he entered his office at the university. He regretted deeply not being a part of the photograph—that desire being trumped by the fact that his absence was required for the element of surprise.

He touched the glass of the photo, as if that in some way connected him to that place and time. It was small consolation. Returning the photo to its place on his desk, he exhaled deeply.

Tony looked at his watch. He gathered the slides necessary for his lecture to the Rotary Club on malignant melanoma. Tony looked once again at the family photo as he turned off the light. He shut and locked the door and headed off to the cafeteria of Western Psychiatric Hospital for his lunch meeting with Sean.

Sean was already sitting at a table away from the flow of foot traffic, off to one side of the cafeteria, when Tony arrived. He saw Tony enter and waved his hand high in the air for Tony to see.

"Have you been waiting long?" Tony asked as he set the slide carrousel on the table and his briefcase on the floor next to the chair across from where Sean was sitting.

"Only about a minute or so. I finished my rounds early. I didn't expect you this soon," Sean said as he put the journal he had been reading down in front of him.

"My last interview disappointed."

The two friends walked to the cafeteria line as they continued the conversation.

"How did the others go?"

"Let's just say that I'm still in the market."

"The right one will come along, I'm sure."

"I've decided to lower my standards. I'll take a warm body that can turn on the computer, so long as they refrain from phone sex on my second line."

Sean laughed as they approached the deli section of the cafeteria.

"I'll have hot pastrami on pumpernickel, with onion, a slice of red pepper, lettuce and horseradish. Also, give me a corned beef on focaccia with melted Swiss and Dijon mustard," Sean said to the woman behind the deli section.

"Where do you manage to put it all?" Tony asked, in reference to Sean's appetite and small stature.

"I'll meet you back at the table. I'm just going to have a bowl of soup," Tony said.

Tony was crushing some crackers into his minestrone when Sean returned to the table.

"You are so predictable, Tony. You always get the minestrone when we eat here."

"Minestrone was my father's favorite soup. Go ahead and clog your arteries. Let me sit here and be nostalgic."

"You mean *that* tastes like the minestrone that your mother made for your father?"

Tony looked up at his friend.

"You're kidding, right? This doesn't taste ANYTHING like my mother's soup. In fact, that pastrami probably tastes more like my mother's soup than this does. I don't get this because it tastes like my mother's minestrone. I get it because it's a lesson in contrast. Compared to this, my mother's soup is heaven's soup. It just reminds me how good her soup really is!"

"I see," Sean said, as he took a large bite out of his pastrami sandwich.

Tony took a spoonful of the soup. He made a face, showing his displeasure.

"I'm getting pretty tired of hospital food." Tony remarked.

"We should have gone down to *Primanti's* or the *O,*" Tony said, referring to an Italian deli and *The Original Hot Dog Shop* down the street from the hospital.

"What were you saying about clogging arteries?" Sean asked.

"You clog your arteries the way you want. Let me clog mine the way I want!"

Tony took another spoonful of the soup. He made another face.

"So, tell me. How are Cathy and the kids?" Sean asked, hoping to change the subject.

"The kids are great! I tell you—that Rob! He never ceases to amaze me! He's so bright! I swear—he takes after my father!" Tony said in reference to his deceased father, who, Tony often said, was the most intelligent man that he had ever met.

"Dominick and Joseph are still fighting like cats and dogs. Troy, your godson, is—well, Troy is Troy. Angela's as cute as ever—and Kathleen made the dean's list last term and…"

Tony caught himself in mid-sentence.

"I'm sorry, Sean. That was a rhetorical question wasn't it. You know that I can talk about my kids for hours!"

"And Cathy?" Sean said, without changing expression.

"Cathy has been…preoccupied, to say the least, Sean. She's in line for a partnership, and all of her energies, as you can imagine, have been focused on that."

Sean said nothing, his silence and stare being a psychiatrist's ploy to get the other person to open up and tell him more.

"I guess that you can say that our relationship has been strained, lately," Tony confessed.

"Strained?" Sean asked, using another psychiatric ploy of turning a client's statement back on itself, in the form of a question, in order to get the client to elaborate.

"Yes, strained, Sean. What are you—hard of hearing?" Tony said, seeing through Sean's approach.

"Go on."

"Look, Sean. I know that you are an eligible bachelor with a bachelor's pad and no relationship tie-downs. There's no lack of women in your life. You breeze in and out of relationships like the wind. If you find emotional support lacking in one relationship, you just move on to the next. So, please excuse me for saying this, but how in the hell could you possibly understand what I'm talking about when I say that the relationship that I've had with Cathy for the last twenty-two years is feeling strain? How could you possibly understand the magnitude of that statement? It has no meaning within your frame of reference."

"Well, then define 'strained' for me within your frame of reference."

"I don't know if I can, Sean. It's experiential. It's like trying to define love, or hate, or comfort. All that I can say is that it's multi-factorial. The strain is fueled by many things and many events. Cathy's preoccupation with her job, I've already mentioned—her placing me and my feelings on the back burner. Then there's her near-peri-menopausal state, and all that those hormonal influences bring to bear. There's the natural stagnancy that creeps in. *My* midlife crisis issues and outside pressures placed on us by my practice. I could go on and on. Hell, she couldn't even use my name and *dear* in the same sentence this morning! It all adds up to us growing further and further apart—emotionally AND physically." Tony pushed his soup bowl away from him as if to punctuate his statements with a metaphor of separation.

"I see," Sean said, almost more clinical than concerned.

"Look, I've got to go. Our family portrait is being delivered today, and Cathy asked me to come home as soon as I've finished. I'm sorry for being such terrible company, Sean. It's just that I've had a bad day."

"I understand, Tony. I think that we should talk more. Meet me for a drink later?"

"I don't know. We'll see. I'll call you."

Before Tony could get up to leave, Mary Jo, Sean's secretary, approached the table.

She was a woman in her early thirties. She wore a beige business suit, with pants covering her shapely legs. Black open-toed high heels revealed red polish on her toes that matched her manicure. Tony always thought that she resembled the actress Sandra Bullock and told Sean this often. Mary Jo also possessed a throaty, sexy telephone voice that Tony enjoyed. He called Sean often at the office, half kidding him that it was because he just wanted to hear Mary Jo's impersonation of Kim Carnes.

"Hello, Dr. Cipullo, how are you?"

"Hello, Mary Jo. I'm fine, but not nearly as fine as you are. How are you doing?"

"I'd be better if your friend would give me a raise."

"Come work for me, Mary Jo. I'll give you a raise. What's Sean paying you now—minimum wage?"

Sean rolled his eyes back.

"You two deserve each other!"

"Are you honestly looking for a new staff person, Dr. Cipullo?" Mary Jo asked.

"Yes. Joan's leaving me for motherhood. Do you believe it?"

"Joan's pregnant? How wonderful for her!"

Tony smiled.

"Listen, I just ran into an old friend of mine that I used to work with when I was with Radiology Associates. She might be interested in getting back into this rat race that you two call health care." Mary Jo took her Palm Pilot out of her purse. "I just got her new phone number. We were supposed to get together for a drink."

Mary Jo touched the small screen with the stylus.

"I hate those damn things! I got Kathleen one for her last birthday. $250.00! She lost it after two days! What's wrong with those little notebooks that you can get for a dollar?" Tony said, looking at the tiny computer that Mary Jo held in the palm of her hand. It displayed the names, addresses and telephone numbers of dozens of people. They were alphabetized. She touched the M.

"Here we are: Hanna McDowell."

Mary Jo wrote the name and telephone number down and handed it to Tony.

"You'll like her a lot! She's a real looker too, Dr. Cipullo."

"I don't need a looker, Mary Jo. I need someone who knows her way around the front desk!"

"She's both! Call her!"

Time would reveal that this benign conversation in the cafeteria of Western Psychiatric Hospital would lead to events that placed Tony at decision forks in the paths of his life.

Chapter 4

That same morning, at Cathy's office

Cathy walked into the foyer of the large office building where the public relations firm she worked for had a suite on the sixteenth floor. She had been with them for six years now and held a position as senior account executive. She enjoyed her work very much. She needed the intellectual stimulation that her work provided—it being good therapy for her. It was unimaginable for her to be a housewife and stay-at-home mother. Watching soap operas, attending garden club functions and other underemployment activities offered no stimulation for her. She had graduated cum laude from Bucknell, and she did not expend those intellectual energies to one day have her talents go unused. As her many talents became evident, more and more responsibilities were placed on her by the firm, until she was now in the partner stream. Becoming a partner in the firm was a goal that she had set for herself, and her fixation on that goal as well as the time and energy demanded by this quest was the source of no small amount of tension between her and Tony.

Tony tried to be supportive, but the time Cathy had to spend away from home grew, as did the strain that the relationship felt. *All marriages feel stress,* Tony thought often. *Our love will carry us through this and any future stress that we may encounter,* he would say to himself, half hoping, half believing.

The problem that Tony failed to realize, was that the love of twenty years ago, or the love of ten years ago, or the love of even last year, was tempered and reinforced differently than the love of today. Stresses take their toll, as if they were eroding tides—subtle yet consistent erosion forces that if examined at any given point in time seem to exert no harm, yet in the grand scheme of things and over time, if permitted, can undermine even granite cliffs.

So it was with Tony and Cathy, as with all married couples. From the

43

moment that they said, "I DO," and turned to walk down the aisle as Dr. and Mrs. Cipullo, the erosion began. That is not to say that marriage is a bad thing. On the contrary! What it is meant to say is that marriage is something to cherish, and work for and sacrifice and shed sweat and blood for—forsaking all other things.

Sadly, these things are best viewed in hindsight. The subtle effects, spoken of, are often hidden from the eyes of those living in the present—with present obsessions and present distractions and present goals, clouding one's view.

Cathy walked up to the lobby security desk thinking of little else but the McTigh account, what it meant to the firm, and what it ultimately meant to her. A uniformed security guard stood behind the desk. In front of him was a logbook. Everyone who entered or left the building had to sign the book.

What a royal waste of time! Cathy thought.

The truth was that the security persons never checked for identification, so what was the point of signing in? If someone wrote *John Q. Public*, but never produced an ID, verifying that they were, indeed, John Q. Public, then what was the point?

If a tree falls in the woods, but there is no one there to hear it, does it indeed make a sound? If a person writes John Q. Public *but there is no one there to identify him, does John Q. Public indeed exist?* Cathy thought, reflecting on and extrapolating on a basic question asked in all philosophy 101 courses.

If he indeed doesn't exist, then why expend all this money on security personnel?

She smiled at the guard, nodded, and said hello. She picked up the pen and under *name* wrote, *Phuque Hugh.* She placed the pen down, and walked toward the elevator bank. A pregnant moment passed.

"Excuse me, miss!" the guard called after her.

Uh-oh! Cathy thought. *Busted!*

"Listen, Officer, I was just—"

"Miss, you need to write the time of day and office location."

"Oh yes, of course. How silly of me, Officer! What was I thinking?"

She picked up the pen and wrote, *13:00 p.m.* and *Nowhere special.*

"Thank you, miss," the guard said, not looking at the logbook. "Have a good day!" he said, as if that fulfilled his job obligation.

Cathy walked to the elevator bank, pushed the "up" button and smiled, smug in her exploits.

"Cathy? Cathy Mathias? Is that you?" a male's voice came from over her left shoulder.

44

Cathy turned, anxious to see who it was who referred to her by her maiden name.

"Charlie? Charlie Vantare?"

Walking toward her was a middle-aged man wearing a blue pin-striped Armani business suit. His once jet-black hair was graying on the sides—salt-and-peppered on the top—making him seem more distinguished than aged. He was a couple of pounds too heavy around the midriff, a result perhaps of too many three-martini power lunches, too many entrees laced with Alfredo sauce, and not enough exercise. His shoes were Italian leather, and expensive. His briefcase matched his shoes. He was tan and could still turn a few heads, she thought, as he approached.

They embraced, not so much as old friends, but as former lovers—the realization of what was happening surprised Cathy. She blushed. He didn't.

"You look great!" he said with candor.

"Bullshit! I'm ten pounds too heavy, and my hair looks like shit!"

"Don't be silly! You haven't aged a day!"

"You are too kind!"

It was amazing to her how much his flattery meant to her. It was true that Tony flattered her as well, but to hear it from a former lover—one you haven't seen for over twenty-four years—was something special. She blushed. He didn't.

"What's gong on with your life?" he asked, as if this were the next thing to say.

"Do you have a year or two?"

"I once told you that I had a lifetime for you!"

She glanced down and saw the wedding ring on his hand.

"So tell me what's going on in *your* life!"

"I don't want to bore you," he said in his smug way.

She looked at him as he spoke. He was still very attractive, with Italian good looks. He was shorter than she remembered, perhaps because she was accustomed to Tony's six-foot, two-inch height. He still had the spaces between his front teeth, and she wondered why he never had them fixed. They offered character to his smile, even though they were mildly distracting. It was, however, how she remembered his smile.

His cologne was a little overpowering. Tony never wore any at all, so any cologne was more than she was used to. He had a confident manner about him. He always did. It was part of his charm, she thought.

"I haven't seen you since your third year at Georgetown Law School. What was that, back in seventy-seven?" Cathy asked, already knowing the answer.

"My goodness, that seems like a lifetime ago! " he said, with a faraway look in his eye. "Can we get a cup of coffee somewhere? I have some time before my appointment," he said as he looked at his watch.

"Come up to my office," she said enthusiastically. "We can talk there. I have a little time before I have to get home. Our family portrait is being delivered this afternoon, and I have some work to do beforehand."

They entered the elevator, pushed the button for the sixteenth floor, and smiled at each other as the door closed.

She looked into his hazel-green eyes as they spoke small talk. She had a tug of guilt. Was she supposed to look into another man's eyes this way? Was she supposed to have these feelings—almost as if she was a schoolgirl again? The memories came—nonetheless—regardless of whether it was right or wrong.

There is a certain pleasure reliving fond memories. Endorphins are released, and synaptic re-uptake inhibitors kick in, creating a unique euphoria. No one is immune to its effects. Cathy was no exception.

Slowly, she was transformed back to the early seventies—back to Bucknell's campus. Back to her college days and how she was pursued by two eligible young men. These had been the best years of her life, she thought. It had given her great joy to have two handsome men vying for her attention.

"I see that you two have met Tony," Amy said as she entered the commons room with a cup of coffee in one hand and a bud vase in the other.

Tony reluctantly let go of Cathy's hand and turned toward Amy.

"Why, Amy, is Tony here with you?" Barb asked, somewhat surprised.

"Yes. He is here to talk about Rush policy with me. If you two will excuse us."

Amy handed Tony his coffee, took him by the arm, and led him away to another table, as he looked back over his shoulder toward Cathy.

"He was cute!" Barb said, as she looked at Cathy for a response.

"Cute and interesting." Cathy said, as she looked at her watch.

"Shoot! It's almost nine thirty. Charlie's going to call me tonight. I've got to go!"

Cathy got up and ran towards her room, looking back over her shoulder at Tony as he looked blankly past Amy in the direction of Cathy's exit.

As Cathy approached her room, she thought about Charlie. It was her first serious relationship, and she thought about him often. He was romancing her, and she liked the attention. He would send her flowers. He would send her telegrams with nothing more than X's and O's in the message. He would call and tell her how much he missed her—how cold it could be in South Bend, not because of the latitude, but because she wasn't there with him.

She thought also about this past summer—about his parents' cottage up at Lake Arthur—how they would take long walks in the moonlight. How he made love to her on the screened-in porch, with the cicadas chirping in the background. How it was her first time—the wonder of it all locked in her contemplation.

Cathy opened the door to her room as the phone was ringing. She slowed her pace as if to send a message of not being too eager. She took a deep breath, counted to three, and picked up the receiver.

"Hello. Oh Charlie, it's you. What a surprise!"

"Hi, sweetie. Didn't you remember that I was going to call tonight?"

"Was that tonight that you were supposed to call? Silly me!" she said with a touch of indifference in her voice, playing the game that all women play.

"I've been thinking of you all night," he said, pretending to not be affected by her response.

"Really? How sweet!" She would rather die than let him know that she was thinking of him as well, or that she checked her watch every hour until 9:30.

"How was your day?" he asked, a little upset that she didn't tell him that she had been thinking of him as well.

"My day was very interesting! I went to my first college anti-war rally today."

"You mean with all of those long-haired hippies and revolutionaries?"

Charlie was very buttoned down. He was Oxford cloth and Brooks Brothers—the family *golden boy*, who was being primed for a career in the law, and perhaps even politics. He wore his straight black hair short, in a modified Princeton cut. He would fit in at an anti-war rally as well as Spiro Agnew.

"Charlie, it wasn't like that at all," Cathy protested, a little taken aback by his conservative bias. "Of course, some people fit that description, but by and large, it was a cross section of concerned college students," Cathy said, taking a defensive posture.

"Concerned about their ass, maybe. Concerned that they may be drafted next!" Charlie said with marked insensitivity.

"War is wrong, Charlie! Killing is wrong! Dropping napalm on innocent babies is wrong! What's more, Charlie, YOU'RE wrong!"

"Look! I don't want you attending those things! I can't be associated with people like that!" Charlie's tone was firm and demanding, like a self-centered father talking to a child.

"And just who the hell are you to tell ME what I can and can't do? What am I—a possession, like one of your cars, that has to fit into your image? Besides, if your father hadn't pulled some strings to get you into the National Guard and out of the draft, you'd be there protesting too—only for all the wrong reasons!"

Cathy slammed the receiver down with enough force to be heard down the hall, not giving Charlie time for rebuttal. She picked up a stuffed animal from her bed and threw it hard against the wall, causing a picture of her and Charlie to fall, breaking the glass as if she AND fate were making a statement.

"Lover's quarrel?" Barb asked, entering the room.

"I don't want to talk about it!"

"Sure you do," Barb said as she sat on her twin bed, knee to knee with Cathy.

The roommates sat and talked for an hour. They talked about men, how self-centered and self-serving they could be. How superficial their attentions can appear when looked at in a different light and under different circumstances. They talked about a woman's needs, wants and desires. How maybe it wasn't such a good idea to only date one person at such an early age—to be so vulnerable. They bared their souls to one another, and Cathy thought how grateful she was to have a friend like Barb. Their friendship was taken to a different level that evening. They had remained close ever since.

The telephone rang, and Cathy asked Barb to answer it, not wanting to speak to Charlie at this time.

"Hello? … Oh hi! Just a minute, I'll see if I can find her." Barb put her hand over the receiver. "You'll never guess who this is! It's that Tony from the rally today."

"Hello. Yes, this is Cathy. No, it's not too late, Tony," Cathy said, looking down at her wristwatch, then up at Barb. "Barb and I usually don't go to bed until late. Yes, it was nice to meet you as well. Tomorrow night? I'm afraid that I can't. I have a philosophy test to study for. Existentialism. Yes, with Rabbi Sheffield. You took that course? Yes, I find it depressing as well. Yes, I probably will need cheering up after dwelling on Sartre and Camus. Friday night? Yes, I think that that's doable. Seven p.m.? Fine, I'll see you then. You have a good night, also, Tony. Thank you."

Cathy raised her eyebrows at Barb. The phone rang again. Barb answered it.

"Hello? Charlie? Cathy's asleep. OK. I'll tell her. Goodnight, Charlie."

The elevator doors opened when Cathy and Charlie reached the sixteenth floor.

"Cathy, are you all right?" Charlie asked with a puzzled look on his face. "You had this blank stare, and you seemed miles away."

"Many miles and many years," she answered.

They walked down the corridor towards Cathy's firm's suite. It was carpeted with low-nap Berber. High-wear, low-maintenance, with a color pattern that only an industrial designer could love—the pattern with shades of brown and gray that will hide dirt and look none the worse for wear.

They came to a set of double six-paneled walnut doors, with half-width trim doors on either side. A brass plate to the right read, *Donahue Public Relations. Suite 1640.*

Cathy turned the brass levered handle and led Charlie into the suite.

Behind an impressive reception desk sat a well-dressed young lady in her apparent mid-twenties.

"Good morning, Ms. Cipullo." The receptionist handed Cathy a stack of papers and a manila envelope.

"Good morning, Susan," Cathy said as she glanced, not at her, but at the correspondence. "Could you please bring two cups of coffee to my office?" Cathy didn't bother to introduce Charlie. It was as if he and the receptionist were non-persons—perhaps just supporting actors in the play that she called life.

"Yes, Ms. Cipullo. Will there be anything else?"

"Yes. See if my secretary left the updated McTigh account folder in the conference room, and check to see if my PowerPoint slides are ready."

Cathy led Charlie into her office. It was large and impressive, as one would expect someone on the cusp of partnership to have. It was a self-contained suite unto itself, with a sitting area complete with an Italian leather couch and love seat. A wet bar with a small table and chairs were tucked into the corner. A large desk with a leather chair that matched the sofa and love seat completed the furniture.

"Very impressive, Cathy! You have done well for yourself, my dear!" Charlie said as he looked around Cathy's office.

"Thank you. The powers that be moved me into this office suite after I landed a seven-figure deal with the local professional hockey franchise. It's all about perks and incentives in the business world. Do you think that I would ever want to move back into my old 8x10 office after this?" she said, extending her hand over her new digs. "I will kick ass to stay here. I know it and they know it."

If power and creature comforts are addictive, then Cathy was hooked.

Charlie saw it. What's more, he *understood* it as well—having sold out to the power gods long ago. He wondered if she saw it as clearly as he did.

The receptionist knocked and entered with a tray and two coffees. She placed the tray on the table. She handed Cathy the requested folder and the PowerPoint slides. She left without saying a word.

Charlie knew that Cathy would do well in life. She had so much going for her. She was bright and industrious, with movie star good looks and an endearing personality.

Charlie sipped his coffee.

"Colombian—very nice!"

"Of course! Nothing but the best—especially for such a dear old friend."

Cathy sipped her coffee as well, looking up from her cup to see Charlie's response.

"I remember when we were more than just friends!"

Charlie thought back to his days in the early seventies with Cathy.

"Howie, you were so very right! She is so damn hot!" Charlie said to his roommate as they pissed into adjacent urinals in the restaurant's men's room. "I want to fuck her right now, right here!"

"Would I steer you wrong, my friend? Barb told me about her, and I said, 'This one's for Charlie'" Howie said, as if he were talking about a dog in the window of a pet shop, or a piece of prime meat hanging in a butcher's case.

Charlie was the type of person who knew what he wanted and went after it. He was denied little in his life, and it spilled over into the way that he looked at all things that he wanted—people and things. He had pursued and cornered dozens of women. When he set his sights, he was not to be denied. Cathy was a trophy that he wanted.

Charlie and Howie walked back to the table where Barb and Cathy were sitting, looking pretty and talking small talk.

Charlie sat down next to Cathy and put his arm around her.

"You are incredible! I want you so bad, that I can taste you! I want to taste you! Let me taste you! Take me to your room and let me taste you!"

Cathy didn't know what to say. No one had ever been *that* direct *this* soon with her before. The way that he said *taste* came across as vulgar, not sensual. She thought that he was cute, and intelligent, but to run off with someone that she hardly knew and let him *taste* her was a little overwhelming.

"Well, wants are sometimes strong, and sometimes needs are complex and difficult to understand," Cathy said, being tactful and philosophical while trying to not be hurtful. "Call me sometime after you've regained your sobriety, and maybe we can talk!" Cathy said with authority.

She got up and left the table and the restaurant—not looking back. She was not an object, nor did she want to be treated as such.

Charlie ran after her.

"I'm sorry. Please, can we begin again?"

"Of course we can. Tomorrow!" Cathy turned away from Charlie and hailed a cab, again, not looking back.

The next day a bouquet of flowers were delivered to Cathy's room. Pinned to the tissue paper was a card. They were from Charlie. The card read,

Please accept my sincerest apologies. My forward actions were both uncalled for and inappropriate. If you find it in your heart to give me another chance, I promise to behave as the gentleman that you deserve.

"How sweet," Cathy said to Barb, who was reading the card over her shoulder.

"Howie says that Charlie's gaga over you."

The phone rang. It was Charlie, asking for another chance, in person. Cathy agreed, and Charlie rejoiced to himself, and in himself. The conquest was on.

Chapter 5

Back at Bucknell. Early seventies.

The scene had been set. Here was Cathy, the beauty, with two suitors—Charles Dante Vantare and Antonio Dominick Cipullo.

Charlie, the Notre Dame student with a bright future in the law and/or politics, coming from a well-to-do background, was used to getting what he wanted, and he wanted Cathy. The fact that she didn't fall over and play dead to his pursuit antics only fueled his desire for her. His pursuit was somewhat shallow—transparent to those who knew him well. Cathy did not know him well.

Tony, the pre-med student from a working-class background, with family values as deeply seated as his principles, wanted Cathy as well. What you saw was what you were going to get with Tony. Meeting Cathy touched his entire being. He needed her, because life without her would be unthinkable. Those who knew him well could not understand his feelings—the depth of his desire—nor were they supposed to.

And so the stage was set.

She first met Tony in the fall term of her sophomore year. She had been seeing Charlie since just before the spring break of her freshman year—a little over six months now. She and Charlie continued to date over the summer as well. It culminated in a weekend together at his parents' summer cottage at Lake Arthur. It was there, on a warm August night, that Charlie reached the summit of his pursuit—or so he thought. For Cathy, it had been a spontaneous event—a naturally occurring crescendo of their feelings for one another. It was her first experience with carnal knowledge—coupling with another human being. It was as much an emotional joining as it was physical. For her, it was she and Charlie making love in the heat of passion and in the heat of the August night, with a backdrop of chirping cicadas. For Charlie, it was the planned reason why he brought her here in the first place —to romance a beautiful woman in a romantic setting—to fuck her on the porch of his parents' cottage at the lake. He had done it before with a dozen

52

other faceless forms on the same sofa in the same screened-in porch. The fact that he had developed a relationship with Cathy did indeed add a dimension to the act that heightened his pleasure.

When it was time to say good-bye—for him to go back to South Bend and for her to return to Bucknell—they each desired to continue the relationship to explore what depth of feelings the passions of August had wrought in their lives.

It was in that fall term of her sophomore year that she encountered the insensitive side of Charlie, had the heart-to-heart with Barb, and had her first date with Tony.

Cathy came down to the living room of the Kappa house at 7:15, where Tony was waiting for her. He stood up immediately upon her entering the room, not the least bit upset that she chose to be fashionably late. He held a single long-stem red rose, unwrapped. He handed it to her.

"You look terrific!" Tony said with obvious sincerity.

"Why, thank you Tony—how sweet," Cathy said, the economy of her statement covering both his greeting and the rose.

He couldn't believe that he was here with her—sharing time and sharing her space.

They left the house and walked toward the curb.

"How was the existentialism exam?" Tony asked with interest.

"It was better than I expected. It consisted of a single essay question," Cathy said, happy for the opportunity to discuss her exam. "The question was: 'If only nature is real, and if in nature only desire and destruction are legitimate—then what is the ultimate goal of humanity as it relates to this truism?'"

"Albert Camus!" Tony said without hesitation.

"You're right! That's a quote by Camus. How did you know that?" Cathy asked.

"I took Rabbi Sheffield's course, remember? One of the problems that I have with existentialistic thought, and believe me, I have many, is the total absence of hope and the apparent passive acceptance of a joyless existence," Tony continued.

"Oh Tony, I agree! Could you even imagine life without hope?" Cathy added.

Tony looked her straight in the eye and, after a pregnant moment, said, "Not even for a minute!"

In that brief moment of suspended time, Cathy came to see Tony in an entirely different light.

"There are places where the mind dies so that a truth which is its very denial may be born" Cathy said, quoting Camus once again. "What do think he meant by that, Tony?"

"I think that Camus was full of shit!" Tony said, still looking into her eyes. "The mind should never—CAN never deny the truth!"

Tony had Cathy's full attention now.

"Camus also said, '…the only paradises are those we have lost…'" Tony held her hand. "He never held your hand or looked into your eyes, Cathy, because if he had, then he would have known that the only paradises are those that I have found—with you!"

"Tony, what a romantic thing to say!"

Cathy could not help but compare her first meeting with Charlie and this first date with Tony. She also now knew why modern man should study Camus—not to learn from him, but to apply one's life as a means to disprove him.

They reached the curb, and Cathy turned to Tony.

"Which car is yours?"

"I don't have a car. I have my bike."

Tony extended his hand toward his 450 Honda motorcycle.

"Tony, I've never ridden on one of those things!"

"You are in for a real treat, then, Cathy!"

Tony took the spare helmet off the handlebars and handed it to Cathy.

"Here, put this on."

"My hair!"

"Your hair looks great! Do you really think that a helmet could ever make you look bad?"

Cathy laughed. "I can't believe that I'm doing this!" she said, as she stretched the helmet over her head. "Where are we going, anyway?"

"It's a surprise!" Tony replied as he put his helmet on. "Listen, the strap between the front and back seat is broken. You'll have to put your arms around my waist and hold on tight," Tony said with a smile.

"How convenient!" Cathy said, laughing.

"Exactly! One more thing. Lean INTO the turns! Ready?"

Tony hit the kick-start and revved the engine repeatedly. With Cathy holding on to Tony as tightly as possible, they headed down Main Street towards the edge of town.

At first, Cathy was terrified. As she realized how unfounded her fears were, she became more relaxed. After a few moments she began to enjoy it. It was exhilarating. The wind on her face and the vibration between her legs was a unique experience for her. She began to enjoy it very much!

They reached the edge of town in just a few minutes—Lewisburg, Pennsylvania, not being a very large town. They continued to ride out into the surrounding farm country. Now, away from the Lewisburg lights, with only the stars, a near full moon and the wind on her face, Cathy felt like she was flying. A sense of freedom and detachment came to her. She tightened her grip on Tony, now not out of fear, but because she wanted to draw him closer, sensing that he was, in part, contributing to her exhilaration.

After about twenty minutes, Tony turned down a dirt road and up a driveway that led to a farmhouse on top of a hill, overlooking a meadow and an apple orchard. Tony pulled in front of the house, put the kickstand down, and he and Cathy dismounted the bike.

"Tony, that was fantastic!" Cathy said as she removed her helmet.

"Told ya!" Tony said, smiling.

On the porch of the farm house was a shingle that read, *Dr. Evan Frick, DVM*

"So where are we?" Cathy asked as she read the sign.

"We are going to have dinner with my friend Evan and his wife, Rebecca. You'll like them a lot."

As Cathy and Tony walked up the porch steps, the front door opened. Out to meet them came a man in his early thirties, with long dark hair tied back in a ponytail. He was thin but athletic and was wearing a plaid long-sleeved cotton shirt and clean blue jeans.

"Tony! Qué pasa?" The men embraced in a hug, tapping each other on the back several times.

"Evan, this is Cathy. Cathy, Evan."

Evan took a long look at Cathy.

"Nice! I approve! So tell me, what is a babe like you doing with THIS guy?" Evan said with a straight face.

Dr. Frick was a doctor of veterinary medicine, specializing in livestock/large animal medicine. He and Tony had been friends for almost three years. Tony needed some extra cash and responded to an ad that Dr. Frick ran for a vet assistant. Tony had no experience, but a sincere desire to learn and be of use. Dr. Frick taught him everything that he needed to know. Tony was a quick study, and both benefited from the relationship, as did the animals that they treated. They were now good friends, as well.

"Please come in, Cathy."

They entered the modest farmhouse. There was incense burning and the Beatles' *Abby Road* was playing on the stereo. Evan's wife, Rebecca, came to meet them. She had long strawberry-blond hair that rested against a Laura Ashley cotton dress. She wore no makeup to enhance her natural beauty and looked as if she would fit in just as well in Haight-Ashbury as she would in a farmhouse in central Pennsylvania. She was holding her baby on her left hip.

"Cathy, this is my wife, Rebecca, and my son, Caleb. Rebby, this is Cathy."

Rebecca held out her available hand.

"So very nice to meet you, Cathy."

"It is my pleasure, Rebecca," Cathy said with sincerity. "What a beautiful baby! May I hold him?"

"Of course you may!" Rebecca said, happy to give her hip some relief.

Cathy took Caleb into her arms and held him against her as she kissed the top of his tiny head. Tony looked on and thought how maternal she looked.

"So, what can we get you two?" Evan asked as Rebecca went into the kitchen, after she greeted Tony with a friend's kiss on his cheek.

"White wine?" Tony asked, looking towards Cathy for a response. She nodded approval, and Evan left to retrieve it.

Cathy rocked Caleb. She had a natural rhythm, it seemed, almost as if God placed this innate ability in all women.

"You've done this before!" Tony said as he watched her with Caleb.

"What, hold a baby? Of course I have!" Cathy punctuated her statement by again kissing the top of Caleb's head. "Come here, Tony," Cathy said as she continued to rock, now quietly humming a lullaby—its lilt keeping with the rhythm of her motion.

"I want you to smell him. There is no sweeter fragrance on earth than the scent of a baby!"

Tony approached them, placed his arm around Cathy's waist, pressed his cheek against hers, and inhaled slowly and deeply. The combination of her soft skin against his face and the complementary mixture of her perfume with Caleb's sweet scent were almost more than he could handle.

Evan and Rebecca returned with a bottle of California Chablis and three glasses. Evan nudged Rebecca and smiled.

"So, what have you two been up to while we were gone?"

Caleb woke from his nap at the sound of his father's voice. He yawned widely and began to whimper.

"Someone's hungry," Rebecca said as she took Caleb from Cathy's arms. "Come with me, Cathy, while I feed this big guy. We can get acquainted"

Rebecca and Cathy retreated into the kitchen. It was a large country kitchen with a wood-planked floor. A brick fireplace took up one entire wall. Two cherry rocking chairs faced the fireplace and sat on the flat fieldstone hearth. A large black cast iron pot hung from a wrought iron bracket that allowed the pot to swing inside the fireplace. A brick-lined bread oven occupied a niche to the right of the firebox.

"Is this functional?" Cathy asked.

"As functional as we let it," Rebecca said with a smile. "Evan and I used to cook in it all the time—mostly game stews after a hunt. But since Caleb joined us, we've gotten away from it, relying more on the conventional oven. This remains our favorite spot in the house. Sitting in front of the fire, especially during the long Pennsylvania winters, reading a good book, and spending quality time with Evan, and now Caleb, is bliss."

Cathy and Rebecca sat in the rockers. Rebecca opened the front of her dress and began to nurse Caleb. Caleb took to her breast with vigor.

"Just like his dad!" Rebecca kidded.

"You seem so happy here, Rebecca."

"I have never been as content in all my life, Cathy." Rebecca kissed the top of Caleb's head. "After Evan finished vet school, we joined a commune in Oregon. It was back in the sixties. We were the original flower children. At the time, I thought that was true happiness. Living in community, sharing everything with one another. Holistic sharing. Body, mind and spirit sharing. During the day, we'd work in community for the common good. In the evening, we'd smoke some dope and solve the world's problems.

"One day, Evan and I came to the realization that the only community that was necessary was the community of him and me. We left that life and not even for one second did we look back."

Evan brought Cathy her wine. He handed her the glass.

"I need to see some ID," Evan said, laughing, as he turned, bent down and kissed Rebecca on the top of her head. "Can I get you some juice or something, dear?"

"Maybe later, hon."

The telephone rang. Evan walked over to the phone on the opposite wall.

"Hello? Yes, this is Doc Frick. How long has she been pushing? Is this her first foal?" Evan looked at his watch. "I'll be there in ten minutes, Sam." Evan hung up the phone. "I've got a mare in trouble. I'll be back as soon as I can." He kissed Rebby on the cheek and turned to Cathy. "I hope you don't mind if I take Tony with me."

Evan and Tony got into his Jeep Wrangler and headed for Sam's farm. The ragtop was down on the Jeep as it was a pleasant Indian summer night. They drove down past the apple orchard, where the Red Romes were full and heavy on the branch, begging to be picked.

"Almost time to make some cider." Evan inhaled the sweet night air of the orchard. "I love this time of year out in the country. Pity the poor city folk. They don't know what they're missing!"

Evan pulled up to the barn at the McCabe farm.

Sam was waiting for them.

"Thanks for coming, Doc! She looks pretty bad."

"Bring my bag, and the lantern, Tony," Evan said as he hurried into the barn.

Tony opened the back gate on the Jeep and removed a large leather satchel, and a dry cell lantern. He followed Evan into the barn.

The mare was lying on her side, and breathing heavily. She was lathered as if she had been running in the hot sun.

Evan opened his bag, took out a flashlight, and checked her pupils.

"She's in shock. Give her 100 mg of Morphine, Tony! And get some Epinephrine ready."

Tony took the vial of Morphine out of the bag and held it up to the single bare light bulb hanging from the overhead rafters above the mare.

"There's less than 5cc in the vial, Evan."

"OK, then give her Talwin!"

Tony took the vial of the narcotic, aspirated the appropriate dose into a large syringe and gave the mare an IM injection into her upper shank

Evan gloved and reached into the mare, feeling the foal's position.

"She's breach, all right! These things are all legs! When they get twisted, it's like trying to pass a grappling hook through a pop bottle!"

Evan attempted to correct the breach but couldn't.

"Start an IV, Tony! We're going to have to C-section her!"

Tony started the IV and handed Sam the bag of ringers, instructing him to hold it high, and not crimp the line. Evan prepared another syringe with lidocaine and attached a spinal needle. He palpated the horse's lumbar vertebrae. Between lumbar 2 and lumbar 4, he inserted the needle and slowly gave the spinal injection.

Evan checked the mare's pulse, holding two fingers along her carotid. He rechecked her pupils. He tapped her on her side.

"That a girl. You'll be fine!" Evan said, more for Sam's benefit than for the mare's.

Evan tested for analgesia with a sharp probe. He and Tony positioned themselves for the procedure, with Tony standing behind Evan, shining the lantern onto the surgical site as Evan swabbed her abdomen with a betadine-soaked gauze sponge. With a quick stroke of the scalpel blade, the arced incision was made. Evan pushed upon the mare's lower abdomen. Uterine access was gained and the foal exposed. Evan quickly extracted the foal, who immediately struggled to get free.

He placed both foal and placental sack next to the mare. Tony handed him the needle holder and suture, having prepared it while Evan re-approximated the incision.   .

He quickly closed, impressing Tony with his speed in suturing.

Evan gave the mare a carpule of Penicillin G, and then rechecked her pupils.

He degloved, as Tony took the bag of ringers from Sam.

"Good job, Sam!"

Tony attached the bag to a nail in the rafter above the mare, making sure that the flow rate was correct, and the line was not crimped.

Evan gave some post-op instructions to Sam, as he covered the mare with a blanket.

"Stay with her, and call me if there is any concern, Sam. I'll be back later tonight to check on her."

Tony finished tying and cutting the cord as the foal began to nurse.

"That reminds me how hungry I am, Evan."

Evan put his arm around Tony as they walked back to the Jeep.

"Are you sure that I can't talk you out of going to med school? I could use an associate like you!"

"Thanks, but no thanks, Evan. I want patients who have Blue Cross/Blue Shield."

On the way back to the house, on a winding country road, a white-tail deer appeared out of nowhere, jumped through the brush on the side of the road and directly in Evan's path. He hit the brakes and tried to swerve out of the way, but he couldn't avoid it. The Jeep hit the hindquarters and the right flank of the deer with a loud thud.

"Shit! I can't believe that just happened!"

Evan pulled onto the shoulder and put on his flashers. He opened the back of the Jeep and retrieved the lantern. The deer had made it to the side of the road before collapsing. She had complex fractures of both hind legs. Her abdomen was beginning to distend. Tony brought Evan's bag and set it beside him. He took out his stethoscope and placed it on the fawn's flank. Gurgling sounds came from her lungs. Froth formed on her mouth and blood poured from her nostrils. Her breathing was labored and irregular.

"Can we move her?" Tony asked.

Evan shook his head. He took a vial—Tony couldn't see what it was— filled a syringe and injected into the fawn's femoral vein. The deer went limp, and expired.

"Euthanasia?" Tony asked.

Evan nodded. "She wasn't going to make it, Tony. She sustained liver damage. Hepatic hemorrhage is tough to deal with. When pulmonary edema occurs that quickly the only recourse is to put them down."

"How do you make sense of this?" Tony asked, realizing as he did that he had just come face to face with a great irony. He had just witnessed Evan's gifts, skill, and energy bringing a life into the world. At the same time, his skill maintained an existing life. Moments later, he witnessed those skills being used to remove one.

Life's ironies are rarely presented so graphically, and in such a short time frame—served up for people with caring thought to ponder.

"I don't even try, Tony. Life is laced with irony. There is also no great shortage of tragedy. What I have learned is to always try and apply the best of yourself to any situation. Sometimes the best is to choose the lesser of two evils. Sometimes the best is extreme self-sacrifice. Sometimes the best is knowing when to throw in the towel. Always, the best is to rest in the comfort of your decision."

The two men drove in silence for several minutes—Tony, reflecting on the wisdom of Evan's statement; Evan, resting in the comfort of his decision.

Evan pulled into his garage. He walked around the front of his Jeep and looked at the right fender. Dried blood and fur stuck to the paint. Tony opened the back gate and removed the satchel.

"I'd better replenish the drugs and supplies that we used."

"Thanks, man! Then let's get cleaned up and enjoy the rest of the evening."

Tony went into the clinic. The clinic area was a structure that was added to the once detached garage. It occupied the space between the garage and the house. The local carpenters that Evan hired matched the Early American saltbox architecture of the farmhouse, so that it looked more like an extension of the original house than an addition.

He replenished the satchel's contents and then used the washroom to clean himself before dinner.

He entered the house through a door that led to a hallway just off the kitchen. He found Cathy and Rebecca setting the table.

"Tony! This is for you!" Rebecca said as she handed him a glass of the Chablis that Evan opened earlier.

"I understand that you earned it!"

"I didn't do anything, really. Evan may need one though. He's an incredible guy, that husband of yours!" Tony said with sincere admiration.

"I just sent that incredible guy upstairs to shower! He was incredibly messy!" Rebecca said with a smile. "I hope that you two don't mind if we eat here in the kitchen. It's so much homier than the dining room," Rebecca continued as she lit the candles in the center of the table.

The kitchen table was antique cherry and went with the early-American décor. It was round and about four feet in diameter. Four ladder-back chairs were equally spaced around it. Cathy was folding the last of the linen napkins. She picked up her glass and walked over to Tony.

"You have some wonderful friends!" She tapped his glass with hers. "Rebecca and I really got to know each other while you were gone."

"Terrific! You'll have to tell me all about her sometime, Rebby!" Tony said, turning to Rebecca.

Evan entered and accepted the glass of wine offered by Rebecca, as he kissed her on the cheek. He looked at his watch.

"Wow! It's nearly ten p.m. I am so sorry, you two!" Evan said to Cathy and Tony.

"If you marry a doctor, you'll have to get used to eating at strange hours!" Rebecca said to Cathy, as she winked at Tony.

The four sat at the table. Evan said grace—thanking God for the bounty as well as for the gift of family and friendships. For the next hour and a half, the four ate, laughed, and got to know each other as only people can by breaking bread together. Intermixed with small talk of recipe exchanges and polite comments about "how ever do you get your rice to not stick so" were deep conversations and sharing. Debates and dialogue flowed on life's important issues and philosophies as well as on politics and the economy. They talked about Camus and modern thought; about veterinary medicine and public relations; about pre-med classes and rug weaving; about the importance of laughing and the need for weeping. About OPEC and cats.

At the end of the evening, as Tony and Cathy prepared to leave, they all hugged as old friends do when saying good-bye.

Evan took Tony aside as Cathy and Rebecca walked to Tony's bike.

"She's a keeper, man!"

"Tell me something that I don't already know, Evan!"

Tony and Cathy pulled up to the Kappa house. He walked her to the door.

"Tony, I really enjoyed myself tonight. More than I can ever remember on a first date. I hope that you will call me again."

Tony held her hand and kissed her gently on her full lips, caressing her cheek with his other hand's open palm.

That first kiss, as innocent as it was, was everything that Tony imagined it to be, and more. Over the course of the next year, Tony would come to a fuller awareness of what Cathy would mean in his life. His joy that night was complete. Not in the sense of his reaching the fullness of what his relationship with Cathy could be, but complete in the sense that he could not have handled any more bliss at that given point in time.

He kick-started his motorcycle, revved the engine repeatedly and drove home—the wheels never touching the ground. Or so it seemed.

Chapter 6

Christmas break 1973

Charlie tossed his duffel bag into the trunk of his 1970 Porsche and started on the seven-hour drive to Pittsburgh. He finished his last final exam at eleven that morning, turned in his paper on "Ethical Choices in Twentieth-Century Thought" to Professor Peterson at noon, and was now ready for Christmas vacation. The air was crisp, clear and cold. The sun, low in the northern Indiana sky, glistened off of the golden dome as he drove through the Notre Dame campus. The red Porsche was a gift to Charlie from his older brother, Robert, when Charlie received his acceptance to Notre Dame. Robert, a judge in the third circuit court of appeals, had always wanted to go there. He was, in a sense, living his life through Charlie, as is often the case when either children or younger siblings fulfill one's own shattered dreams.

Charlie took the ticket at the tollbooth and headed east on the Indiana turnpike towards Pittsburgh. He was looking forward to spending some time with Cathy during the Christmas break. Their relationship had cooled somewhat during the fall term due in no small part to the fact that Cathy was now also seeing Tony. Charlie disliked the idea of sharing Cathy with anyone. It was a major blow to his enormous ego. In the past, it had always been Charlie who ended or cooled a relationship. He had no prior experience at being on the receiving end of what he perceived to be mild emotional exile. He did not enjoy it. He vowed to change things. He intended to turn the heat up on their relationship, and the three-week furlough from classes, books and study provided the opportunity for his undivided attention to be focused on Cathy.

Back home, Charlie's parents were preparing for his return with excited anticipation. He was the youngest of their four sons, born late in their life—a surprise pregnancy, when Mrs.Vantare was in her mid forties and Mr. Vantare was approaching fifty. The older siblings would often tease Charlie, telling him that he should have been named Joseph and been presented a multi-colored coat.

Mr. Vantare was comfortable in his retirement, having invested well the money that he made in life through business-leverage deals. It's amazing how money can grow.

He spoiled Charlie shamelessly. The entire family did. Charlie not only loved it, he grew accustomed to it and expected it. This expectation spilled over into all areas of his life.

The Indiana turnpike in mid-December is a colorless, monotonous drive. Charlie's thoughts turned towards Cathy. How could any other man hold a position in her heart? How dare she throw him crumbs when Charlie was used to only the first fruits? Charlie shifted into overdrive and leaned into the accelerator with a heavy foot. The highway divider stripes raced towards him with increased frequency as he sped towards Pittsburgh in the hopes of regaining Cathy's undivided attentions.

Mrs. Irene Vantare was preparing a late lunch for her husband, Alfonse. Her spacious kitchen was a comfort zone for her, not so much because she enjoyed cooking, but because it provided her with her own space—away from her demanding and domineering husband. She was a dutiful wife—not because she desired to please Mr. Vantare, but because he expected it. Mr. Vantare was used to getting what he expected.

Irene and Alfonse had raised their four sons in this large house in the Upper St. Claire suburb of Pittsburgh. Even though the nest had emptied, Alfonse refused to downsize. He insisted on maintaining the five-bedroom residence, expecting his family to gather there on every holiday. He was used to getting what he expected.

Irene melted butter in a cast iron skillet. She removed the centers from two one-inch thick slices of Italian bread, leaving a halo one inch wide encircling the space, contained by the hard crust. She buttered these as well and placed them in the hot skillet, flipping them over when the downside had turned a light yellow-brown. She broke an egg into each bread center and added salt, pepper and a pinch of oregano. Bird's nest eggs were Alfonse's favorite.

She set a place for one at the table, poured a glass of Cribari vino rosso and stationed it next to the plate. She filled a carafe from the gallon jug and placed it on the table as well.

"Alfonse! Lunch is ready," Irene called out with a degree of indifference.

She turned back toward the stove as Alfonse entered the kitchen. He was a ruggedly handsome man. Many thought that he reminded them of Anthony Quinn, the actor.

"Are the eggs cold? I hate cold eggs, Irene!" Alfonse said, without any other greeting.

64

"I just took them out of the skillet when I called you, Alfonse. If they are cold, it's not my fault."

Alfonse took a knife and fork to the bird's nest. Steam rose from the eggs. He blew on his fork as he lifted the bread and egg to his mouth, without saying a word of apology.

"So, what time is Charlie due home?" Alfonse asked as he chewed his lunch, not looking up at Irene.

"He left Notre Dame at around noon. He should be home by seven p.m. or so." Irene poured another cup of coffee for herself, not looking in Alfonse's direction.

He took a sip of the wine and continued to speak, with his mouth open—full of the wine, bread and egg mixture.

"It will be good to see my son. I miss him so much!"

"Yes, Alfonse, it will be good to see *our* son," Irene countered.

"Robert is coming over tonight to see Charlie. He was in court all day yesterday and today, hearing testimony, yet he's coming over to see Charlie," Alfonse said as he took another sip of the wine.

Robert was their first-born, and the brightest of their four sons. He was twenty-five years older than Charlie and Charlie was more like a son to him than a younger brother. He treated him as such.

Alfonse's business ventures were struggling early on, bringing him to near bankruptcy twice. Therefore, Robert grew up in an entirely different environment than his youngest sibling. He worked all through high school and college, where he attended the University of Pittsburgh on a full academic scholarship. After graduating summa cum laude, he attended the Georgetown University School of Law—graduated with honors and was named to the *Law Review*. He was clerking for a state supreme court justice when Charlie was born. Even though he was twenty-five years old and a member of the Bar, Robert still came home on weekends to the family home in Upper St. Claire that his father bought when Robert was a sophomore in college. Alfonse expected it. Alfonse was used to getting what he expected.

"Frank and Vinny will be over tomorrow night with the children. It will be good to have everyone together." Irene looked out of the kitchen window, pushing the curtain aside with an open hand.

"I hope that it doesn't snow. At least not until Charlie gets home," Irene said as she stared blankly at the cold and overcast December day. Sandwiched between the gloom of a sunless winter's afternoon and a loveless marriage, she gazed at the large oak tree that stood in the center of their backyard. She could feel winter's chill through the insulated glass pane as she stared at the oak's leafless branches reaching for the gray December sky. She let the curtain fall back into place as a light snow began to fall.

Tony rang the doorbell at the Kappa house. He pulled his collar up to block the cold December wind as it blew across the Bucknell campus. Mrs. Smyth opened the door and smiled.

"Hello, Tony! Come in before you catch your death."

Tony loved her English accent and told her often that he did.

"Top of the morn'n to you, darl'n," Tony said in an attempted Irish accent, just to tease the housemother.

"If I've told you once, I've told you ten thousand times, Mr. Cipullo, there's no love lost between we Brits and the Irish!"

"You know that I love you, Mrs. Smyth. I only tease the ones that I love!" Tony said with a smile.

"I'll forgive you this one last time, mister. One day, that charm of yours may run out!" she said as she closed the door. "Now behave yourself, or I'll not be ring'n for that lass of yours!" she continued, mocking an Irish accent of her own.

Mrs. Smyth went to ring for Cathy as Tony went into the living room to wait. He held a business-sized envelope tightly in his left hand as he paced back and forth in anticipation.

Cathy entered the room. Tony turned and stared at her for a brief moment, as he was accustomed to doing whenever they met.

"Do you ever look bad?" he asked in all seriousness.

"Quit it! Why do you always have to be so melodramatic, Tony? It's embarrassing!"

Tony approached her and they embraced. He kissed her gently on the cheek.

"I've got some fantastic news," he whispered, punctuating his statement by blowing gently into her ear.

He handed her the envelope as she shivered slightly from the stimulation of his breath. It was from the University of Pittsburgh School of Medicine, addressed to Mr. Antonio Cipullo.

"Tony! You were accepted?"

A look of excitement and joy for him lit up her face.

"How wonderful!"

Tony put his arms around her waist, picked her up, and spun her around, drawing her close to his body as he did so.

"Oh, Tony, I'm so very, very happy for you! I know how much you've wanted this!" Cathy said as Tony set her down and wiped a tear from his eye.

66

"...Since I was ten years old!"

"What a great Christmas present, Tony!"

"I know! So, what did YOU get me?" Tony added, injecting his sense of humor into the scene, almost as if some comic relief was necessary, lest he break down and weep fully.

"I'm also so very proud of you, Tony! You're going to be a very good doctor. Those people at the University of Pittsburgh really know their beans, picking you!" Cathy said as she hugged him again.

"I still can't believe it!" Tony said, holding up the letter. "Pinch me, Cathy! I must be dreaming. I can't believe how my life has been enhanced since meeting you—I mean things have just fallen right into place for me. Here I am halfway through my senior year, all my core courses have been completed for my degree, my acceptance to the program of my choice realized—now I'm coasting, taking electives that I can do standing on my head. No more cutthroat competition for grades—no more all-nighters. I have a couple of weeks off to do nothing but chill, recharge and spend time with you. Go ahead, pinch me!"

Tony walked with Cathy out into the hall, where Cathy had set her two suitcases.

"Did I miss a memo? Were we supposed to take ALL of our clothes back home for the Christmas break?" Tony teased.

He picked up the bags, uttering an exaggerated grunt to punctuate his statement. They said good-bye to Mrs. Smyth, wishing her the merriest of Christmases. She thanked Tony for the bath soaps that he had given her as a gift as she opened the door.

"You two have a wonderful Christmas as well. Behave yourselves!" Mrs. Smyth added maternally.

Tony and Cathy walked to the curb, where Dan was waiting for them in his 1960 Chevy Bellaire, with the engine running. Dan was driving home to Akron, Ohio. He was giving Cathy a ride to Youngstown, Ohio, and dropping Tony off in Pittsburgh on the way.

"You two know what OPEC is doing to gasoline prices? What have you and Dr. Kildare been doing in there, while I'm out here with my engine running to keep from freezing my ass off?" Dan kidded.

"One more word out of you, and we'll not grace you with our presence for the ride back home," Tony retorted.

Tony and Dan had been the best of friends since they were freshman roommates, which in and of itself is the college equivalency of a sibling relationship. As in life, so it is with roommates—some brothers are closer than others. Tony and Dan were close.

They pledged the fraternity together, going through all the harassment that the "hell week" process entailed: from swallowing live goldfish, being "tarred and feathered" with maple syrup and cornflakes, carrying bricks tied around their necks everywhere they went, to not bathing for the entire week. The kind of ordeals that form a bond between fraternity brothers that non-participants can never fully understand.

"Has he been drinking?" Cathy whispered to Tony.

"Of course not! It's noon! Danny's not an alcoholic. He parties hardy, I know, but he would never drink and drive. Please don't worry."

Tony lifted the trunk and placed Cathy's bags next to his. He and Cathy got into the backseat.

"What am I now—a chauffeur?" Dan teased, referring to the seating arrangement.

"Now here's an interesting quandary. Whatever shall I do—sit up front with Danny or in the backseat with Cathy? Danny-Cathy. Danny-Cathy." Tony said as he held both hands out, elevating one, lowering the other, as if to portray a balancing scale.

Cathy wrapped her arms around Tony's upper arm and squeezed tightly. "You're not going anywhere, big guy!"

"Boy! A guy gets into medical school, and now all of a sudden, he forgets all about the little shits that he met on the way up!"

"Don't sell yourself so short, Danny. I think that you're a very big shit. Really, I do!"

Dan looked into the rearview mirror and pulled into the traffic. The three headed for Pittsburgh. "With a little help from my friends" by the Beatles was playing on the radio. Dan sang along. Tony smiled at the coincidence.

"You know, Cath, when I was saying how positive my life has been since meeting you, I wasn't kidding. I can tell you something now. A miracle occurred on the day that I met you."

"I don't know if I'd quite call it a miracle, Tony," Cathy interrupted.

"No, listen. I've told you how my mother was making novenas for my application process to medical school. She's a sainted woman, my mother. My grades were good, but so were the grades of the four thousand other applicants vying for the hundred forty positions in the first year class."

"So?"

"So, she was asking for divine intervention—something to set me apart from the other 3,999 or so applicants."

"And?"

"I've never told you this. I didn't think that I should until, when and if, I received an acceptance notice"

"What is it, Tony?"

"The anti-war rally occurred on the ninth day."

"Ninth day?"

"Yes, the last day of my mother's novena. That boy at the anti-war rally —the one that I helped—his name was James Tobin."

"So?"

"I received a thank you letter, from his father, James W. Tobin, MD. He had contacted campus police, who sent him a copy of the accident report. My name was on the report. James' friends told Dr. Tobin what had happened. He thanked me for my immediate attention to his son, and that he was certain that my intervention was exactly what the situation called for."

"What are you saying, Tony?"

"Two weeks later, I had my personal interview at Pitt's medical school. The Dean of Admissions, the one who interviewed me, was Dr. James W. Tobin."

Cathy placed her hand on Tony's knee.

"Oh Tony! I feel shivers."

"That miracle happened on the day that we met. It was also the reason that we met. Everything has been going right in my life ever since."

Dan headed north on Rt. 322 toward the Appalachian Thruway and Christmas vacation.

In her modest kitchen, in the "Little Italy" section of Bloomfield—an ethnic inter-city neighborhood of Pittsburgh—Philomena Cipullo pounded her fist into the bread dough. She took a handful of flour and sprinkled it over the mass of dough and pounded it again. Her mother-in-law, Angelina, sat at the table, cranking the pasta machine. As the linguine emerged, she draped them over her extended hand, leading the strands out and away from the chromed roller. She placed them over the wooden rack to dry. Philomena's husband, Joseph, and his brother, Dominick, were drinking homemade wine and eating dried sweet sausage and Italian bread.

"Is there any mortadella left, Philomena?" Joseph asked, referring to the fatty peppercorn- and garlic-laced lunchmeat.

"Joseph, God gave you two legs. You see that I have flour all over my hands. Look in the icebox!" Philomena said, pointing to the refrigerator.

"My brother, Dominick, looks hungry. That's why I asked."

"Dominick has two legs too!" Philomena said.

Dominick laughed, as he reached for another piece of the sweet sausage.

"Sopprosatta sta bene!"

He knocked over his glass, spilling wine on the table.

"A fa nabila! Managia madigan!" Dominick swore in their southern Italian dialect.

"Dominico, sta ta zee!" Angelina corrected her younger son, in her native tongue.

"Mi scusi, Mama."

"We are in America, Dominick. If you must swear, then swear in English!" Philomena joked.

"Remember, Philomena, Antonio likes his pasta al olio *al dente!*" Joseph said.

"You're telling me, his mama, how he likes his pasta? As if I didn't know! Va fungule!" Philomena shouted.

"If you must swear, Philomena, then please swear in English!" Dominick teased.

Dominick and Joseph laughed out loud, knowing that they set her up nicely.

The Cipullo family was very closely knit. It was not at all uncommon in Italian households for three generations to live under one roof. Zia Angelina, Joseph's mother, lived on the first floor of the modest three-story brick house. The first floor consisted of a small living room, a bedroom and a kitchen. Joseph added a small bathroom, off the bedroom, about ten years ago. Prior to that, Angelina would have to go down to the basement to use the commode. The second floor consisted of a kitchen, dining room, bathroom and small living room. The third floor had two bedrooms, one for Philomena and Joseph, and one for Antonio and his younger brother, Gino.

Dominick, Joseph's younger brother, lived six houses up the street, but he spent most of his time at "the house."

Philomena looked up at the kitchen clock. She continued to kneed the dough.

"Gino will be home from school at three o'clock. I need to send him to the market for more tomato paste. Antonio should be here by four o'clock. I need to make my pizza sauce."

Ever since Tony left for college, Philomena would make his favorite meal upon his return for Christmas break. It was a simple meal, yet rich in tradition and memories. It consisted of homemade linguine in a sauce of olive oil and garlic, served with homemade pizza.

"My nephew deserves the best!" Dominick said, more the wine talking than anything else.

"Then why don't YOU go to the market for the tomato paste?" Philomena asked.

"God gave Gino two good legs. I might have flour on my hands."

Joseph laughed, as did Angelina and Philomena. It was good to have family. It was good to be close. It was good that Antonio was coming home.

It was nearly 4:00 p.m. when Dan pulled up in front of Tony's parents' home. It took him three attempts to finally parallel-park the Chevy.

"I'm not used to these city streets and curb parking." He turned off the ignition.

"Why is it that large cities have such small parking places?" he continued.

"Pittsburgh is hardly a big city, Danny," Tony said.

"It is compared to Akron and Lewisburg!"

Tony leaned forward toward the front seat. "Just admit that you are a shitty parker, Danny—don't blame Pittsburgh's streets!"

"Shitty Parker? Hey, I used to date her cousin, Kitty. Kitty Parker—in high school. I seem to remember that she LIKED my parking!" Dan turned around and exaggerated a wide smile.

Tony turned to Cathy. "I can't believe that you are finally going to meet my family, Cath!"

Cathy had heard all about Tony's family. He spoke of them often. She envied the closeness of his family's bonds—coming herself from an unhappy home life with an abusive, alcoholic father. She had heard all about Tony's younger brother, Gino, who had just turned sixteen and called Tony every week—sometimes from home, sometimes from Uncle Dominick's to keep the family phone bill down. He often would seek Tony's advice for everything important in his life, from unrequited puppy love to how to head-fake a defender in football—whatever THAT meant. She got the impression that he idolized, if not adored his older brother.

She had heard all about the loving relationship between his parents. How they teased one another. How his father allowed his mother to believe that she was in charge of the house—often calling her "boss." How his father's work ethic and love of his children was definitive. How his mother had homespun wisdom and common sense, but little formal education. How she was giving and generous to a fault, often going without for the sake of others.

Cathy had heard all about his bachelor Uncle Dominick—how he was at Tony's house every single day. How close he was to Tony's father. How they labored hard every day together laying brick. How they would come home and sit around the kitchen table—their large, callused hands lifting glasses of homemade wine to their parched lips. How they both insisted that Tony work with them in the summers through high school, moving pallets of bricks and buckets of mortar to the laborers on top of scaffolds in the hot sun, so that he would appreciate the value of an education.

She had heard all about Tony's grandmother, to whom Tony lovingly referred as Zia Angelina. How everyone in the neighborhood called her Zia out of respect, even though Zia literally meant "Aunt." How she lived downstairs in Tony's house. How she spoiled him, not with money or *things*, but rather, tending to the important areas in life, with love and support—nurturing, maternal, accessible love and support.

Cathy had seen photographs—as if one could really come to know someone through a photograph. She was anxious to meet this colorful group in person—her anticipation adding to her excitement.

Tony took his bag out of Dan's trunk. He, Dan and Cathy walked up the concrete steps to the front porch of the Cipullo house at 527 Marta Street.

"You are in store for a real feast, Cath," Dan said as they approached the front door. "My mom doesn't even make me dinner when I come home on break. She knows that I'm stopping here first. No competition! It's all about eating here at the Cipullos'."

Tony opened the front door and followed Cathy inside. Dan closed the door behind him.

The sweet aromas from the second-floor kitchen filled the house and greeted the three friends with the promise of home cooking—a welcomed departure from college cafeteria food.

"I'ma home!" Tony called up to the second floor with an obvious attempt to imitate Zia Angelina's accent.

As they climbed the stairs, Philomena came out of the kitchen to meet them on the landing at the top of the stairs, wiping her hands on her apron.

"Antonio!" She embraced her son on the landing. "My son the doctor! We are so proud of you!" Philomena made the sign of the cross and then kissed the knuckle of her index finger as reverent punctuation. She folded her hands and looked up to heaven. "Grazie, mio Dio! Grazie Jesu Cristo! Grazie Santa Jude!"

"I could not have done it without your prayers, Mama!" Tony said as he kissed her on the cheek. He turned to Cathy. "Mama, this is Cathy, who I told you about."

"Hello, Cathy." Philomena wiped her hands again on her apron and shook Cathy's hand.

"Very nice to meet you, Mrs. Cipullo. I've heard so much about you!"

"Hello, Mama Cipullo!" Dan said as he embraced Philomena.

"Danny, you look too thin!"

"Mama, you always say that Danny looks too thin!" Tony laughed.

"Come, Cathy, meet the family. Danny, you need to eat more. Veni qua. A mangia!"

An Italian woman's credo is that the way to a man's heart is always through his digestive tract. It was the best way that Philomena knew how to show her love. It came easily to her.

She loved Danny like another son. He stayed with the Cipullos in the summer between his and Tony's freshman and sophomore year, working construction with Uncle Dominick and Papa Cipullo.

"He'll last one week!" Uncle Dominick had said when he saw Dan for the first time in that summer of 1971.

"Too skinny. No muscle. Madigan!"

The Cipullo brothers worked Tony and Dan like dogs that hot and humid summer—trying to either break them or give them the opportunity to show their "stuff," whichever came first. It was for their own good, they rationalized. Work ethic. Value development. Prioritizing choices in life.

The higher they set the bar, the more the boys responded. Tony, because he was a Cipullo. Dan, because he wanted to be. After three weeks, Papa Cipullo was convinced. When they completed the PNB job in Lawrenceville, he put his arm around Dan as they walked to the truck.

"Good work, *son*. You moved more mud and bricks today than I could have done at your age! Let's go eat!"

It was a rite of passage for Dan. He felt that he belonged—survived another pledge's hell week and now was admitted into another fraternity of sorts. He turned and looked back at Tony, who gave him the "thumbs up." It was a good day. All was right with the world, and with Dan's self-esteem. He had never felt as good—before, or since.

The three friends walked into the kitchen behind Philomena. Joseph and Dominick got up from their seats at the table. Angelina remained seated. Tony embraced his father, and then his uncle.

"Dr. Antonio Cipullo. I like the sound of that, my son!"

"My arm hurts, Tony. Can you fix it?" Dominick joked.

Tony then went over, bent down and hugged Angelina as he kissed her on the cheek. She whispered something in his ear.

"I know, Zia Angelina…I know!"

Dan repeated Tony's actions as Tony spoke.

"Papa, Uncle Dominick, Zia Angelina, this is Cathy, my friend from school."

"Hello, Cathy," Joseph said as he shook her hand. Dominick did the same.

Cathy approached Zia Angelina and extended her hand to her. "Buon giorno, Zia Angelina."

"Buon giorno, signorina." Angelina smiled at Cathy's attempt to speak

Italian. She turned to Philomena. "Madigan?"

"Si, Mama. Madigan."

Whether one's name was Smith, whose ancestors came over on the Mayflower, or Kosikowski, fresh off of the boat from Poland—if you were not of Italian descent, then you were a madigan—southern Italian dialect for an "American."

Angelina shrugged as if to say that one can't win them all.

"Tony, Danny, Cathy, a glass of wine to celebrate!" Joseph said as he poured three more glasses from the gallon jug on the table.

"Where's the sopprosatta?" Joseph asked, looking at the spot on the table where the dish had been a minute ago.

"I hid it when Danny came in," Dominick teased. "I don't like to waste good sopprosatta on madigans like him!"

He then grabbed Dan around the neck and rubbed the top of his head. "Maybe I should bring it back out. You're getting too skinny, Danny!"

"Uncle Dominick. Haven't you heard? I'm no longer a madigan. I'm changing my name from Dan Vincent to Dan Vincenzo," Dan teased back.

Dominick grabbed his crouch. "It takes more than an Italian name to make you an Italian, Danny!"

"Dominico!"

"Mi scusi, Mama."

Tony looked at Cathy as if to apologize for his uncle's crude gesture.

Cathy felt out of place, and Tony saw this.

"Cath, have you ever had sopprasatta?"

Tony took the plate of the dry sweet Italian sausage from the chair where Uncle Dominick had hid it from Danny. He cut her a slice, along with a slice of the Reggianno parmagiano cheese, and broke a large piece of the hard-crusted home-baked bread at the table.

"It's so fatty!" Cathy said as Tony handed it to her.

Angelina looked at her as if she had insulted her directly.

"It's not as bad as it looks. Trust me." Tony took the knife from the table and cut a slice from an orange and a wedge from a peach that were in the basket at the center of the table. "These will cut the fat taste. Guarda!" Tony took the sausage and, placing it on the bread, took a bite. He chewed slowly to release the flavors. He took a sip of the wine, a bite of the cheese, and another sip of the wine. He took a bite of the orange and then the peach and another sip of the wine.

"It's all about chemistry! The flavor combinations and the release of the flavors—the pork, the garlic, the fennel , the peppercorn, the spices of the sausage and the sharp bite of the cheese—as you combine them with the wine and citrus—they just explode in your mouth! The sweetness of the peach is needed as if to bring you back down to earth, and complete the sensation, almost as a dessert."

Cathy took a bite of the sausage. She made a face. "Maybe it's an acquired taste."

"No, Cath. La trippa, polipo and calamari are acquired tastes. Sopprosatta is a *required* taste."

Cathy took a sip of the wine. She made another face. "That's strong!"

"It's homemade. Here, try this."

Tony took the knife and sliced more of the orange and the peach. He placed them into her glass, stirring it with the knife. "Let it sit for a moment."

This all was a bit of a cultural shock for Cathy. It was a huge departure from her home life. When she would arrive home from break, she would expect to be greeted by her unhappy mother. She would greet Cathy, with a clinging embrace—not unlike one would expect observing someone clinging to a life vest after a boating accident. Cathy found it to be more sad than anything else. If her father were sober, he would be distant, quiet—a million miles away, mentally and emotionally, if not physically. They would sit in the living room in silence punctuated with meaningless small talk.

"So how are your classes this term, dear?"

"Fine. Just fine, Mother."

"Have you made any new friends, dear?"

"Not really, Mother."

"Anything new at the sorority?"

"No, Mother."

Mr. Mathias would stare blankly toward the wall. He would not say a word, as if he had lost the ability or the desire to communicate. Cathy would look at him. "Sober," she would say, experienced as she was in the differential diagnosis between sobriety and drunkenness—between behavior not in the "grasp" and being in the clutches of the netherworld, as she would come to call it. If he had been drinking, his behavior, depending on the amount of alcohol consumed, would range from verbal abuse and rude condescension to actual physical acts, such as throwing objects. Either way, he was not the father that she knew growing up—the man who took her to the zoo or to the park, to swing and slide. "Could chemicals alter a man's person—redefine him?" she would often ask. Obviously, they could, and did. They redefined the family as well.

They were all trapped within the web of substance abuse—pawns under the control of unknown as well as distilled spirits.

Tony's brother, Gino, came in the front door and ran up the steps to join everyone in the kitchen. Tony got up from his seat and they embraced, slapping each other on the back several times.

"Tony, I'm so glad you're home! Mama had me run some carciofi over to Coomahda Madronne's. I told her that you were coming home, and that I couldn't stay, but she insisted that I eat some of her mulignon."

"Man, her mulignons rule!" Tony said. "Did you bring me some?"

"I finished them."

"Gino!"

"Sorry, Mama. I didn't want to insult Coomahda!" Gino said, shrugging.

The sounds of laughter and antipasti conversations continued until they were interrupted by Mama Cipullo calling everyone into the dining room for dinner. Cathy discovered that mealtime at the Cipullo's was not merely a time to ingest food, but rather, it was truly a social event—a time to communicate and to bond. A time for instruction and debate. A time for questions and answers. A time for teasing and for laughter. A time for remembering and for prediction.

"May I help you, Mrs. Cipullo?" Cathy asked.

"Thank you, Cathy, but you are a guest. Please go sit over there, next to Tony." Mrs. Cipullo looked over at Zia Angelina and nodded, as if to give her approval of Cathy's offer.

Mr. Cipullo said grace after everyone was seated—a sign of the cross and a brief blessing.

"E Cattolica ella?" Zia Angelina whispered to Mrs. Cipullo.

"Si, Mama."

Tony leaned and whispered to Cathy, "My grandmother wanted to know if you were Catholic. I guess that one out of two ain't bad! I shudder to think what would have happened if I brought a Protestant madigan home to meet the family!"

Mrs. Cipullo placed what appeared to be a stale toasted piece of Italian bread into Cathy's bowl. Cathy looked at Tony in moderate disbelief. She whispered, "I was expecting a little more elaborate fare."

"What, you don't like prison-camp cuisine?" Tony joked. "Aspetto. We are going to show you how we recycle day-old bread."

Cathy watched Mr. Cipullo drizzle some olive oil onto the bread. Mrs. Cipullo brought in a large dish of cooked greens and set it on the table. Mr. Cipullo motioned to Cathy. "Mange, Cathy."

"Oh, please, Mr. Cipullo, you go first."

Mr. Cipullo took a large forkful of the cooked escarole, canaloni beans and sliced sausage, and placed it on the Italian bread. He sprinkled black and red pepper and a generous spoonful of grated cheese on top of the dish. Cutting it with a knife and fork, he took a large bite. He motioned with a wave of his fork for Cathy to proceed. "Scarole sta bene, Philomena!"

Dominick served Angelina and Philomena, then himself. He passed the dish to Tony.

"It's *verds and beans* or *scarole,* Cath. It's almost like a hot salad. You'll like it!" Tony said as he served Cathy.

"Mama Cipullo, you read my mind. How did you know that I wanted some of your scarole?" Dan asked. "They don't serve this up at Bucknell."

"Looking at you, they don't serve ANYTHING up at Bucknell. You'd better eat two bowls!" Uncle Dominick kidded.

"It's delicious, Mrs. Cipullo," Cathy said with sincerity.

"Thank you. It's very simple to make. It's what we call depression food. During the Great Depression, when food was scarce and money was short, you could feed a family of six for pennies, without the pork, of course."

The conversation began with stories of the Depression, and then moved on to happier subjects. They ate and conversed for more than an hour. After the last course, a bowl of fruit and a dish of nuts were placed in front of Cathy, as Mrs. Cipullo went to get the cake and espresso. Angelina helped clear the table.

"I'm stuffed! I couldn't possibly eat another thing, Tony."

"Rookie!" Dan teased.

More pleasantries were exchanged, until Cathy looked at Tony. "I really have to be going, Tony. I told my mother that I'd be home by eight p.m."

Cathy and Dan said their good-byes with promises of returning sometime soon. Tony walked them to the car.

"Thanks for coming. I hope you enjoyed my family."

"I did. I really did, Tony."

Tony kissed her and told her that he would call tomorrow. He instructed Dan to be careful. The car pulled out and headed toward the Pennsylvania Turnpike and Youngstown Ohio.

The flower delivery truck pulled up to the lower middle-class suburban home in Youngstown, Ohio. The delivery person opened the double swinging doors of the van. He checked his invoice and removed two items—a long-stem white flower box—the larger variety, with a red ribbon and bow securing the lid to the box proper—and an arrangement with a porcelain vase.

He walked up to the front door at 1233 Rosemount Drive. He rang the bell. The door was answered by a middle-aged woman in a housedress. She looked tired—a fatigue that goes beyond mere physical spending. She appeared to be emotionally spent as well—as if she had been crying.

"Is this the Mathias residence?" the delivery person asked as he looked down at the invoice.

"Yes, it is."

He handed her the arrangement and then the long white box. "Have a very happy holiday!"

"Thank you—same to you." Mrs. Mathias closed the front door with her foot and walked into the kitchen, where she placed the arrangement in the center of the table. She placed the flower box on the chair. Opening the card pinned to the tissue paper covering the arrangement, she reached for her reading glasses.

The arrangement was from Charlie to Mathias. He told her how much he looked forward to seeing her over the holidays.

"What a nice boy! Notre Dame, too!" she thought out loud.

She poured another cup of coffee and sat at the table waiting for Cathy's arrival, staring without expression towards the flower arrangement.

Charlie saw Robert's Mercedes in their parents' driveway as he pulled in. Robert greeted him at the door with a firm handshake. "Welcome home, Charlie! Mom and Dad are in the kitchen waiting for you! Before we go in, I've got some great news for you! I wanted to be the one to tell you!"

Robert reached into the inside lapel pocket of his suit coat, which was draped over the banister in the large foyer. He pulled out a business-sized envelope addressed to Judge Robert Vantare.

"It's from Dean Coyne at Georgetown Law. Congratulations! You've been accepted! You, young man, are going places—the sky's the limit!"

Charlie took the envelope but didn't read it. He had expected the notification as one expects the morning newspaper delivery—wondering, not if it would come, but when.

Dean Coyne and Robert were classmates together at Georgetown. They remained close and in contact with one another. This notification was a given, and Charlie knew it.

"Let's go tell Mom and Dad the good news!" Robert put his arm around his younger brother's shoulder as they walked into the kitchen—mentor and legacy, side by side, walking towards a bright future as well as towards the kitchen.

That Christmas break of 1973 saw Cathy's time divided equally between Charlie's and Tony's attention and affection.

There were romantic evenings with Charlie at expensive restaurants that overlooked the Pittsburgh skyline from high atop Mt. Washington—Charlie picking her up in luxury cars with soft leather seats—sending her long-stemmed roses with cards expressing even softer words of love and regard. They attended parties at homes with large white pillars outside and people with tuxedo shirts and bow ties inside—serving drinks and canapés on silver trays. All these attentions allowed her to move in affluent circles that were not only new and exciting to her, but addicting as well.

There were endearing, if not colloquial evenings with Tony, who showed her a softer, warmer side of life—slower-paced and more familiar evenings. Tony picking her up in a red pickup truck with *Cipullo Construction* stenciled in yellow paint on the side. Dates allowing more time for talk—verbal intimacy and soul revelation rather than self-serving conversations laced with swaggered boasting. These were dates with more substance than cost—appealing and addictive in their own right.

So it was, in that Christmas break of '73—Cathy alternating nightly between Charlie and Tony. One day, choosing the one and imbibing in what he had to offer—the next day allowing the other one to show her the other side. To not make a commitment—either way—was part of the pleasure, as much as it was a part of the problem.

Cathy's indecision instilled an increased desire in both of them, to the point that if Cathy wasn't the object of all of their thought-energy before Christmas break, she certainly was all that they thought of afterwards. This emotional pursuit continued for Charlie and Tony through the remainder of their senior year—wanting her but never fully having her. A taste of paradise with a chaser of purgatory. Could anything be more cruel, yet at the same time give the taste of ecstasy as it did?

The blessing was that each was now available to give their full attention to Cathy—their undergraduate page now essentially turned, awaiting to embark on the next chapter in their academic, if not their emotional, lives.

"Do you know how unusual this is?" Barb asked late one night during one of their heart-to-hearts.

"Lots of girls date more than one guy," Cathy countered.

"You're in love with more than one guy, Cath. There's a huge difference!"

"I don't know if I'd call it love. I don't know what I'd call it, really. It's so very hard to explain. I feel very deeply for each of them. They each attract me so intensely, yet so differently. When I'm with the one, I never think of the other. When I'm alone, I think of them both. Charlie has asked me to choose. It upsets him so. His jealousy is flattering, but it's also an unattractive side of him. His nature is to be controlling, but I see that he fights it, sometimes succeeding, sometimes not."

"You once told me that Charlie's 'bad boy' image was part of what attracted you to him."

"Definitely! I sometimes feel naughty, being with him. It's also his swagger, his self-assurance. He's good, and he knows it!

"Tony, on the other hand, is so sweet, so giving. The difference is, he's good and *I* know it!"

"So, what are you going to do?"

"I'm not going to do anything, Barb. This summer, I plan to work in Pittsburgh at a PR firm, and stay with my cousin Carol. I will continue to date them both, and see how it plays out. This fall, when Charlie goes to DC and Tony to Pittsburgh, I will be between them geographically as well as emotionally, and I'll see how THAT plays out."

"That seems to me to be in Charlie's favor."

"How so?"

"Well, for one thing, he'll be a lot closer, being in DC.... I mean, weekend visits closer, instead of being ten hours away in South Bend. Tony, on the other hand, will no longer be available for lunch between classes."

"I'm actually looking forward to the change. It will be interesting to see how the relationships evolve under different circumstances."

Cathy turned off the lamp on her nightstand as the telephone rang. It was Tony. He knew that she'd be going to sleep about now and he wanted his voice to accompany her into slumber. He didn't speak his own words. In fact, he didn't speak at all. Instead, he sang her favorite Lennon/McCartney song, "I Will," to her in a soft, lullaby-like tone.

Who knows how long I've loved you? You know I love you still.
Will I wait a lonely lifetime, if you want me to, I will!

Chapter 7

Mid-December 1978

It was seven months since their graduation from medical school. The frustrations and release of eight long years of study and competition for grades and favor now behind them—Sean and Tony faced the challenges of their respective residencies. The elation of achieving their lifelong goals quickly faded with the new pressures of residency training upon them.

Sean was a first-year resident in psychiatry at Western Psychiatric Hospital across the street from Presbyterian University Hospital. Tony was at Presby, doing his first year of internal medicine. His goal was to complete an internal medicine program and proceed with a fellowship in hematology/oncology.

Tony walked into the cafeteria of Presby—the pockets of his knee-length white lab coat filled with patient status notes and drug formularies. Embroidered over the left breast pocket, in blue script stitching, was *Antonio Cipullo, MD, Internal Medicine.* A stethoscope was draped around his neck. He looked tired—sleep being a stranger to him, as it is to all residents. He went through the line, choosing only a bowl of soup, crackers and a paper cup of water. He looked for his friend Sean.

Spotting Sean sitting at a table by a window, Tony walked toward his friend, tray in hand.

"That's the problem with you psychiatrists. Tell the loonies that they need to get in touch with their feelings. Tell the poor rich bastards that their guilt lies not with them, but with their sexually frustrated mothers. A quick change of the rubber wallpaper, and…ta da!…an early lunch!"

"I just got here myself, smart shit!"

Tony sat down and crushed the crackers into his soup. He tried to sink the floating fragments repeatedly with his spoon.

"So, tell me. How's it going over in the loonie bin?"

"Piece of cake! How about you? Find a cure for cancer yet?"

"I'm working on it! If they'd only give me some time for reflective thought."

"Residents aren't expected to think!"

"Ain't that the truth? Fourth-year med school was a cakewalk compared to this gauntlet."

Tony took a spoonful of the soup as his pager went off. On a pillar next to their table was a house phone. Tony dialed the extension from the pager.

"I gotta go, Sean. It's Danny," Tony said with a pained look on his face.

"How's he doing?" Sean asked, knowing that Tony's best friend from undergraduate school was in house.

"Not well. The pancreatic tumor has metastasized to his liver. Donaldson is going to do a belly tap, to drain some fluid and reduce the pressure from the ascities. When I saw Danny this morning, he looked nine months pregnant!"

"Who's Donaldson?"

"He's the chief hematology/oncology fellow. He's very, very good. He knows that I want to do hem./onc., so he's taken me under his wing—allowing me to participate in Dan's care."

"Want me to come with you?"

"No. Thanks anyway, Sean. I'll call you later."

Tony picked up his tray and walked towards the exit.

He was having a difficult time dealing with Danny's illness. They stayed close since graduating from Bucknell. Tony was the best man at Dan's wedding, and godfather to eighteen-month-old Jenna. Dan was family.

Dan's wife, Judy, maintained a facade of strength in Dan's presence but broke down frequently to Tony. Today would be no different.

Tony exited the elevator on the eighth floor and turned down the corridor. Judy was standing just outside Danny's room. The door was closed. She was sobbing into a crumpled wad of Kleenex. He approached her slowly, uncomfortable and unsure of what to say. He embraced her, telling her that it was good to let it out. He rubbed the top of her shoulder blade as he told her that everything would be all right. He knew that it wouldn't. She knew it as well.

"Dr. Donaldson is in with Danny. He asked me to wait out here. Oh, Tony. He is suffering, so."

"We are doing everything that we can, Judy. You must understand that."

"Tony, you've got to help him. Please, help him." Judy's voice trailed off as she cried into Tony's shoulder.

"I'll do whatever I can, Judy. Whatever I can. Now I have to get in there with Danny. I want you to go to the family lounge and wait for me. I'll come down when we've finished."

He kissed her forehead and watched as she walked reluctantly toward the lounge. He took a deep breath and entered the room.

Dr. Donaldson was opening a surgical pack. "Tony, we're just about to start. Give me a hand with this guy. He looks like trouble to me," Dr. Donaldson kidded.

"His middle name is trouble, Frank. Daniel Trouble Vincent! That's who this guy is!" Tony said as he knelt on one knee next to Danny's bed.

"It's Daniel Trouble Vincenzo, and don't you forget it!" Dan whispered—his voice strained and shallow.

"He thinks he's Italian, Frank—but he's hung like a madigan!" Tony said, looking into Danny's eyes—the inside joke remaining between the two of them. Tony took his hand. "Roll over on your side toward me, big guy. Dr. Donaldson is going to drain off some of that beer belly of yours." Tony pulled Dan towards him, allowing Frank access to Dan's rib cage.

"Uncle Dominick should see me now. He wouldn't dare call me skinny if he got a load of this gut!"

Dan's stomach was distended and full of fluid—his body's response to the liver damage. The fluid's pressure not only created pain to his damaged organs, it made it difficult for him to breathe as well. He felt like he was drowning and climbing Mt. Everest at the same time—short, shallow and rapid breaths resulting in poor oxygen exchange that lent a blue cast to his lips and fingernails. The near constant crescendos of pain were punctuated by intense waves of nausea. His jaundiced skin contrasted against the white hospital linens and gave Dan an almost ghoulish look.

Tony wiped the sweat from Danny's brow. His skin was cold and clammy.

Dr. Donaldson swabbed Dan's skin with betadine antesepic. "This is going to pinch for a second, Dan," he said as he injected a local anesthetic into Dan's skin under his ribcage. "Now just a little burning sensation."

"Go ahead and squeeze my hand, Danny," Tony said sympathetically.

Dr. Donaldson waited a moment, palpated the area with skilled fingers, and quickly made a small incision with a scalpel blade. He dabbed the area with a large gauze pad, applying pressure at the same time. Dan winced. Tony squeezed his hand, as much for distraction as for support.

Dr. Donaldson then took the long rubber drainage tube and carefully inserted it into Dan's fluid-filled abdomen, guiding it into place. He placed the other end of the tube into a large jar on the floor next to him, continuing to apply pressure to the gauze. When he released the clamp blocking the tube, an amber-colored fluid drained into the jar.

"Do you want to suture this drain wound, Tony?" he asked rhetorically.

Tony went around to the other side of the bed and placed two sutures, closing the wound on either side of the tube.

"Very good. Thanks for not nicking the hose. When you tape the hose, make sure that you don't crimp it and that you maintain the flow," Dr. Donaldson said as he showed Tony, by looping the tube in a wide arc and taping it in place to Dan's stomach.

"OK, Dan. All finished. You can turn over onto your back now. You did great!"

Dan rolled onto his back and looked down at the amber fluid draining into the jar. "So that's where all that beer I drank in college was hiding!" Dan's sentence trailed off as he grabbed his right flank and moaned.

Dr. Donaldson looked up from the chart he was writing in. "Do you need something for pain, Dan?"

Dan nodded.

"I've written the order for PRN Demerol, Tony. I've authorized you, as the resident working with me on this case, to have access. Do you understand?"

Tony nodded as Dr. Donaldson handed him the chart.

"I've cleared it with the attending. He understands the situation. Why don't you give him his meds? I wrote for Tigan suppositories for the nausea as well."

Dr. Donaldson checked the wound area once again. "You'll feel much better as soon as some of this fluid drains, Dan." He turned and left the room.

"I'll be right back with the kick-a-poo juice, Danny."

"Please hurry, Tony."

Tony trotted to the nurse's station, catching up to Dr. Donaldson halfway there.

"He doesn't have much longer to go, Tony. A few weeks, max. All we can do is try to keep him as comfortable as possible. It's the metastasis to the spine now that presents the biggest problem from the standpoint of pain control. I'm sorry." He looked at Tony—into his glassy eyes—and placed a firm hand on Tony's shoulder. "Do you still want to be involved in Dan's care?"

Tony nodded, and then as Donaldson left he went into a vacant room just before the nurses' station and cried into his open hand.

Judy was staring blankly out of the window in the family lounge when Tony walked in.

"How is he, Tony?" Judy asked, not even looking at him—continuing to stare out the window.

84

"I just gave him something for the pain. He wants to see you."

"How many tears can a person have, Tony? I mean, do they teach you things like that in medical school?"

"They teach you very little about how to deal with this."

"He looks so pitiful, Tony. I mean, a human being wasn't meant to have all of those tubes in him—wasn't meant to have his dignity stripped from him so cruelly—wasn't meant to have people who love him watch helplessly as he suffers so." She brushed her hand against the sill, as she continued. "Last night, he held my hand and asked if I would lie next to him in his bed. He said that that was the worst of all that's happened to him—to not be able to lie next to me in bed. To not be home with me in our bed, with Jenna lying between us, each of us taking turns stroking her hair and kissing her forehead. Do they teach you about such things in medical school, Tony?"

Tony put his arm around her shoulder. "They teach you so very little about so much."

"To lie in bed with me—our bed. The bed that we came together in, and held each other so closely that we were no longer two people, but one—co-creating that beautiful baby. Is that too much for someone to ask for, Tony?"

She turned to Tony, and he now also saw the pain in her eyes as well as heard her express it. From the depth of her pain, she couldn't see his. She wasn't supposed to.

Tony took her by the hand. "He's waiting for us."

When they entered the room, Dan was humming a song that was unfamiliar to either Tony or Judy. His eyes were half-open. He did not appear to be in any distress.

"The amount of time that he has relief from pain seems to get shorter and shorter," Judy said as she stroked his cheek.

"Donaldson increased his dosage. He should be comfortable for a longer time now."

Dan opened his eyes. "Tony, is that you?"

"It's me, big guy."

"Tell Uncle Dominick that I'll bring him more 'mud' in a little bit. The mortar mixer is on the fritz again!"

"We need to get a new one. Did you kick it in the arse, like he showed you?"

"Twice. Once for me and once for him!"

"While you're over here playing with mortar mixers, Papa has me hauling bricks up the scaffold."

"I'll give you a hand in a minute, buddy. Let me kick this sumna bitch one more time."

"No one can kick mortar mixers like you, Danny. No one!" Tony looked at Judy. She smiled back.

"I hope Mama Cipullo is making la trippa tonight, Tony!"

"…with fresh baked bread," Tony added.

"…and homemade wine…" Dan's voice trailed as he dozed off.

"He'll sleep for quite a while now, Judy. Why don't you go home and get some rest. Is Jenna at your mom's?"

She nodded as she stroked Danny's cheek. "It's almost like he isn't even sick now. He's so peaceful when he's out of pain—when he's sleeping." She adjusted his nasal canula so that the oxygen hose wasn't pressing on his nose. She looked at the other tubes and hoses going into and coming out of his body. She shook her head and began to cry once again. Tony tried to comfort her but knew that she was far beyond comfort—at least any that he could provide, even if he knew how.

Tony turned on the light in the resident's on-call room and looked at his watch. It was 3:00 a.m. He couldn't sleep, despite the fact that he was exhausted. First-year residents have to learn how to function on little sleep—learning how to grab pieces of sleep here and there when the opportunity presents it. They must learn how to reset their biological clocks—now determined not by any circadian rhythm, but by the chief residents, the attendings and of course the patients.

He rubbed his eyes as he got up from the cot, stretched and yawned, then put on his lab coat over his green scrubs. He took the stairwell to the eighth floor—not riding elevators being the only exercise he had time for.

Hospital corridors at 3:00 a.m. are dark, eerie places. Quiet moans and stirring, restless patients' noises. Bubbling oxygen and beeping monitors. *The place even smells differently in the middle of the night,* Tony thought as he reached Danny's room. He could hear his groans through the closed door.

"Fucking cancer," Tony whispered as he entered the room, as if swearing at it would help in some way.

On seeing Tony, Dan tried to sit up in bed but couldn't—his upright progression halted by a sharp piercing pain in his spine.

"Oh, shit!" Dan shouted as he grabbed his flank. "Motherfucker!"

Tony grabbed Danny's hand and squeezed hard, in the hope of distracting some of the pain.

"Tony. You've got to help me. I can't take this any longer, buddy. I can't take this shit!"

"Do you see this?" Tony raised his voice in frustrated anger at his friend, as he held up the call button to the nurses' station. "Use this when you need something for the pain!" Guilt overcame Tony as he regained his composure.

"I've been ringing. No one has come."

"Hang on, buddy. I'll be right back!"

Tony hurried to the nurses' station. He arrived at the same time as the heavyset RN. She was coming from the opposite corridor.

"I need the keys to the narcotics cabinet," Tony said, as he wrote in the narcotics logbook. She unlocked the cabinet and initialed Tony's entry as he prepared a syringe of Demerol.

"8312 has been ringing," Tony said as he looked up at the night nurse.

"I'm the only RN on the floor tonight. I only have two hands, Doctor." Her tone was unfriendly and abrupt. "I wasn't on a coffee break. I was tending to another patient."

"I understand."

"I've been an oncology nurse for over twenty-five years. I know my job. I do the best that I can."

Tony said nothing else. He hurried back to Dan's room. As he inserted the needle into the IV port, he looked Danny in the eye. "This will work very quickly, Danny!"

"Tony. You've got to help me."

"I am, buddy, I am!"

"No...I mean you have to end it! I can't take any more. I can't take the pain. I can't take the nausea. I can't take the humiliation.... Judy's suffered enough."

Dan's voice started to trail off as the drug took effect. Groggy now, he continued. "Do you hear me, Tony?"

Tony heard him but did not answer.

"End it, Tony...please, you've got to...end...it."

Dan fell into a deep sleep. Tony checked his drainage tube for kinks. He sat down in the visitors chair and rubbed his eyes. He rubbed them long and he rubbed them hard. He sat and looked at the shell of the person who used to be his vibrant friend. He reminisced about their freshman year at Bucknell—how fortunate he felt in getting Danny as a roommate. How well they got along. How caring and generous Danny was. How his sense of humor lifted Tony's spirits.

Tony walked down the hall of the freshman dorm looking for room #16. He was nervous about so many aspects of starting college. He felt the tug of separation anxiety that most freshmen feel—being away from home for the first time. He wondered what it would be like sharing a room with someone other than his brother Gino.

Arriving at #16, Tony put his large duffel bag down and opened the door.

Danny was sitting on one of the twin beds, tossing playing cards into a baseball cap across the room.

"Hi! I'm Tony Cipullo." Tony extended his right hand in Dan's direction.

"Are you my roommate?" Dan asked in deadpan.

"I believe so."

"There must be some mistake. I specifically asked for a female roommate—one with big boobs. This fucking administration can't get anything right! Heads will roll!"

Tony smiled.

"You're Italian, aren't you?"

"Yes, I am."

"You're not going to bring any goats in here or anything like that, are you?"

"Of course! I left her downstairs with my trunk, other bags and stereo. How about giving me a hand?"

"No problem." Dan got up and walked downstairs with Tony. "I guess there is something to be said for fresh goat's milk in the morning!"

Tony reminisced about them pledging the fraternity together.

"Welcome to hell week, gentlemen!" the pledge master addressed the group of ten pledges as he lined them, stripped naked, against the wall in the fraternity's basement—in firing squad fashion. If only the administration knew what went on behind closed fraternity house's doors.

"Cipullo, as president of this pledge class, I want you to know that more will be expected of you!"

"Sir, yes, sir!"

"Fine! I then want you to know that there was an error in the order that we put in to the pet shop. Instead of sending us ten goldfish—they sent us fifty goldfish. That comes to one live goldfish for each of you to swallow, with forty left over. You wouldn't mind swallowing the other forty, would you, Cipullo?"

"Sir, no sir! It would be an honor, sir!"

"Permission to speak, sir!" Danny interrupted. "The nine of us insist on splitting the other forty fish, sir!"

The pledge master walked up to Danny. "So we have pledge class unity, do we?"

"Sir, yes, sir, oh omnipotent one!"

"It so happens that in our chapter's manifesto, it is written that the pledge who first speaks up for pledge unity during hell week must eat every olive used in the pledge class olive races! So let's begin those now, shall we?"

The pledge master took ten olives and placed them on the floor across the room from the ten pledges.

"On my signal, each of you will bear-crawl over to the olives, turn around and pick up an olive in his asshole, and then bear-crawl back to your starting point, dropping the olive into the cup on the floor. Mister Vincent will then have the privilege of eating all ten olives."

"Permission to speak, sir. As pledge class president, I insist on eating the ten olives, sir!" Tony interrupted.

"Sir, we choose to eat our own olives, sir!" the other pledges chimed in.

Pledge unity. Brotherhood. Friendship.

Tony reminisced how Danny was with him when he saw Cathy for the first time at the anti-war rally. How he was there for support and encouragement during their senior year as Tony vied for her affections. How they embraced on the day that Tony received notification of admittance to medical school. How they cried at graduation.

Tony also reminisced how Danny was there for him during the toughest time in his life—when he and Cathy decided that maybe it was best not to see each other anymore. The pressures of starting medical school had been brought to bear. Tony could not devote the time required in their relationship. They drifted apart as Cathy and Charlie's relationship heated up. It was best to end the relationship and go on their separate ways. It was the toughest decision of Tony's young life, and Danny was there for him.

Danny groaned in his sleep, bringing Tony back to the present and back to reality. Dan's breathing was labored, a combination of the fluid pressure on his lungs and the respiratory suppression of the Demerol. Tony increased the flow rate of the oxygen to compensate and tilted Dan's head back to make his airway patent. He returned to his seat.

He reminisced on taking the Hippocratic oath at graduation. His first vow— an oath. A promise to God and to his fellow man: *First do no harm! Practice the art and science of medicine to heal the sick. Abstain from whatever is deleterious and mischievous. Give no deadly medicine to anyone if asked, nor suggest any such counsel. Into whatever house I enter, I will go into them for the benefit of the sick, and abstain from every act of mischief.*

How could he justify Danny's request to "end it" in light of the oath that he took?

But Hippocrates wasn't here in Danny's room. He wasn't here to observe the degree of suffering—the humiliation. Even if he were, he couldn't know how much Tony loved him—how he was a brother to him. He couldn't possibly feel Judy's pain, as Tony did.

"Fucking cancer! Son-of-a-bitching-bastard—fucking cancer!" Tony closed his eyes and rubbed them again with the fingers of his right hand. He was exhausted. He leaned back into the chair and fell asleep. It was a shallow, restless sleep—but it was sleep, nonetheless.

Dreams came—R.E.M. sleep and dreams. They came quickly—almost as soon as his eyes closed. He dreamt of Danny in healthier, happier times. He dreamt of his mother's kitchen and Zia Angelina. He dreamt of Uncle Dominick teasing Danny. There was laughter. There was peace. There were no signs of distended bellies or pain. He dreamt of Danny's wedding and his toasting to friendship and brotherhood. He dreamt of Danny carrying Judy out of the reception hall towards the waiting limo and towards a lifetime of happiness and bliss. He dreamt of Jenna's birth—her baptism—her first steps—the first time she called him "Uncle No-nee." He dreamt of Cathy and Bucknell. He dreamt of Mrs. Smyth. He dreamt of Evan.

Evan took him aside—almost outside the dream. He put his arm around him.

"Tony. There is no great shortage of tragedy in life. What I have learned is to always try and apply the best of yourself to any situation. Sometimes the best is to choose the lesser of two evils. Sometimes the best is extreme self-sacrifice. Sometimes the best is knowing when to throw in the towel. Always the best is to rest in the comfort of your decision!"

Tony awoke at the end of Evan's words—almost expecting to see him there in the room with him. The dream was that real.

He remembered the night that Evan actually spoke those words to him—the suffering deer on the side of the road—Evan's mentoring wisdom.

Morning light was now filtering into the room through the window blinds. Danny began to stir. Tony went to his side. He held his hand, as Danny opened his eyes.

"How are you feeling, Danny?"

"Like I probably look. Maybe worse. Very groggy. Nauseous."

Tony took one of the Tigan suppositories from his lab coat's side pocket. He put on a surgical glove. "Here, this will make you feel a little better. Roll onto your side."

Tony helped Dan to roll away from him. He parted the hospital gown and inserted the bullet-shaped medication.

"Maybe I can return the favor some day and stick something up your ass!" Dan kidded—a defense mechanism to hide his humiliation and vulnerability.

Tony saw this and was as embarrassed as his friend. "I would have finished sooner, but there was this olive stuck in there."

"Don't tell that fuck'n pledge master that I only pretended to eat it. I've been hiding it in there all these years for fear of discovery." Dan's voice was hushed—almost a whisper.

"It'll be our secret, buddy."

"What time is it?"

"Almost eight a.m."

"The pain is starting to creep back in. It's not too bad now, but I can tell it's knocking at the door."

In the beginning, Dan would test his pain threshold—see how long he could go before buckling, giving in and asking for his medication. It was a way that he stood up to this disease—standing up to it as he would to a bully. He was long past that approach. He was beaten down—the bully was winning and Dan was giving up.

"Do you remember that course that we took together from Rabbi Sheffield?" Dan asked, rhetorically.

"Of course I do. It was your idea that we take it. Existentialism."

"We read Sartre's *No Exit*. Remember that?"

"Of course I do."

"That's what this fuck'n cancer is. I'm stuck in hell with no apparent exit, Tony. You can open the door and let me out, Tony. Please let me out!" Dan squeezed his hand tightly.

"Danny. I can't. You must understand! I can't."

"You must!"

"I'm not God, Dan."

"You're as close as I have right now. Please."

"Do you need something for the pain now?"

"That's not opening the door, Tony. It's its own hell in and of itself. You tease me by showing me the door—letting me go partway through, then pulling me back into hell again. Open the door, Tony, and set me free of this hell! Please, set me free." Danny now grabbed Tony's arm and squeezed it—hard.

"You have no idea what you are asking, Danny!"

"You have no idea what I'm going through, Tony. If you did, then you would agree that I'm not asking much at all. But don't do it for me—do it for Judy. Do it for Jenna—my baby. Do you want her to go through life remembering her father as this invalid shell of a man?"

"These are half-truths, Danny! I must embrace what I believe in! I cannot sway! I must not sway!"

91

Danny held his side as he let out a loud groan. "Then fuck you! Leave me alone in my anguish and my pain. Get the fuck out of here! Take your fuck'n pain medication and stick it up your fuck'n ass! I don't want to ever see you or your fuck'n self-righteous face again!" Danny tore his patient gown at the neck as punctuation—a Jewish metaphor for total separation from the other party.

"So you are going to play that card, are you? This is so unlike you, Danny."

Dan looked down at his jaundiced body with the distended belly and the tubes and hoses. "You've got that right. You've finally got it, Tony. This is so unlike me. It is not me at all!"

Tony embraced his friend. He kissed his cheek. He wept. "I can't do it, buddy. I can't."

"You must!" Dan let out another load groan. "There's no exit, Tony. You have the key!" Dan belched and vomited bile onto the pillow—a brownish green foul-smelling slime. He then doubled over in pain.

Tony went to the nurses' station. A morning clerk was doing paperwork.

"Where's the on-duty nurse?"

"The day shift has not checked in yet. The night nurse is in 8327. She's not a happy camper!"

Tony went to 8327. The RN was tending to a patient going through chemotherapy purging—projectile vomiting.

"I can see that you have your hands full. I just need the keys to the narcotics cabinet."

"I can't leave just now, Doctor!"

"I understand. Just give me the keys. I'll fill out the log. You can initial it later. I'll return the keys in a couple of minutes, nurse."

The patient went through a series of dry heaves, gasping for breath in the interim.

"In my pocket." The nurse tilted her hip in Tony's direction.

Tony took the keys and hurried to the nurses' station. He unlocked the cabinet. He dispensed a dose of Demerol, nine times the allotment. He then filled a syringe with Phenobarbital. He misrepresented the drugs in the logbook and returned the keys to the nurse in 8327.

When Tony entered his room, Danny was doubled over in pain. His sheets were soaking wet with urine and sweat.

"Tony. Don't take me to the door. Take me through. End it, Tony. End it."

Tony accessed the IV port. He injected the Phenobarbital and then the overdose of the narcotic. Danny's eyes rolled back.

"Unlock the door, Tony. Unlock…the…door…set me…free…"

Danny's breathing became slow and labored. Then it stopped altogether. After a moment, Tony searched for a carotid pulse. There was none.

He kissed Danny on the forehead, then closed Danny's eyes with his right hand. He closed his own and saw Evan standing on the roadside next to the fallen deer.

"I don't try to make sense of it, Tony. There is no great shortage of tragedy in life. What I have learned is to always try and apply the best of yourself to any situation. Sometimes the best is to choose the lesser of two evils. Sometimes the best is extreme self-sacrifice. Sometimes the best is knowing when to throw in the towel. Always the best is to rest in the comfort of your decision…"

There was no comfort in Tony's decision. He wept like a small child— embracing Danny's lifeless corpse as he did so.

Chapter 7B
A chapter epilogue

Tony was uncertain how long he remained in Danny's room. He was sure that it seemed much longer than it actually was. He looked down on Danny's remains—still not certain that he had done the right and proper thing. He thought how peaceful Danny looked. How free from pain and suffering he was.

He soul-searched. He made a career decision in that death-room in the early morning light. If this is what oncology was all about—the majority of your patients being trapped in a story by Sartre—you showing them the door, allowing them to go part of the way through, and then pulling them back into hell—then he wanted no part of it.

He was going to the director of resident training and inform him of his desire to leave the program. He would finish out the year—using it as a transition year in medicine, and then apply to a dermatology program somewhere. Something safe. Nine-to-five work. No weekends. No on-call. No terminal cases. No IV ports to inject into. No night nurses not answering call buttons. No best friends asking you to play God. No bile vomited onto your lab coat. No wives to console.

He felt small and inadequate—nothing like someone should feel after playing God. *Isn't that the irony of it all, though?* he thought. He never intended to play God—yet never once did he seek His counsel.

He had made one vow—one sacred promise in his life. In less than one year's time, he found out that he was not strong enough to keep it. He would be near reluctant to make another vow ever again.

Tony picked up the telephone and dialed Judy's number.

"Judy, it's me, Tony. I'm afraid that I have some very bad news for you." Judy began weeping into the phone. "Danny's passed on. He went very quietly in his sleep. He's not suffering any longer."

"Oh, Tony. I should have been there," Judy said in between sobs.

"I'll come right over, Judy."

"No, Tony, don't. I want to be alone for a little bit. Meet me over at my mother's house in a couple of hours. I want you to be there when I tell Jenna."

"I understand. I'll see you there around eleven."

Tony walked out of Danny's room. He went down to the OR suite and showered—washing away the sweat and grime if not the guilt. He put on new scrubs. It was his day off. He planned on spending the day sleeping—but now, how could he possibly sleep? How could he ever sleep again?

His stomach rumbled and he felt lightheaded. It occurred to him that he hadn't eaten since yesterday morning, save for a spoonful of soup.

The late breakfast crowd was starting to thin when he entered the cafeteria. He chose scrambled eggs, a bagel, juice and coffee. He pushed his tray towards the cash register, taking a bite out of the bagel and licking his thumb where it had touched the scrambled eggs.

"Hello, Tony."

He turned to see Cathy in the cafeteria line behind him.

"Cathy!" He didn't know what else to say—shock not permitting the brain to send words to his mouth.

"You look great, Tony! And look at you, a doctor now! Imagine that!"

"Cathy! What are you doing here?"

"I have a meeting this morning with one of the hospital's administrators. My PR firm has been contracted to do some promotional work."

Tony put her coffee on his tray. "Let me get that. Aren't you going to eat anything?"

"Thanks, Tony, I ate breakfast before I left my apartment. You always were such a gentleman."

They walked to an empty table. Tony held her chair for her, then sat across the table, looking at her as she drank her coffee.

"So, you're doing public relations work, then," Tony said, thinking how bad he was at small talk.

"Yes. We plan to do some radio spots, a little bit in the print media. More subtle advertising for the hospital than true public relations."

"So hospitals are advertising now."

"It's the seventies, Tony. Even hospitals have to maintain a client base. Get used to it!"

"You don't have to sell me. You had my attention at 'Hello Tony'!"

"Still the same Tony, I see," Cathy said with a smile. "I can't believe that it's been four years since we've seen each other."

"Four years, two weeks, and twelve hours," Tony kidded. "But who's counting?"

"Twelve hours and twenty-two minutes," Cathy added without skipping a beat.

They both laughed, and Tony felt like he hadn't felt in a very long time.

It was early December of Tony's first year in medical school when they decided that it would be better to end their relationship. It affected Tony more than she would ever know.

"We have so much to talk about, Tony." Cathy wrote her phone number on the yellow legal pad that she took from her briefcase, tore off the page and handed it to him. "Call me." She looked at her Rolex. "I've got to run, or I'll be late for my appointment."

"Nice watch. You must be doing well for yourself," Tony said, perhaps in the hope that further small talk would keep her here with him a little longer.

"Thanks. It was a gift from Charlie, last Christmas," Cathy said, not thinking.

"If you're still seeing Charlie, maybe it would be best if I didn't—"

"I'm not. It's over. He broke my heart," opening up to Tony as she always could.

"I'm a doctor. Perhaps I can fix it!"

"Call me!" Cathy got up, kissed Tony on the cheek and hurried toward the exit.

Tony sat there holding the phone number in his hand. He touched his cheek as he watched her leave the cafeteria. His heart was pounding like it hadn't for a very long time. He finished his breakfast, then walked to his car. He drove back to his apartment to change his clothes before going to meet Judy at her mother's house.

On the drive back to his apartment, his wheels never touched the ground—or so it seemed.

Chapter 8

Tony left the cafeteria at Western Psychiatric Hospital, after his lunch date with Sean. Sean's secretary was very kind to direct him toward a former co-worker from her days at Radiology Associates. It eased his mind a little bit as he was beginning to become mildly concerned about the impending vacancy at his satellite office. The interviews that morning and the quality of the people applying for the position left him a little depressed. He tried not to think of it.

He promised Cathy that he would be home around 3:00 p.m. to see the family portrait being delivered that afternoon. Being dutiful, he did not want to upset her. As he walked to his car, his cell phone rang.

"Hello."

"Tony, it's me, Barb."

"Hi, Barb. Is everything all right with the kids?"

"Yes, of course. They are really enjoying themselves. It's a perfect day to be at the pool. Troy wanted to talk to you. Troy, your dad's on the phone."

"Dad?"

"Hi, buddy, what's up?"

"Dad, I've been really worried. I saw Bobby Campbell here at the pool today. He said that the police called his parents about his spud launcher and the damage that he did to the Bonner's house."

"Yes, son. Go on."

"Well, Dad, I just wanted to tell you how much I love you, and in the event that the police call you, nothing will change that!"

Tony laughed out loud, then catching himself put his hand over the receiving plate of the cell phone. He waited a moment to regain his composure.

"Troy, the police did call me this morning at my office. I know all about spud launchers and the damage that they can create. The police told me about the Brunswicks' house, but I didn't know the Bonners were shelled as well!

97

Quite frankly, son, you are in some deep doo-doo. I can't tell you how happy I am that you love me and that no phone call from the police can change that, because when I get home you and I are going to have some serious words! Now put Barbara back on the phone."

"Tony?"

"Barb, I'm sorry if the children caused you any inconvenience."

"They're no problem, Tony."

"Like I said. I owe you one!"

Tony closed the front plate of his cell phone and got into his car. Traffic was light in Oakland and he made it home before 2:00 p.m. As he pulled into his driveway, Claudia was saying good-bye to Cathy at the front door. She put his check into her briefcase and walked to her car as Tony approached her.

"Hello, Claudia. We are all a little excited about the portrait!"

"I think that it is my best work to date, Dr. Cipullo. I'm excited as well!"

"Well then, I should go in and see it!"

"Yes, you should, Dr. Cipullo! Yes, you should."

"Good-bye then and thank you." Tony extended his hand toward Claudia.

"Good-bye," Claudia said, shaking Tony's hand.

I don't think she likes me, Tony thought as he opened the front door.

Tony entered the house to find Cathy standing in the family room, facing the wall behind the sofa.

"Honey, I'm home."

He entered the family room. The portrait was on the wall facing Cathy and away from Tony's view. He looked at Cathy. He couldn't read into her expression. He was puzzled by the look on her face.

When he fully entered the room he kissed her on the cheek and turned in the direction of the portrait.

He was not prepared for what he saw.

On the wall behind the sofa was a portrait of the family posed in the living room in front of the baby grand piano. Cathy was seated in the winged-back easy chair. The children were posed behind and on either side of Cathy. Behind the piano, looking into the room from outside the large bay window was Tony.

"What the hell?" Tony said half in disbelief. "What the hell is this?"

"It's our portrait, dear."

"I know it's our portrait. I can see it's our portrait. I want to know why the hell I'm outside, looking through the window."

"It's artistic expression, dear. It's Claudia's subjective reaction to how she sees our family. It's true art. It's not meant to represent objective reality, Tony. It's not a photograph."

"And you approve, Cath?"

"Art sometimes has to grow on you, Tony."

"That's easy for you to say, Cath. It's growing on you because you're sitting inside with the children. I'm outside looking in through the damn window."

"I admit I was a little shocked at first, Tony. You must understand that Claudia is a true artist. Her works will be worth something one day. The fact that we have a Claudia original should mean something to you."

"Oh, it means something, all right. It means that I've been ripped off!" Tony walked to the wet bar and poured himself a drink. "It's a good thing that Andy Warhol is dead, or else you might have commissioned him to do our family portrait. Then I'd be a Campbell's soup can looking in through the window!"

"Isn't it a little early for Jack Daniels, dear?"

"Consider it *my* artistic expression." Tony went into the kitchen for some ice.

"I've invited some people over tonight for cocktails and to unveil the portrait. If you start with Jack Daniels now, what kind of shape will you be in tonight?"

"Don't worry, I can just stand outside and look in through the bay window."

"Tony, be serious."

"I can't believe that you are going to invite our friends over to share in my humiliation." He took a sip of his drink and winced.

"Tony, you need to broaden your approach to this whole thing!"

"Be patient. I'm only on my first Jack."

"Really. If you wanted to, you could put some very positive spin on this."

"And exactly what have *you* been drinking?"

"I can't believe that you're being such a baby. Why don't you grow up?"

"Cathy, I can't believe how insensitive you are to my feelings on this."

"What about MY feelings, Tony? I want this portrait. I like this portrait!"

"You want me to be on the outside looking in?"

"Maybe Claudia saw something in our relationship that you're not seeing. Artists are very sensitive and observant people."

"So what are you saying? Claudia's now a marriage counselor?"

"I'm saying, grow up! I've got some work to do on the McTigh project," Cathy said as she took her briefcase and left the room.

Tony took another sip of his drink and looked at the portrait. "Positive spin? There's not enough Jack Daniels in the bottle for that!"

Justified or not, Tony spent another few minutes looking at the portrait and feeling sorry for himself. Forced isolation is an unhappy feeling. How could this person outside of the family separate him from his family? What's more, his wife was now also justifying this isolation, it seemed. He felt separated physically, and now, as if by default, emotionally as well.

He took the last swallow from his glass and set it down on the wet bar. He walked into his study and took the paper from Mary Jo with Hanna McDowell's telephone number out of his inside jacket pocket. He sat down at his desk and put both feet up on the desktop. He dialed the number.

"Hello?"

"Hello. Is this Hanna?"

"Yes, this is Hanna. May I help you?"

"I certainly hope so! I got your name from Mary Jo Murdy. She works for a friend of mine—Dr. Sean Dempsey."

"I just saw Mary Jo this morning."

"Yes, I know. She told me all about you—how you might be considering coming back into health care."

"I don't know. I had a bad experience with Radiology Associates. I decided that maybe it was time to move on to other things."

"You may have had one bad experience. Don't let that sway you away from the field altogether. Can we get together and at least talk about your options?"

"I suppose so. I mean, it's always good to explore one's options. To be honest with you, I didn't know that I had options."

"From what I've heard about you from Mary Jo, you have many options!"

"She's so sweet!"

"So we can get together and at least discuss this?"

"I suppose. What do I have to lose?"

"Great! How about Monday? You can come to the office, I'll introduce you to the staff and show you around, and we can discuss this over lunch. How does that fit into your plans?"

"It's workable for me, Doctor."

"Fine. My office is in the professional building across the street from *Tai Pei* on Freeport Road. How's noon sound?"

"Noon's fine. Freeport Road. No problem. I'll see you then."

Tony hung up the phone, leaned back in his chair and put his feet back up on the desk in his study. It was no small consolation for him that he may have found a quality person to run his business office. It eased the pain and disappointment over the portrait, if not the hurt of Cathy's insensitivity. He picked up the phone and dialed Sean.

"Sean. Let's get together for that drink you mentioned at lunch today."

"There was a message on my service from a staff person at Cathy's office. I'm invited over to your place for cocktails at 7:30 tonight."

"I know. I may need a drink beforehand."

"A drink before a cocktail party? What's up?"

"I'll tell you all about it. How's six o'clock at Franco's sound? I want to get some psychological insight into something."

"Sounds serious."

"Is six o'clock doable for you?"

"I'll see you at Franco's. Six p.m., Tony."

The study was Tony's favorite room in the house. It occupied an area off to the far right side of the house's floor plan and was away from the traffic flow. With the door closed, it provided the peace and quiet one would expect from a study. It was his fortress of solitude and he did his best thinking there.

The L-shaped study consisted of two rooms. A floor-to-cathedral-ceiling cherry wood bookcase occupied one wall of the main room. Various medical textbooks and journals filled the bookcase to capacity. A matching cherry desk faced the bookcase. A sofa, end table and lamp occupied the wall to the right of the desk. This is not how Tony had wanted to furnish his study. It was to be his room when he built the house, and he wanted it furnished in a more colloquial manner—not with sissy Queen Ann furniture. In fact, he had wanted to place a dining room table to be used as a desk—something that he could spread some papers out on. Cathy had other ideas, and one day when Tony was at the office she had the room decorated as she felt a doctor's study should look. As was always the case, Cathy got her way and Tony learned to live with her choice.

The extension room contained Tony's computer desk, a high-backed swivel chair and bookcases filled with slide carrousel boxes. An X-ray view box hung on one wall. A fluorescent slide sorter was positioned on a short table along the opposite wall. A slide projector sat on an end table that Tony purchased at a garage sale. The projector was pointed toward a blank white cardboard poster that Tony thumbtacked onto the wall. Tony used this room for lecture preparation and Internet research. He could keep it as messy as he wished by closing the door and therefore hiding it from guest scrutiny. Out of sight, out of mind. Cathy gave him this much. It didn't take much to make him happy.

Tony took the slide carrousel that he had retrieved earlier that day from his university office. He placed it on the projector and focused the first slide. With the remote control in hand, he leaned back in his swivel chair and went through the lecture for the Rotary Club. He was lost in his work and he was, for a moment, happy.

Tony finished his lecture preparation. He turned off the projector as he heard the children coming into the house: Laughter and commotion coming into the hallway leading into the kitchen from the garage. He became revitalized, hearing the children's laughter as he did. He opened the study's door.

"Hey, guys!"

"Daddy!" Angela came running into Tony's arms. "We had a wonderful time with Barbara at the club, Daddy!"

Tony caught her as Angela leapt up into his arms. He spun her around, squeezing her close to him. "I'm glad, sweetie!"

"You're not going to yell at Troy, are you, Daddy? He told Barb that he didn't want to come home with us—that you were going to yell at him!"

"Where is Troy?" Tony asked as he looked past Angela and into the kitchen.

"He ran up to his room. Are you going to yell at him, Daddy?"

"I want to talk to him pumpkin. I'll be right down."

Tony put Angela down and walked upstairs to Troy's room.

"I knew that you were going to yell at him, Daddy. I just knew it!"

Tony knocked on Troy's bedroom door. "Open up, Troy. I know that you are in there!"

"You're going to yell at me."

"Open the door, Troy!"

"Promise that you won't yell at me first!"

"I'm going to count to three!"

"It was an accident, Dad!"

"One…"

"Honest, Dad. It was an accident!"

"Two…"

"Promise that you won't yell at me…"

"Two and a half…"

Troy opened the door. He extended the spud launcher towards Tony.

"Here, Dad. Take it. I don't want to get in any more trouble!"

Tony took the plastic bazooka-like object constructed of schedule-40 plumbers pipe from his son. Troy reached behind his headboard and handed Tony two potatoes that were hidden there.

"Here's all of my ammunition too, Dad. I've learned my lesson."

"Have you? Maybe after you pay for the Brunswicks' window AND the flowers out of your allowance, you will convince me of that, son."

102

"Yes, sir."

Tony extended his hand toward Troy. "Let's just learn from this experience, son. Be grateful that nobody was hurt!"

They shook hands like men. Troy felt ten feet tall.

Dominick came running up to Troy's room. "Dad, come look at the family picture. Wait till you see!"

Gathered in the family room, the children were standing in front of the portrait.

"Look at Joseph, he looks like a dork!" Dominick kidded.

"I look just like you, so you must look like a dork too!" Joseph responded.

"We're not identical twins, dork-face, so you don't look just like me!" Dominick said as he pushed Joseph.

"Stop it, you two!" Tony commanded as he and Troy entered the room.

"Daddy, why are you standing outside?" Angela asked.

"Yeah, Dad. There's plenty of room next to Mom," Troy joined in.

"Looks like some kind of statement being made to me," Rob said.

"Well, I think that the artist captured Kathleen's inner beauty," Tony added, hoping to divert the conversation.

"It's a good thing that it's not raining, Dad. You'd be pretty wet if it were," Troy said.

"Your mother looks exceptionally beautiful," Tony stated, as if he hadn't heard the rest of the conversation. "Each of you looks very good as well. I'm very happy with the portrait! Very happy!" Tony lied.

Tony looked at his watch. "Oh boy! I've got to meet Dr. Dempsey in a little bit. I have to take a quick shower. Mom's having some people over tonight. You guys want to order pizza and hoagies for dinner?" Tony reached into his pocket and handed Rob two twenty-dollar bills.

"Are you and Mom having little sandwiches on trays, Daddy?" Angela asked.

"Probably, pumpkin," Tony said, smiling.

"I like the ones on pink bread," Angela continued.

"I'll make sure nobody eats the pink ones, honey!"

"Please take the green olives off first, Daddy."

"I always do, monkey face."

He kissed his daughter and hurried upstairs to take his shower. He passed Cathy in the upstairs hallway. She didn't say a word. He returned her silence.

Tony got to Franco's just before 6:00 p.m. He arrived just as Sean was getting out of his car. Tony parked beside his friend and greeted Sean with a hug. The two friends entered the restaurant and took a seat at a table in the bar.

"So, what's up?" Sean asked as he leaned forward toward his friend.

"Our family portrait was delivered today."

"And?" Just then the ringing of Sean's cell phone interrupted the conversation. He glanced down at the incoming number. "It's Mary Jo. I'd better get this."

Tony smiled at the waitress as she approached the table and Sean spoke with his secretary.

"Hi ya, Doc. Will you two hunks be joining us for dinner this evening?"

"Judy, I bet that you say that to all the hunks that come in here," Tony said.

She smiled as she placed the cocktail napkins down and set a Jack Daniels on the rocks first in front of Tony and then Sean. "I took the liberty of bringing your regular drink."

"You are going to go places in this world, Judy."

"Are you going to take me?"

"Why, Judy, shame on you. I'm a married man."

"So, bring her along. I'm not the jealous type," she said as she winked at Sean and set a bowl of salted peanuts on the table. She walked to the next table, exaggerating her hip sway as she went.

"Nice ass!" Sean said as he flipped the cover plate closed on his cell phone.

"She had an ass? I didn't notice," Tony said with a smile.

The two friends sat and talked about Tony's feelings of isolation in his marriage. They talked about the family portrait and Tony's response to it—how the two shared some intimate yet difficult-to-explain connection. They talked about Tony's inability to deal with the jealousy issues of sharing Cathy's attentions with her career. They talked about lost intimacy and insensitivity.

Sean offered psychological input but mostly just listened and gave presence support. It was what he was good at doing. It is what friends do. Good friends do it well. Sean was a good friend.

"Look, Tony, that was Mary Jo on the phone a little bit ago. She called to tell me that Hanna just called her and asked about you."

"Yeah. She has an interview with me on Monday."

"No. She didn't ask about your office. She asked about you."

"Meaning?"

"Tony, I'm just a little concerned. I think that you may be, well... vulnerable right now."

"What are you saying, Sean?"

"After you left us at lunch today, Mary Jo told me a little bit about this

Hanna. I don't know if this is a good idea."

"Sean. I'm interviewing for a staff position. Nothing more."

"Your mouth is saying one thing, Tony. Your subconscious is saying something else entirely."

"You psychiatrists are always reading into people's subconscious. Can't you look at the surface—how we normal people look at the world?"

"Normal, Tony? Excuse me, but aren't you the one who called me to have a drink before a cocktail party—to discuss how a family portrait defined your marriage relationship? And how 'normal' is that?"

Tony smiled widely at his friend. "Touché!"

"Seriously, Tony, this Hanna seems to me to be the wrong prescription for what is ailing you right now. It is my duty as a friend to tell you this."

"Just what did Mary Jo tell you about this Hanna?"

"Let's just say that she fits a certain pattern. Be careful."

Driving to his office on Monday morning, Tony tried to put the embarrassment of Saturday's cocktail party for the portrait's unveiling behind him. It had been insult added to injury—salt in an open wound. Fortunately, most of the people that Cathy had invited were her friends, not his. Sean was an obvious exception. Cathy had tried to get Sean to offer his approval of the portrait, either as a way of proving her point, or as a means to further embarrass Tony—he wasn't certain which. Sean, however, maintained neutrality that the Swiss would envy, offering only benign yet complimentary statements shy of subject matter endorsement.

"The artist used interesting and pleasing color combinations. Her brush stroke is soft…"

Tony arrived at the Fox Chapel office at 8:40 a.m. and entered through the employee entrance in the rear of the building. He walked up the one flight of stairs and entered his office suite through the door marked *Private*.

Once in his office, he glanced at the day sheet of scheduled procedures. It was a light day, and Tony preferred that on Mondays. There were six Lrs—lesion removals—two CONs—consultations—and three ACANs—acne patients—before lunch.

"Good morning, Doctor," Mitch, his office manager, greeted him. "You have to make these calls this morning," she said as she handed him memo slips with the words *While you were out* printed on the top.

"Good morning, Mitch," Tony answered, taking the memos but not looking at them. "I am interviewing a young lady for the Oakland office job today. She'll be here before lunch."

"I take it that your Saturday interviews didn't go well, then."

"You could say that."

"How's Joan feeling?"

"She's hanging in there. She's such a trooper. I'll miss her."

"Your ten o'clock L.R. canceled. Dr. Robins referred her for you to remove a suspicious lesion from her forehead, but she called and said that her husband thought it was OK."

"That's what this world needs, Mitch—more armchair dermatologists! Please call Tim Robins' office and inform them, so they can keep an eye on it for her. Jeesh!"

Tony closed the door of examining room three, having finished his last consultation before lunch. He was washing his hands when Mitch approached him.

"Your interview is here, Doctor. She's waiting for you in your private office." Mitch handed him the applicant's résumé. She looked at him with one eyebrow raised.

"What?" Tony asked, somewhat surprised at the look

"Nothing." Mitch turned and walked back to the front office.

Tony glanced at his watch.

"Right on time. Excellent!"

He walked down the hall towards his private office, reading the résumé as he went. The door to his office was open and Hanna was standing in front of Tony's desk, her back to him, looking at a picture of Kathy and the children that hung on the wall. She was wearing a gray business suit with a skirt that fell to just above her knees—professional and attractive. Her long golden-brown hair had subtle highlights as if created by the sun—not a salon—just shy of a brandy red—to call it auburn would not do it justice.

"Good afternoon, Hanna. Thank you for coming."

Hanna turned at the sound of Tony's voice. His first impression was of her height. He was six feet and two inches tall, yet she looked him straight in the eye—her natural height supplemented by her four-inch heels. She was not only tall, she was slender as well—her stature making a statement of long legs supporting a torso fit from exercise if not genetics. Her tailored suit jacket highlighted a tight tummy and narrow waist.

"Good afternoon, Doctor. So very nice to meet you."

She extended her delicate hand and, grasping his softly, smiled warmly. Her eyes were intensely blue—almost a midnight blue. A deep ocean blue. The color of blue that one can get lost in, if one were fortunate enough to take them in for any length of time, as Tony now did.

"Have we met before?" Tony asked in all sincerity.

"I don't believe so." Hanna looked at Tony's features. "No, I'm certain that we haven't. I would have remembered you."

"It's odd. You look familiar to me."

"I get that a lot. I have a familiar face. People say that I remind them of the actress Angelina Jolie." Hanna's tone was matter-of-fact and not the least bit pretentious.

"Now that you mention it. I can see the resemblance." Tony remarked as he admired her high cheekbones, flawless complexion and amazingly full lips—not as a physician who dealt with the aesthetics of the facial form, but as a man who recognized and appreciated true feminine beauty. "My grandmother's name was Angelina," he added, as if they now had something in common.

"You have a very nice office," Hanna said in an obvious attempt to change the subject.

"Thank you. Let me show you around."

Tony extended his hand toward the office proper, and as Hanna passed him her scented hair invaded his space. Her perfume complemented her appearance and enhanced an already pleasant presentation.

"Pardon me, Hanna, but what is that scent that you are wearing?" Tony asked in a complimentary tone.

"It's called Patchouli. It's a throwback to the sixties. When I was a little girl, I had an older sister who was a flower child. I adored her. She always wore it and it reminds me of her. It brings me good luck," Hanna said, seemingly pleased at Tony's inquiry.

"You are far too young to have any recollection of the sixties."

"I'm forty-three," Hanna said matter-of-factly.

"You look great for forty-three. I would have guessed early thirties," Tony said with an affirmation not so much centered in casual compliment but rather, a sincere observation by a physician trained to help people look more youthful.

"Thank you." Her reply's inflection suggested that she was accustomed to hearing that on a regular basis.

Tony introduced her to his staff and showed her the facility.

"My Oakland office is slightly smaller, but similar," Tony offered. "My support staff travel to the Oakland office and are cross-trained to assist at the front desk. Mitch stays here to run the business office. You are interviewing for Mitch's equivalent position at the Oakland office."

"I see." Hanna looked at the business office program running on the computer screen. "This is Windows based, I see. I prefer that to DOS. May

I?" Hanna leaned over Mitch's shoulder and, with a quick motion of her wrist, slid the mouse on its pad. She moved the cursor to highlight an item on the tool bar and right-clicked on it, bringing up another screen illustrating insurance claims.

"Are you doing e-claims?" Hanna asked Mitch while looking over the information displayed on the screen.

"We just started. You look like you've done this before," Mitch replied.

"I'm very computer literate. You have to be with three children. As far as medical business office software is concerned, they are all pretty similar." Hanna did not look at Mitch but continued to study the screen.

"You have three children?" Mitch inquired as she looked over her shoulder at Hanna's figure, then down at her own.

"Yes, I do." Hanna's tone was laced with mild swagger as if everybody should look like her at forty-three and after going through three pregnancies. She turned back toward Tony. "I should have no problem adjusting to this system."

Tony smiled widely. "I'll bet." He looked at his watch. "Mitch, we'll be at Franco's for lunch. If you need me, I have my pager on."

After Tony and Hanna left the office, Mitch turned toward the other staff members standing in the business office. "I don't like her. Not even a little bit."

At the lunch meeting, Tony and Hanna talked about her experiences at Radiology Associates—what her responsibilities were and what she could offer his practice. They talked about her career move as a representative for a cosmetics line, and how it provided some flexibility in her schedule—something that was important to her as a single parent of three young children. She liked her new job but disliked the traveling—taking her out of town more than she wanted. They talked about salary and benefit needs. At the end of the meeting, Tony knew that he wanted her in his practice.

"I'll need a day or two to consider your offer, Doctor." Hanna tapped her french manicure against the white linen tablecloth almost as if to draw attention to her bare left ring finger. She then applied fresh lip gloss as she looked up at Tony for a response.

They agreed that Tony would call her in two days. She thanked him for the lunch and the opportunity to explore her options as they shook hands and left the restaurant.

Tony entered his private office with a little spring in his step. He was whistling a tune as Mitch walked in.

"Well, how'd it go? Did you hire her?"

"She wants to think about it, but I think it's safe to say that she'll take the job."

Two days passed and Tony called Hanna, only to find that she was still undecided. She asked some specifics regarding the hours relative to flexibility and her children's activities. Tony reassured her that adjustments could always be made, understanding as he did how involved children can become with school and outside interests. As a single parent of three young children, Hanna often had to juggle work with brownies, boy scouts and after-school sports, and she wanted him to understand this. She asked for another day to decide.

When Tony called on Thursday, he could tell that Hanna was still unsure of making the change in jobs.

"I understand that change can be difficult and that the status quo can be a comfort zone at times. I can tell that you are torn between giving up the comfort of your present routine and coming on board with us. Let me help you make the decision. Just say yes. It's the right thing to do." Tony's voice was comforting and persuasive.

There was a pregnant pause.

"All right, Doctor. You've convinced me. I'll need to give two weeks' notice to my present employer."

"No problem. So you can start on the eighteenth then?"

"Yes, Monday the eighteenth will be fine."

"Excellent. Call Joan at the Oakland office tomorrow and introduce yourself to her. Tell her what size you wear and she'll order some scrubs for you. Welcome aboard, Hanna. You've made the right decision."

On Monday the eighteenth Hanna reported to Joan for training at the Oakland office. Joan called Tony at lunchtime and told him that things were going well and that Hanna was having very few problems learning the system.

"She should be ready to solo long before my due date, Doctor."

"Excellent. I'll see you both tomorrow, Joan. How are you feeling?"

"Tired."

"You sound tired. Are you getting enough sleep?"

"I suppose. I can't wait until I can sleep on my stomach again. Men have no idea what it's like, being pregnant."

"Hang in there, kiddo, and thanks again for everything, Joan."

"Tony..."

Joan got Tony's attention. She only referred to him by his first name on rare occasions—when she allowed the closeness between them to overcome

109

the more proper salutation of doctor that the doctor/staff member relationship demanded.

"Yes, Joan…what is it?"

"I just…"

"Yes, go on…"

"It's just that…"

"Yes, Joan, honey. What is it?"

"Nothing, really. I just…never mind."

Tony wondered what it was that Joan wished to tell him. It became for him one of those mysteries in life that puzzle you briefly in the present and then haunt you occasionally the remainder of your life.

Chapter 9

As the months passed, Tony and Cathy grew further apart. Cathy was named a partner in the PR firm and was spending more time away from home. She became more and more consumed by her work, placing Tony on some back burner—if he was even in her life at all. Her work consumption also placed barriers between others in her life. Pauline, the nanny, who had been with them since Angela was three years old, handed in her resignation. She stated the wish for retirement as the reason, although Tony knew it was because Cathy was becoming more and more difficult to deal with.

Out of desperation, Tony contacted an agency that was recommended to him by the prosthodontist in the office suite next to his. The agency dealt with the placement of au pairs from Europe. In the ensuing weeks, he interviewed and accepted the commission of a young girl from France named Claire.

Claire was a twenty-year-old college student at the University of Paris studying art history. She took an extended sabbatical to become an au pair in order to make some money and have an opportunity to see the United States. Claire was petite and spunky. She was an obvious brunette with bleached-blond shoulder-length hair. The children loved her. She read stories in English as well as French to Angela and taught her how to make quiche. She even seemed to have a calming effect on the twins.

Joan had a baby girl in early September. They named her Aubrey. There were mild transition woes at the office when Joan left—none that were not expected. Hanna handled the transition better than Tony had hoped. Despite the fact that Tony missed Joan tremendously, he admitted to Sean that Hanna brought a vitality to his office that was delightfully refreshing for him. He looked forward to the days when he would go to his Oakland office. It was more than just a change of pace and scenery. It was a changed ambiance. Hanna possessed a warm and endearing personality as well as a striking physical presence. Tony not only felt refreshed on the days when he was in the Oakland office, he felt restored.

"Be careful!" Sean would often say to his friend, with a tone not unlike one would use when speaking to a child about to light a match for the first time. "Be wary of the winds of change. Unstable foundations quiver at the hint of the winds of transition not unlike the quivering brought on by the winds of war! Sirens continue to intoxicate, dear Ulysses."

"Sean, I know that you are Irish, but James Joyce, you're not!"

"Do not discount the given wisdom of Dubliners! If nothing else, remember this: Keep the Trojan on your horse!"

"Very punny, Sean. Very punny!"

Tony left for the office earlier than usual, intending to catch up on referral correspondence before his first scheduled patient. He was halfway between his home and the Fox Chapel office when his cell phone rang. It was Claire.

"Claire, is everything all right?"

"Oui, Doctor. It is just that Angela woke up just now and is complaining of—how do you say it—sore throat?"

"Is Mrs. Cipullo there?"

"No. She just now left for her office."

"Does she feel warm?"

"Mrs. Cipullo is not a very warm person, Doctor."

"No, I mean does Angela feel warm to you—you know, does she feel like she has a temperature?" Tony laughed at Claire's misunderstanding.

"I am sorry." Claire laughed as well. "Come here, mon petit chou." Claire pressed her lips against Angela's forehead. "Oui, Doctor, she is very hot."

"I'll be there in a few minutes. Give her some juice and keep her warm."

Tony pushed the programmed button on his cell phone that dialed the Fox Chapel office.

"Good morning, Dr. Cipullo's office. Hanna speaking. How may I help you?"

"Hanna? Did I dial the wrong office?"

Tony was surprised to hear Hanna's voice answer the Fox Chapel phone.

"No, you dialed correctly. Mitch phoned me this morning and asked me to cover for her here. Her son had an emergency appendectomy in the middle of the night."

"Wow! Thanks for covering. I like team players."

"I know you do. What's up?" She sounded mildly annoyed, as if she was in the middle of something important and his call interrupted it.

Hanna was a complex, multifaceted individual. It wasn't that she was a moody person, but she would show you different sides of her nature. She could be warm and extremely approachable or distant, if not barriered. Her attention could be focused on you at any particular point in time, thereby making you feel as an important part of her life, or be detached and as distant as another galaxy, setting you adrift and feeling discarded. Fortunately, the warm side was predominant.

"Mitch was supposed to put my referral correspondence file on my desk."

"It's right here. I'll put it there for you."

"Thanks. I'm going to be a little late. I've got to go back home. Angela's not feeling well."

"OK. See you when you get here."

Hanna did not inquire about Angela. Tony perceived her apparent disregard as self-centered and mildly hurtful.

Tony pushed the programmed button for Mitch's cell phone. "Mitch. How's Tommy?"

"He's all right now, doctor. He really had me frightened though. We rushed him here to Children's Hospital at three this morning. He's out of surgery now and everything's OK. The resident assigned to the case said that you taught him in med school. His name was Dr. Mauer."

"Bud Mauer was a good man. I remember him well. I'll call him and thank him for taking such good care of Tommy."

"Thank you, Doctor."

"Now you just get some rest. I'm sure everything will be all right."

"I called Hanna to cover for me at the office."

"I know. Don't worry about the office. Just get some rest!"

Tony closed his cell phone as he pulled into his driveway. The middle door of the attached garage was open. He entered the house and walked into the kitchen, where he found Claire sitting at the table with Angela on her lap. Angela was wrapped in a blanket and looked like a papoose.

"How's my pumpkin?" Tony walked up to Angela and kissed her on the forehead.

Angela moaned. It was a get-attention moan. A Daddy-I'm-glad-to-see-you-please-make-me-feel-better kind of moan.

Tony walked to the cabinet above Cathy's recipe desk across from the kitchen's island. He retrieved the liquid Tylenol and a thermometer. He dispensed the proper dosage into a teaspoon and gave it to Angela, kissing her once again on the forehead as she swallowed the medication. He peeled back the blanket and unbuttoned her pajama top enough to place the thermometer under her armpit. Using the spoon as a tongue blade, he tilted her head back and depressed her tongue. Taking a penlight out of his shirt pocket, Tony looked at Angela's throat. "Say 'ahh' for Daddy." With two fingers, Tony palpated her tiny neck and assessed her lymph nodes. "We have white-speckled basketballs where your tonsils should be."

Going back to the cabinet, Tony took a bottle of Penicillin and checked the expiration date. Using a glass as a pestle, he crushed the tablet and mixed it with a spoonful of orange sherbet. "Down the hatch."

Tony turned to Claire.

"Thank you for calling me. She should be fine now. I'll phone in a script for liquid antibiotics and have the druggist deliver it. She needs a teaspoon every six hours." He looked at the thermometer. "She should get a teaspoon of the Tylenol every three hours or so. Keep her warm and give her all of the fruit juice, popsicles and sherbet that she'll take. I'll call at lunch to see how she's doing."

He kissed Angela once again. "You be a good girl for Claire now, monkey face. Don't give her a hard time about drinking your juice. I'll bring you home a surprise."

Angela moaned as Claire rocked her on her lap. Tony smiled as he left for the office, comfortable in Claire's caring attention.

Tony entered his office suite through his private entrance. He arrived twenty minutes before his first patient despite the delay.

As soon as he entered the hallway that led to his private office, he knew that Hanna was there within the office suite. Her scent permeated the office. "Patchouli," he said out loud. He inhaled deeply through his nose. "Damn, she smells good!"

He fought the temptation to go up to the front office area to see her—still mildly annoyed that she was distant and seemingly uncaring regarding Angela's status. "She heard me come in. If she wants to speak to me, she knows where to find me." Tony whispered under his breath—as if to justify his sophomoric behavior.

Tony went to work on his correspondence, trying to focus, but thinking of Hanna instead and her apparent reluctance to come back and speak with him.

Tony, grow up! he thought, not believing the way that he was acting. *You're a grown man—a doctor—a professor—an educator of doctors. Why are you thinking and acting like a schoolboy?*

He opened the next patient file and stared blankly at it for several minutes before putting it back onto the desktop. He leaned back in his chair and once again inhaled deeply through his nose.

The morning passed slowly—almost dragging, it seemed. At about 10:30 a.m., Hanna came back into the treatment area and caught Tony as he was about to enter a treatment room.

"Dr. Reilly wants you to call him regarding Mrs. Ludwig at your convenience," she said as she handed Tony a note with Dr. Reilly's telephone number on it. "How's Angela feeling?" she added with a sincere tone as she touched Tony on the arm.

"She'll be fine. Acute tonsillitis. Thank you for asking." Tony held back a smile, not certain if his pleasure was from Hanna's interest in Angela or the fact that she came back from the reception area to make contact with him. "This can probably wait until lunch," Tony added.

"I'm certain it can. I thought that I could kill two birds with one stone and use the opportunity to stretch my legs and give you the message now. I heard you speaking to Mona in the hallway, so I thought that I could catch you before you went into the treatment room."

Tony looked down at her scrub pants that hid her long, shapely legs. "Yes, it's good to stretch your legs once in a while."

Hanna smiled at Tony. "This office is a little different from the Oakland office."

"A little bit. Step into my office for a second," Tony said, extending his hand down the corridor toward his private office.

"It's a little busier and the patients are a little more upscale and demanding," Hanna offered as they entered Tony's office.

"It's Fox Chapel. You fit in well here."

"I wish I could fit in Fox Chapel," she said in reference to the affluence of the area.

"You've been with us for several weeks now. Can we do lunch today and talk about your performance?" Tony inhaled once more through his nose.

"Of course. You're my boss. I'll do whatever you say." Hanna smiled.

After he finished his last morning patient, Tony changed out of his scrubs. He called home and Claire told him that Angela was resting comfortably and lying on the couch watching something on the Disney Channel. She promised to call if there was any change. He then called Frank Reilly concerning Mrs. Ludwig.

"Tony, thanks for calling me back. I wonder if you could do me a huge favor."

"Of course, Frank, what do you need?"

"Could you squeeze Anna Ludwig in this afternoon?"

"Sure, what's up?"

"She's certain that she has a squamous cell lesion on her face. She's sure that she's going to die."

"Last time I saw her, she had a piece of dried cereal under her lower lip. I couldn't find an insurance code for a cornflakectomy. So as to not embarrass her, I told her she had a very common dry skin condition and gave her a sample of moisturizer."

Frank laughed. "I know. You were great with her. She loves you. I wouldn't bother you, but she's my mother's good friend. She had my mother call me about it."

"No problem. I mean, how long can it take to remove another corn flake?"

"Thanks, pal. I owe you one."

"Actually, you owe me six, but who's counting?"

"Very funny, Tony. By the way, who's the new person answering your phone?"

"Name's Hanna."

"She sounds very sexy on the phone."

"I know!"

"Does she look as good as she sounds?"

"Better."

"You lucky duck. How come I always hire staff that looks like Jabba the Hut?"

"Maybe you should open your eyes during the interview, Frank. Listen, I've got to go. As a matter of fact, I have a staff lunch meeting with Hanna in a couple of minutes."

"Watch yourself, Tony."

"Why do people keep saying that to me?"

Tony took Hanna to a small Italian restaurant in Sharpsburg. The five-minute drive took twice as long due to the heavy traffic in Aspinwall.

"This place is a little off the beaten path, but the food is outstanding," Tony said as he parked the car.

"I love Italian food!"

"Doesn't everyone?" Tony asked.

"I suppose, but I grew up eating Italian," Hanna added.

"You did?" Tony said, with a surprised look on his face.

"Yes. My mother's an F.B.I.—you know, a Full Blooded Italian."

"I'm familiar with the acronym." Tony laughed, pointing to himself. "So your mother's Italian. I knew there was something that I liked about you when I hired you!"

Hanna laughed out loud.

"So we have something in common. Actually, we have two things in common."

"Two things?" Hanna inquired.

"Yes. I had an Italian mother too."

"What's the second thing?"

"We both stop traffic with our incredible good looks!"

Just then the traffic light turned red and they crossed the street in front of the stopped traffic.

"See what I mean?"

"You're too funny!" Hanna said as they crossed the street and entered the restaurant. "My stepfather is Italian as well, so you see, I grew up in an Italian home."

"It's the only kind of home to grow up in. Oh, how the rest of the world envies us!" Tony looked at Hanna. "Speaking of the world, you know that there are only two types of people in it, don't you?"

"Yes. Italians and those who wish they were. My stepfather says that all the time!"

"I think that we are going to get along just fine!"

The two sat and talked about everything *but* the office. Tony spoke of his travels through Italy, about the university, about his passion for cooking. He spoke of his children and his tastes in music and theater. Hanna spoke of her life's situation—of being the single parent of three young children, how so little time existed except for children-related functions. How she had a burning desire for the "other" things in life—the things that would bring her gratification and pleasure, not to mention lust-fulfillment.

This subject got Tony's attention. He inferred that she was not in the least bit intrusive in mentioning her need for lust-fulfillment. Although it was obvious to Tony that Hanna was a sensual person—that sense being telegraphed by the way she carried herself and her mildly flirtatious demeanor and "come-hither" eyes—he did not interpret her statement to be the least bit lecherous. It was a sincere statement. It indicated that she had done without those things that brought joy and self-indulgence—suppressing them for the sake of her children's needs and wants.

"So tell me, what are some of the things that you lust after?"

"You know, lust isn't necessarily a bad word."

"I never implied that it was," Tony was quick to add.

"It can mean a strong craving for something or a desire to possess and enjoy something."

"Hanna, I understand that. I got a 1400 on my college boards."

Hanna laughed. "I didn't want you to get the wrong idea." She looked at him with a mocked innocence in her gaze—almost pouting.

"Oh, I have a feeling that you can get your ideas across very well!"

"OK then. Maybe I meant that sometimes I just lust after taking a nice long hot bath. To pour scented oils into a hot bubble bath and have a nice long soak. No interruptions, no fighting children—just me and perhaps a glass of wine and the aroma of scented candles burning in the solitude of a locked bathroom. Maybe I meant to go out and buy something that I don't need, but that I want. Maybe I meant that I would like to be swept off my feet by a knight in shining armor on a white horse, with my colored silk scarf tied to his lance."

Tony watched her as they spoke. He tried hard to disregard the phallus reference—that was his interpretation and not, he was certain, her intent. She looked beautiful in the subdued light of the restaurant, the highlights in her hair catching the candle's glow as it burned in the center of the table. Her fragrance carried across the table and he knew that her scent would linger long after the workday ended, if nowhere else than in his reverie. *That lip gloss was made for candlelight.*

A sobering thought struck Tony. This was more like a first date than a staff lunch. He was looking at her and listening to her as if she were not an employee but an object of his affections. He found himself saying things to impress her and commenting on her statements with a degree of caring concern. He had not felt this way since long before he and Cathy married—over twenty years ago.

Hanna ran her middle finger around the rim of her glass in a slow, almost sensuous motion. She looked up at him with large expressive eyes—deep blue and penetrating—framed by mascara lashes, liner and subtle shadow.

"Thank you for lunch and the conversation. I enjoyed it very much."

Tony looked at his watch. "Wow! Where did the time go? We'd better hustle back. Good thing I know the boss!" Tony kidded.

Over the course of the next few months Tony and Hanna had lunch frequently. To the surprise of many of his staff, he added an extra half day at the Oakland office, and had Mitch and Hanna exchange places one day a week, bringing Hanna to the Fox Chapel office. Mitch's feelings were hurt, but Tony couldn't see it, or chose not to.

"I think that it's important to cross-train our staff, so that both can run either office," Tony rationalized.

There were rumblings among the staff that Tony wrote off as petty jealousy. He was spending more and more time up in the business office area. He enjoyed leaning over Hanna and smelling her hair as he pretended to be interested in ledger cards or appointment books—an area of the practice that up until now did not interest him in the least.

In early January Tony sent Hanna to a two-day staff enhancement seminar that he had sent Mitch to the previous year. He attended it with her. In was in Niagara on the Lake, Ontario. The cold Canadian winds off the lake could cut one in two, yet Tony hadn't felt this warm in longer than he chose to remember. The two of them walked down the quaint streets, stopping in and browsing through the shops, admiring the old-fashioned prettiness of their wares.

They shared dinner for the first time. Tony remarked how it felt so different, it being dinner and not lunch. They sat and talked at the charming French-Canadian restaurant until near closing. They were the last two in the restaurant. Tony ordered another bottle of the Pouilly-Fuisse they had been drinking and they moved to a settee in front of the roaring fire. There with the flames of the burning hardwood warming their flesh and the white burgundy warming their affections, they had a deeper conversation than the situations of their previous meetings could or would allow.

Hanna revealed sides of her complex self that surprised Tony, yet interested him keenly. She had been married four times. Her first husband was a male stripper and part-time bartender. She married him as soon as she turned eighteen, under much protestation from her Italian mother. He was into drugs and would involve her in the strangest scenarios, that Tony had a hard time seeing Hanna in. It lasted six months. One day, Hanna saw the light and walked out the door. She never looked back.

Tony had a hard time understanding how anyone could just let Hanna walk out of their lives and not do absolutely anything and everything to attempt reconciliation.

Her next boyfriend got her pregnant when she was twenty and became husband number two. He was immature, self-centered and also into drug use. They were married in June. She miscarried in August, in the fourth month of her pregnancy.

Tony looked across the settee at her with no small degree of disbelief. How could anyone as bright and apparently together as she seemed allow this to happen to them? *Did she not see a pattern here?* Tony wondered. He could tell almost from the moment that they first met that she possessed a kind of energy—an alluring energy that almost seemed to shout: *I am destined for greatness!* She had a certain grace that attracted people to her and made them want to share her space—to be in her life, if only for a brief time. Tony could more easily see her married to a C.E.O. of a large company, or to a successful doctor, than to the losers she chose.

Newlyweds, even with some sense of stability and a steady income, are faced with struggles. Tony could only imagine the rocky road that she and husband number two must have gone through. One day, after three years of living hand to mouth and with little more than the clothes she was wearing, she walked out of the door and again, never looked back.

There are people who live in the mistake-prisons that they create for themselves, either because they do not know how to break out, or because, for the want of the limited comfort offered, they choose not to. Hanna was above that. She was a survivor.

Next in her life came a series of "lovers"—a rogue's gallery in and of itself. She seemed attracted to "bad boys," liars and cheats—bartenders, hustlers, petty crooks, gamblers and people on the fringe of the underworld. Guys who sold counterfeit Rolexes out of the trunks of their cars and sleazy well-to-do guys who led her on with promises of support yet were engaged to be married to other women even as they spoke their lies.

It all seemed more than a waste to Tony. It was like someone driving a classic Mercedes in a demolition derby to fulfill some sick self-serving need.

Among the many lovers in her life was a car dealer named Enzo Gamboni. Enzo lived the high life of fancy cars and good tables in popular restaurants. He was a showy tipper and a loudmouth with a square-cut diamond pinky ring who wore Hanna on his arm like another piece of jewelry to draw attention to himself. Unfortunately, Hanna was just window dressing that he bedded behind his fiancée's back. Regrettably, she fell in love with this deceitful person. She even thought that they would marry. When she found out that he was engaged to be married already, it brought great pain and disappointment into her life.

Soon after that aborted relationship, she became engaged to an individual who was a step in the right direction for her. He was gainfully employed and apparently stable—an industrial engineer. He fell—understandably—head over heels for her. Unfortunately for him, she said yes to his proposal not out of love, but out of a combination of rebound effect from breaking up with Gamboni and a desire to regain some self-respect. She returned his ring after only a few weeks when she regained her distorted senses.

After a series of relationships, some self-serving, others self-destructive, and perhaps during a time of some vulnerability, she met husband number three. He was a cocky sort, and of course, this attracted her attentions. The combination of his persuasive pursuits and her vulnerability led to another pregnancy. They were married a short time afterward. A twelve-year mistake left her in the end with three children and a cheating husband who had great difficulty keeping his penis in his pants. He squandered any money that he made and left her in a state of financial embarrassment. She deserved none of this in Tony's eyes. However, his assessment was tainted by her presentation.

The contradictions confused Tony as well as intrigued him. Was she self-destructive? Did she suffer from some kind of emotional or inter-personal masochism? Perhaps she had a propensity for making extremely poor life decisions. How else could her actions and the way her personal life unfolded be explained? Was Tony alone in seeing what he saw in her—the potential for grandeur—an almost noble presence? In her he saw a package of unique beauty, intelligence and style. More than that, she had an aura about her. When she walked into the room, he could feel the energy. When she touched him, he felt the warmth of the sun—fire flying from her hands. How could this disparity be justified? Was he supposed to even try?

Husband number three's friend, Ned, from the neighborhood, blew the whistle on him. Ned approached Hanna with the facts of her spouse's infidelity, not so much out of a need for the search of truth, but rather as a means to get closer to her. The times, dates, persons and places that Ned provided afforded Hanna justification for separation from her cheating husband. It also afforded Ned with access into Hanna's confidence, as well as her bedroom. Their relationship lasted three years. Three years of unbridled sex that was euphoria for Ned but nothing more than carnal release for Hanna.

Time and relationships passed. She refused to talk about husband number four—saying nothing about him or the marriage.

When she entered Tony's life she was engaged in a love affair with what Tony would call another loser. He was a dozen years older than she—a Greek named Gus. He would hustle on the side as he booked numbers in the strip district of Pittsburgh. He had a monkey on his back named oxycotin. She deserved better. Why couldn't she see it?

Tony had called Hanna at the Oakland office one day to talk about nothing important. It was just an opportunity to hear her voice—to be "with her" even though they were apart. Her voice was soothing and, at the same time, stimulating for Tony. Her voice was as alluring to his ears as her scent was olfactory delight.

During the conversation, the other phone line rang. She excused herself as she answered it. Tony could hear the salutation. It was the bookmaker. There was a pause as if her hand had cupped itself over the receiver of the phone line that Tony was waiting on. In a moment she came back onto Tony's line. "It's for me. Can I get it?" she asked.

"Of course you can." Came Tony's response.

"OK. Bye!" Then a click, as Tony's line became disconnected.

In an instant Tony felt his lack of worth. Discarded. Set adrift—an object of little importance in Hanna's world at that particular point in time.

That evening, Tony and Sean met in Sean's kitchen for an evening of culinary creativity. In the company of portabella mushrooms and homemade pasta and white truffle oil, not to mention their second bottle of Pinot Grigio, Tony opened his soul once again to his old friend.

"Am I missing something here, Sean?" Tony said as he took another sip of the wine. "I mean is there even a contest here?" he said, referring to some perceived competition between himself and the bookie.

"Excuse me, Tony, but did I miss something? I mean just when did you become available so as to have a relationship with this woman and be in competition with Zorba the Corleone?"

"Availability can come in many forms, Sean."

"Evidently, some forms of availability count more than others. You may be available in your own mind, while Mr. Underworld is, well, available in the ways that count to her. You may not approve of his lifestyle or his station in life, but you have to give him some credit. He is experiencing more intimacy with her than you are."

"And this makes sense to you, Sean?"

"I didn't say that it made sense. Sense is relative—not necessarily relevant. You have to understand that you are dealing with the mind of a woman. Nobody said that it had to make sense, my friend—at least not in the rational world that you and I live in."

Tony and Sean laughed out loud as they poured another glass of wine. When the second bottle was almost finished, Tony took the phone book from underneath the telephone stand and began to thumb through it.

"What time would you guess that he would pick her up for a movie, Sean? You are experienced in this dating thing. I overheard her say something about the movies in her conversation with him."

"It depends. If they are going to dinner first, then I'd say seven p.m. If just to the movies, perhaps nine p.m. or so. But hell, there are countless possibilities. They could go out for drinks or to a jazz club or something."

Tony looked up from his reading glasses. "Jazz club? Give me a break, Sean. Perhaps you mean if they decided to roll around on the sofa cushions for a while, but do you really think this guy fits the Rosebud's clientele profile?" Tony looked up at the kitchen clock. It was 7:15 p.m. "I'm going to call her and ask her to break her date with this loser and consider going out with me tonight."

Sean picked up the near empty bottle of wine. "What the hell was the alcohol content of this shit?"

Tony ignored his friend as he punched in Hanna's number and got her daughter's recorded message. "Damn, I missed her!"

Sean took Tony by the arm. "Trust me, old friend, it's better that you didn't get through to her! Get a grip, man! This isn't you, Tony. In fact, you haven't been yourself for several weeks now. This woman is fuck'n with your head!"

"Is that a new psychiatric term—fuck'n with the head?" Tony inquired.

"You are sliding down a slippery slope, buddy. I'm just trying to throw you a lifeline! Count the cost, Tony. You are running the risk of jeopardizing all that you've worked for, for some bimbo, and what—am I supposed to look the other way?"

"Excuse me, friend. She is NOT a bimbo. She is as far removed from a bimbo as the night is from the day! If you were to meet her—to stand next to her—to share her space for even a brief moment, you would see."

"Tony, I know you about as well as I've ever known anyone. You are behaving like someone obsessed. Trust me, this is not you! Look at the whole picture!"

"It's a sweet obsession, Sean."

"That is an oxymoron, Tony. Step back and look at this like I'm seeing it."

"Which is?"

"Your relationship with Cathy is strained, and there's an emotional void in your life. The passionate person that you are needs to have that void filled. Combine that with the fact that you are staring straight in the face of middle age. You are trying to recapture passion and hold on to youth—plain and simple. I suggest that you go buy a Corvette or a Porche!"

"You are oversimplifying things, Sean. As if a sports car could repair what is ailing me!"

"Now that is the first step, Tony—admitting that you are ailing!"

"I know that I am hurting, Sean. One of the first things that we learned in medical school was that pain ultimately accompanies disease." Tony opened a third bottle of the Pinot. He turned and shook his head as he began to stir the white truffle sauce in the All-Clad pot on the stove. "For tonight at least, let us enjoy this shared passion." Tony waved the scent rising from the white truffle sauce towards him and inhaled through his nose. "It's not even a close second, Sean. Not even close."

Chapter 10

Tony walked into the kitchen and found Cathy sitting at the table with a cup of warmed milk. It was 1:00 a.m.

"What's the matter, Cath? Can't you sleep?"

She didn't answer. She took a long swallow from the cup. Tony pulled up a chair and sat across the table from her. He looked at her, trying to see the Cathy whom he saw walking toward the grandstand at the anti-war rally—trying to see the person in whose very presence he melted. He looked, trying to see the person who redefined his life—the person who entered his life when the very fabric of time and space was changed—the time that a miracle occurred and she was in the very center of it. It was as long ago as it was far away. Could the passage of time and distance create the chasm that Tony now looked across as he gazed at his wife? Perhaps his inability to see *that* Cathy was not defined by physical laws, but by emotional ones.

"Tony, I'm very confused right now. I don't know what's come over me, but I do see the effect that it has had on our relationship. I have been soul-searching for several weeks now. I'm embarrassed to say this to you, but my career is more important to me than almost anything else in my life. Outside of my work, I find little joy. In us, I find even less."

Her words hit Tony like a brick. "Perhaps some counseling, Cath—"

"Don't play that card, Tony. Don't you dare play THAT card! Don't even go there! Don't think that for a minute that just because you went to medical school, you can suggest ANY treatment for me! You are nothing more than a damn dermatologist—a pimple doctor! You didn't have what it takes to be a *real* doctor. You didn't have it! You went cowering behind creams and acne medication—because you lack what it takes!"

She was pushing Tony's buttons. She always could. She knew where every one was and exactly how hard to push each one to achieve her desired effect.

Tony could not believe how she misinterpreted his statement. The

124

suggested counseling was for them, not her. Tony got up from the table and abruptly walked out of the kitchen, knowing that if he stayed, hurtful words would be exchanged. The last thing that he wanted was for a shouting match to ensue and wake Claire and the children. He went into his study and closed the door. He put on some soft jazz and lay down on the sofa. With his hands cupped behind the back of his head, Tony stared blankly at the ceiling and reflected on Cathy's words.

She told him that their relationship was strained. He knew that. She said that her work was more important to her than he was. With him, there was no joy in her life. That hurt. It cut deeply. Why not just take a hot poker and stick it in his eye? If it were another man, he could fight that. How was he supposed to compete with a career? Then the painful barrage concerning his career choice came. If she had been in Danny's death room and seen the events unravel that led to his tormented decision, she could not make such a demeaning statement. How could she make such damaging and uncaring remarks? How could she set him emotionally adrift like this?

Sade's *No ordinary love* was now playing on his stereo and Tony's thoughts turned toward Hanna. A breath of emotional fresh air—as sentimental as it was welcome. A diversion of thought. A refreshing diversion. A welcome diversion. It was not a difficult transition.

Tony drifted off to sleep there in the solitude of his study—Sade's alluring voice accompanied by his sultry thoughts of Hanna. Sensual thoughts of Hanna accompanying him into slumber. A passionate, sentimental journey into slumber. It was just what the doctor ordered.

Tony entered the Oakland office with a mild spring in his step. It was the anticipation of seeing Hanna more than anything else.

"Good morning. You look happy this morning."

"Good morning, Hanna. Why wouldn't I be happy? I'm here with you, aren't I?" Tony smiled. "You look great this morning. Do you ever not look good?"

"Thank you. How sweet," Hanna purred with a mocked coyness and with a tone that revealed that she was very used to hearing this. She didn't look up from the computer screen.

"Listen, I was wondering. Are you free for dinner this evening?"

She now looked up from the screen and directly into Tony's eyes. "Did you just ask me out?"

Tony turned as if to see if there was anyone else who could have asked her. "I think that was me."

"I mean, it's just that beside that one time in Niagra on the Lake, our encounters have been lunches only—never in the evening."

"Is that a yes or a no?"

"We'll see."

"Do you know what my kids say when I say that? They say: 'Dad, when you say *we'll see*, that means no.'"

"I'm not one of your kids, now am I?"

"Hardly."

"It's just that it's a school night, and I'd have to scramble for a sitter."

"OK, how about Friday night then?"

"This Friday?"

"No, Friday, April 20. Yes, THIS Friday. I'll compensate the sitter."

Hanna hesitated. Tony couldn't tell if it was to not appear anxious or if she was sincerely trying to decide whether to agree to the date. It was an awkward silent moment. She was in control. She knew it and Tony knew it. Tony was about to retract the offer, now feeling foolish—her silence creating an image in his mind of his being an undeserving suitor, she being the prima persona.

With impeccable timing, as if she had perfected the art of control via delayed response, she responded before Tony could retract the offer.

"I suppose Friday will be OK," she answered.

It was a bittersweet outcome. Manipulation of the event turned the desired response into something much less than it was supposed to be, or than it could have been. Tony accepted it anyway, already a pawn in this game.

There is something immensely sad when a knight becomes a pawn. It is a waste of talent as well as potential. It is not unlike lighting a cigar with a fifty-dollar bill. Tony realized this, he just refused to see the full consequences of it all—both the short-term as well as the long-term consequences of it all.

Tony pulled into the restaurant's parking lot a full ten minutes before his agreed time to meet Hanna. He chose a secluded restaurant off the beaten path and on the other side of town in order to maintain a low profile. The restaurant specialized in southern Italian cuisine—recommended by a friend whose opinion both on the restaurant's quality and privacy Tony respected. He was nervous, twice almost turning around on his drive there, but it was not in his nature to be rude and stand someone up. He had made the commitment and he could not renege. He had never done this in his twenty-two years of marriage—arrange a clandestine meeting with another woman. Strange, he thought, how his "commitment" to meet with Hanna trumped his commitment to his marriage—but then, with his world turned upside-down as it was, few things made sense to him. The inequity brushed by him with little reflection. Was he cheating the devil, or was the devil cheating him? Deep, life-changing decisions as this require reflective meditation. At this point in time, Tony was incapable of superficial thought, let alone deep reflection. Tragedies such as this occur when knights become pawns. Knights climb mountains and slay dragons—armed with little more than sharpened steel and desire—when they are not immersed in deep reflective meditation. Pawns are relegated to the world of superficial thought. This time it was no different. The tragedy of it all, like the inequity, brushed by him like the winds of lost innocence.

He tried to rationalize his guilt away by telling himself that there was nothing wrong with having dinner with an employee. He was terrible at self-deception. He knew that this was very wrong—wrong at every level. He glanced at his watch and noticed a mild tremor in his left hand. He couldn't believe how nervous he was, yet couldn't decide if his tremor was due to his fear of being discovered with another woman or the prospect of being alone with Hanna—she affected him that much.

A half-hour after their arranged time to meet, Hanna's car pulled into the restaurant's lot. Tony was beginning to fear that she had become lost, or worse yet, had decided to stand HIM up. He was relieved to see her car. He took a deep breath as if this would have a calming effect on his anxious state or at least quiet the tremor. It did neither.

Hanna chose to wear scrubs at the office for comfort. If anyone could look good in non-revealing scrubs, she could. *Hell, she'd look good in sackcloth,* Tony often thought. The one opportunity that he had to see her play "dress-up," in Niagra on the Lake, when she revealed her figure with fashionable style, made Tony envy those men in her life who got to see her this way on a regular basis. Tonight was no different.

He walked up to her car as she opened the door. She swung her long, shapely legs out and stood up as he greeted her. Her four-inch open-toed black high heels elevated her to near eye-to-eye level with him, as was the case with their first meeting at her interview.

"We fit together differently when you wear heels," Tony said as he embraced her with a long hug, wrapping his arms around her slender waist as he did so.

He wanted to kiss her full lips, sensuous and inviting as they were in outlined pink, but he read her approach as laced with guarded caution.

She wore a black tight-fitting dress that stopped mid-thigh. It had a scooped neckline with spaghetti straps that allowed for a revealing look at the domed top of her breasts—uplifted into view by one of Victoria's miracles. The dress was clinging. He could see her flat tummy and the hollow created by her navel. When she turned to close the car door, her narrow waist and tight ass were presented—with no hint of panty lines, suggesting that she wore thong panties or perhaps none at all.

Tony wondered how someone could go through three pregnancies and still look this good. It must be the work of the devil—or at the very least the result of some gray-magic spell, he didn't know which. She was hot, and now so was he. This much he did know.

"Hanna, you smell as good as you look, if that's possible. What *is* that scent that you are wearing?" Tony said as he leaned forward, placing his cheek against her neck and inhaling deeply through his nose.

"It's called *Michael*. I wear it only on special occasions. You don't pay me enough to wear it more often than that," she added with a smile.

"Perhaps we can talk about that," Tony said. "Thank you for saying that this is a special occasion, by the way."

"I was hoping that you would say that—about the raise, I mean," Hanna was quick to add. Her phraseology and timing were calculating—creating an upper-hand atmosphere. She was very self-assured and extremely comfortable with herself. Tony could see that she had been around the relationship block a few times. She was good at setting ground rules and defining roles—calling the shots in that regard. It is good to do that which one is good at. She was good at this. Tony was good as well—it's just that in her presence, he lost sight of who he was, let alone what he could bring to the table.

The restaurant was only about half-occupied, which suited Tony. Fewer people meant less potential for encountering someone he knew. It would be difficult to explain away—his being alone with such a beautiful and sexy woman in such a secluded and dimly lit restaurant.

That evening was the first of many clandestine meetings.

"You know, I've never been involved with a married man before," Hanna said matter-of-factly one day. Tony tried to hide his surprise.

"I find that hard to believe."

"And why is that?"

"Surely, married men have hit on you before!"

"I never said that married men have not been interested in being involved with me. I just never chose to get involved with a dead-end situation."

"What is it that makes me different?"

"Are we getting involved?"

"What would you call it, Hanna? You said that you are attracted to me."

"I don't know what to call it. I know that you are interested in me—the

128

way that you come on to me—the way that you put your arms around my waist, and smell my hair and kiss the back of my neck. I know that your marriage is strained at the very least, and near on the rocks at best, but you are still married." She paused briefly before she continued. "Yes, I'm attracted to you. You are handsome, intelligent and successful, with a great sense of humor that I find very appealing. In fact, I can honestly say that I have never met anyone like you before."

Hanna let down her guard like never before. It was the closest to her admitting reciprocity that Tony had witnessed. He was pleased and stimulated by her comments. He felt a rush of warm excitement. She sang to him and he was all ears. How he had longed to hear her open up to him as she just now did. He looked into her eyes, in the hope that he would see confirmation of what he was now hearing. He wasn't sure if he was seeing doubt or confirmation. Was she sending mixed signals, or was she just difficult to read? It was this complexity about her that he found frustrating, and at the same time alluring.

The relationship between Tony and Hanna grew in intensity as his damaged relationship with Cathy continued in its decline.

There were confrontational outbursts at home on a more regular basis, initiated by Cathy's frustrations and fueled by Tony's confusion and hurt. The children were now also pawns in the game. This scenario was sadder than the previous pawn creation—more than one dare fathom. Cathy was pushing Tony's buttons on an almost regular basis now. The confrontations became more frequent and more heated—not really because either party desired the head-butting, but because the feelings kept deep inside, and left to steep over the years, dictated behavior unbecoming those capable of rational thought. Visceral reactions now ruled the day. It came to the point where Tony avoided contact with Cathy in order to avoid argument. It puzzled him how things were unraveling so quickly between him and Cathy. Their relationship seemed so strained that Tony could not see how to get back to where it had been. It seemed as unlikely as trying to get toothpaste back into the tube.

As if on cue, Hanna came to Tony one day, entering his private office and closing the door behind her, as she was accustomed to do to afford them the privacy that the moment demanded. This time the situation was a little different.

"I need to ask you something that I'm a little embarrassed about." Hanna was as serious as he had ever seen her.

"What's up?" Tony said as he got up from his desk and placed his arms around her waist. He kissed her gently on the cheek.

"I need a little help. My ex-husband is late in his child-care payments and I'm a little short this month. They threatened to turn off my electricity." She placed her open palms on Tony's chest, resting them there as she looked at him with pleading eyes.

"There's no need to be embarrassed, Hanna. You know that I will do anything to help you out. How much do you need?" Tony said in a caring and sympathetic tone.

"I feel so cheap asking you for money."

"It's not your fault that your ex-husband is a slouch. How much do you need?"

"I need three hundred for the electric company."

"Is that all you need?"

"I feel so cheap. Cheap and embarrassed."

"Don't say another word. I'll go to the bank at lunch and get some cash out. No need to create a paper trail here with a check. I'll get a little extra just in case."

Hanna put her arms around his neck and kissed him. "It's just a loan, OK?"

"Nonsense. I don't expect you to pay me back."

Tony returned from lunch with a $1,000 in cash and gave it to Hanna. The following week Tony opened a separate office checking account earmarked for office supplies and sundries, giving Hanna access. He deposited $1,000 every month. She could draw on it to supplement her income with other staff members being none the wiser of the obvious bias and the salary prejudice and inequity. $1,000 was an easy amount to launder and keep Cathy in the dark about. It also saved Hanna the embarrassment of having to come to Tony and ask for money.

"If you need a little extra cash, it's there for you. If you don't use it, it will be there for the future. We can use it for another trip to Niagara or something like it."

"You are so good to me. I just wish that you were not married. Oh, how I wish that you were not married!"

"Listen. Angela's birthday is in two months. I am trying to keep peace at home for the sake of the children, but I know they sense the tension between Cathy and me. I don't know if our relationship is repairable. I don't know if I want to try anymore. I have been thinking more and more seriously about leaving her. There is absolutely no way that I can even entertain that, thought until after my baby's birthday. Birthdays are very special to her. They always have been. I can't disrupt her little life with this until afterwards. "

"I don't want to be a home-wrecker."

"The strain was there before I even knew that you existed. You are part of the equation, certainly, but there are other factors involved."

"Do you know what you are saying?"

"I am acutely aware of what I am saying. I've known for a long time now that I need to get more of you into my life. I know that our relationship cannot go much further while I'm a married man. I also know that there are no guarantees that you and I will end up together, but I am willing to take that chance. Hanna, you've redefined my life."

It is extremely sad when knights become pawns. The once-knight now stood before Hanna, unaware on the surface of the extent of his wispy state—like a knight in paper armor. Unaware of what consequences his statement had wrought in the grand scheme of things. Perhaps that is how it is when knights become pawns. Perhaps that is how it is when the devil has his way. Sadness has depths that one can only imagine—unless of course, one is in possession of the truth. Tony, at this point in time, was not in possession of the truth—or anything else of consequence.

Tony had shared his thoughts with Sean. Sean told him in no uncertain terms that he felt Tony needed to back off and regroup before making such an important life decision as leaving one's wife and family and running off with a woman about whom, in Sean's opinion, Tony knew precious little. Sean did not like Hanna. What's more, he didn't trust her. He categorized her as deceptive, manipulative and self-serving. Of course, not being enamored with her, she was quite transparent to him. Such was not the case with Tony. He believed what he wanted to believe about Hanna. What was worse, he believed what *she* wanted him to believe. He couldn't see her actions as being self-serving because he refused to see them as such.

"Tony, listen to me. I really think that you and I need to have a serious man-to-man. In our prior conversations regarding this liaison, it is now obvious to me that I have failed miserably in convincing you that you are making a very bad decision here. Perhaps my arguments lack the necessary impact on you because I never really thought that you would pursue this thing this far. I underestimated the degree of your obsession and involvement. I wrote it off as some silly midlife phase that you were going through. I can see now that I made a terrible error in judging how much this woman has affected you. I can't sit back and let this happen without refocusing and intensifying my efforts."

"Sean, you are my best friend. We've shared many joys and pains over the years. Our bond, like the fine wines that we enjoy, took years to become perfected. You also know that I respect your intelligence and judgment more than anyone else's. But I must say that you are totally wrong about Hanna. A person cannot affect another like she has affected me unless there is some cosmic force at work. This is destiny unfolding, Sean."

"Did you ever think that there are powerful negative cosmic forces as well? Negative forces disguised as forces of light? Fraudulent forces designed to deceive?"

Sean's comment impacted Tony as nothing else that Sean had said before. Tony rarely saw Sean's spiritual side manifested as it had just now been.

"I know that you have my best interest in mind, Sean. I really do appreciate it. I really do."

"Look, what I was getting at, is that we have paid this whole situation little more than brief and flitting lip-service. As I said, we need to have a serious man-to-man. Let's take a weekend and go to the Big Apple—just the two of us. No girls allowed. We'll eat our way across that island that they call Manhattan, take in a jazz club or a play and pay this crisis justice."

"Crisis?"

"Crisis!"

"Is it that bad in your eyes, Sean?"

"It is."

"OK, you have my attention. But I want you to know, I'm not about to roll over and play dead about this. I refuse to be spoon-fed. My intelligence and common sense are intact. I have my own perspective on this thing, you know."

"That's the problem. I wish that you could see it as I do. In the interim, I want you to reflect on one small but, in my opinion, relevant and significant fact. I have never, ever heard her refer to you by name. Not once. That's a statement, my friend. A power statement. Perhaps it's an indication of the degree of importance that you hold in her life. Either way, it is significant."

Tony knew that what Sean was saying was true. He noticed it himself. He had never been in ANY conversation with Hanna when she ever uttered the name Tony—to him or anyone else. He was reduced to a pronoun. It puzzled him. He suppressed reflection on it. This issue, now brought by Sean into Tony's conscious state, forced him by the very confrontation of this truth to reflect on it. It was upsetting to him.

Tony brought Hanna two bank signature cards for her to sign. Her signature was required on the documents in order to give her access to the account. The cards had the account number in the upper right-hand corner. It allowed Hanna access into more than an account. It allowed her to cross a threshold and into a realm of financial intimacy with Tony. That intimacy was as out of place as it was undeserved.

There was no hesitation on Hanna's part. She signed the cards as if she were signing her paycheck—without a second thought and certainly without any trepidation.

The foundations that were laid that day had far-reaching consequences. They shook the foundations that had been laid some twenty-two years before. If the truth be known, they shook foundations that pre-dated Tony and Cathy—foundations that existed in the hearts and minds of those who made love commitments long before Tony and Cathy ever met. It was a foundation set in the hearts of those in love. Commitments. Vows. Promises, before man and before God. None of which belonged in the hearts and mind of those whose object was to deceive—those who chose to cheat the lover's vow. Those who chose to strain or, God forbid, tear the fabric of a lover's promise.

Cathy walked into the lobby of the Duquesne Club. Charlie was waiting for her, seated in a wing-backed chair and reading the *Wall Street Journal*. When he saw her enter, he glanced quickly at his watch and rose to greet her.

"I'm glad that you could get away for lunch today."

"It was touch-and-go for a while, but I managed," Cathy replied with a mild sense of relief in her voice.

Cathy had met with Charlie for lunch two other times since they reunited in the lobby of her office building. At first, she was reluctant and resisting. Her reluctance lessened somewhat on the second meeting. This time there was little, if any. She felt compelled—drawn, as if by some magnetic force. Her original guilt was now covered by a sense of titillating pleasure.

"You look lovely, as always," Charlie said while folding the newspaper and placing it under his arm. "Shall we?" Charlie extended his hand in the direction of the doorway that led to the bar.

"I don't usually drink this early in the day," Cathy said as she glanced at the Rolex that Charlie had given her years before.

"Alcohol prepares the palate. Besides, no one said that you had to quaff a stein. You can sip daintily on a nice Chardonnay. Your amateur standing can remain intact."

There in the room where power meetings often took place, Cathy sat across from her former lover, as he held her hand.

"You know, Cathy, I think of you often. I also often think of what could have been between us."

Cathy looked at Charlie as he spoke. She was transformed by his words. Actually, she felt transformed by the entire experience. She was now not the powerful executive and partner of a large PR firm. She was no longer a career woman with a chip on her shoulder out to prove something. She was almost a schoolgirl again, wrapped up in the amorous advances of a former lover. The sense of relief was as welcomed as it was needed.

"You know, Charlie, what might have been was totally in your hands. You were the one who broke my heart, as I recall." Her statement was in your face and to the point—her delivery tempered by years of hardball negotiations in the business world.

Charlie was taken aback for a moment—but only for a moment. He was not accustomed to going mano a mano in an exchange with an opponent as lovely as she. He quickly leveled the playing field.

"You are so very right, Cathy. It was my bad. I dropped the ball in our relationship, and a day has not gone by that I have not regretted it."

Cathy took a sip of her wine. "Do you mean that?"

"Of course I do. I became intimidated by our relationship. I was confused and, frankly, frightened by the prospect of it all. The idea of the commitment terrified me." Charlie sat there, a bit smug by how good his argument sounded. He thought how it would have impressed Robert Duber, his law professor, who lectured in the art of argument and exchange.

"I wish you had conveyed those thoughts to me at that time, Charlie."

"You and me both."

"Look, all that amounts to little more than a reflection on the past, and what might have been. The fact is you and I are married now—not to each other, but to our respective spouses." Cathy looked him in the eye as she spoke.

"That doesn't mean that we have to lose the moment."

"And what exactly does that imply?"

"It doesn't imply anything. What it does, is speak volumes about the way that I feel for you."

Cathy thought back on the last time she heard that phrase: "The way that I feel for you." It was in the screened porch of his parents' cottage on the lake. She also remembered hearing the phrase: "We shouldn't lose the moment." Charlie and his motives became transparent to her now. She leaned forward.

"So Charlie, are you saying—that you want to fuck me?"

She took him off guard. He swallowed hard.

"I want to make love to you, yes."

"Make love to me, or fuck me, Charlie. There is a huge difference. Which is it?"

"Please don't misread me, Cathy. If my approach upset you, I apologize."

Charlie's charm defused the moment.

"Please forgive me, Charlie. I was a bit tough on you. It's just that I have been going through these problems at home with Tony, and I had some guilt issues about our past—it just snowballed there for a moment."

Charlie saw the door open a crack. He got up and moved his chair next to Cathy. He held her hand and kissed her on the cheek.

"I'm sorry if I made more ripples in your pond, Cathy. That wasn't my intent."

"I'm sure that it wasn't, Charlie. It's just that I need someone to understand me on the emotional level right now, not look at me as just a vagina to come into to relieve some carnal urge."

He pressed her cheek against his shoulder and told her how sorry he was for the misunderstanding. She wiped a tear away as the waiter brought another round of drinks.

Chapter 11

Tony walked into the kitchen. It was 8:00 a.m. on Saturday. The children were still sleeping—tucked under the sheets and on their best behavior for the day. He walked over to the coffeemaker and poured a cup for himself and one for Cathy, who was still dressing. He pulled up a chair and sat at the table, waiting for Cathy to come downstairs.

When he came home last night after the Rotary Club lecture on malignant melanoma, Cathy was on the telephone. She ended the conversation as soon as Tony entered the room. There were no good-byes to the person on the other end of the line—just a sudden placement of the receiver on the cradle. It was as out of place as it was sudden. Mystery, not making for comfort in a relationship as it does, left Tony feeling as puzzled as he was suspicious.

Cathy entered the kitchen and, not saying a word, began to pour a cup of coffee for herself.

"Cath, I have one here for you already."

Cathy looked in his direction with some degree of hesitation. She saw the coffee cup that Tony had poured on the table across from where he was sitting. It was an awkward moment—neither knowing what to say next—neither sure how to proceed with the conversation, let alone with those things of greater importance. With no small amount of reluctance, she walked over to where Tony set the other cup on the table.

"I think that we need to talk," Tony said with a lump in his throat.

"About what?" Cathy said, wishing that she could retract her words, hearing them sound as silly as they did.

"You know full well 'about what,' Cath. We are going down some strange path. We are either kidding ourselves or are playing some cruel game here. We don't communicate anymore. We are as distant as we have been in our two decades together. I see it. You see it. The children see it. Hell, a blind person could see it."

Cathy looked up from her cup. She looked through Tony, not at him. It was a look that telegraphed the fact that she really didn't care to discuss this or anything else with him. "Tony, I…"

"Yes? What is it, Cath?"

Cathy got up from the table and left the room, shaking her head as she left. Before Tony could go after her, the telephone rang.

"Who could be calling at this hour?" Tony thought out loud. He looked at the caller ID. It was Cathy's mother.

"Hello, Evelyn?" Tony said, wondering why Cathy's mother would be calling at this hour.

"Tony, I have some very bad news." Her voice was quivering. She sounded as if she had been crying.

Tony and Cathy dropped the children off at Tony's mother's house. Philomena greeted them at the door. She kissed Cathy and offered her sympathies about her father's passing. Cathy, looking at her mother-in-law through tear-filled eyes, accepted her condolences with appreciation.

The drive to Youngstown was long and quiet—Tony not wishing to upset her any more than she already was. Cathy looked out to her right, at the trees and road signs, passing as they did by her car window. They arrived at her mother's house as a steady rain began to fall—punctuation to not only the dark and dreariness of the sky—but also as a backdrop to the events of the day itself.

Cathy walked up to the front door as Tony retrieved the suitcase from the trunk

The rain fell harder now, almost as a confirmation to the gloom in their relationship.

Tony often pitied Cathy's mother, being weak and controlled by her alcoholic husband as she was. She had been controlled for so long, Tony wondered if she could even function without being told what to do and how to do it and when to do it. Her frailty was never more evident to him than it was when he entered the house and saw her that day. During his training, he had witnessed many grieving individuals after a spouse's death. Their reactions to their newfound loneliness varied, from intense anger to inconsolable grief, but the look in their eyes—when he looked past the glassy surface and into their souls—was always the same. When he looked into Evelyn's eyes, he saw something different. He saw intense guilt—sad and undeserved guilt. He had seen guilt before, but never without being accompanied by remorse. Frank Mathias was reaching out from the grave and controlling her still.

Tony embraced her. "I am so sorry, Evelyn." Tony looked up at Cathy and into her eyes. He saw her undeserved guilt as well, but hers was laced with the remorse that one would expect to see in the eyes of a daughter who remembered a happier relationship with her loving father before redefinition by alcohol. "Do you want me to help you with the arrangements?" he spoke to Evelyn with caring concern.

"I don't know what to do, Tony."

"Let me handle it for you. When a decision comes up that I think you should make, I'll define your options for you, in order to make this a little easier. Do you have any specific requests that you can think of now?"

"No. I told the hospital to call McHugh's funeral home."

"That's over on Main Street, isn't it?"

"Yes. Main Street."

"How about you, Cath?"

"I'll go upstairs in a little bit and pick out a suit that Dad should wear. I want to choose the casket also. I can't deal with particulars like services or songs or such. I'll let you handle all of that."

She spoke to Tony as if he were an employee that she held in little regard—a receptionist at the firm, or perhaps at best a lesser-account associate. It dawned on him that this had been her tone with him during the steady decline in their relationship. He was not only *not* the most important event in her life, his position was now relegated to some backroom degree of importance in her life. His ego had been deflated as surely as if she had stuck a knife in it and twisted it cruelly. His mind raced as he reviewed the events that took place and the time frame during which the decline occurred. If there was a focal event in this declination, it had to be the delivery of the family portrait. Their relationship seemed to change from that day forward. But why? There had to be more than met the eye, but Tony did not know what it was. Initially, Tony was affected at a much deeper level regarding the decline in his relationship with Cathy. Initially, he wanted reconciliation and to bring back their union to the point where it had been before the retrogression—he just didn't know how. All of his attempts bore no fruit. He then reviewed in his mind the events and time frame of his attempts at reconciliation. If there was a focal event in the decline of his attempts to placate their unity—a time when he seemed to give up on any attempt at reconciliation—it had to be when he met Hanna. If there was a parallel here, Tony wondered for the first time if there was a Hanna-equivalent in Cathy's life. The thought struck him in the face like a cold slap. Double standards aside, this sobering thought got his attention, not only for the rest of the day, but it haunted him and accompanied him every day like an unwanted dream.

Cathy led her mother by the arm out of her prosaic living room and into the kitchen as Tony thumbed through the telephone book for the funeral home's number, looking in the direction of Cathy's exit as he did so.

Hanna walked into the Aspinwall branch of the bank that Tony did business with. This branch was in the neighboring town to where Tony's Fox Chapel office and his regular bank branch were located. She had an appointment with the branch manager during the lunch hour. She introduced herself to the woman behind the desk and was told to have a seat. She was not wearing scrubs this day, but a navy-blue business suit with a short skirt and high heels. She sat in a chair facing the manager's office and crossed her legs, as her short skirt rose up to reveal her upper thigh. Her makeup was applied as if by a professional. She looked more like a fashion model than a medical office manager.

The branch manager walked out into the reception area and was immediately struck by Hanna's presentation. He looked her not in the eye, but in the thigh. Still not looking up, he extended his hand in her direction.

"Mrs. McDowell?"

"It's *Ms.* McDowell," Hanna said as she rose and extended her hand to meet his, pulling her skirt down in a mocked attempt at modesty.

"Please forgive me, Ms. McDowell. I'm Frank Peterson, the branch manager. Please come into my office," he said as he extended his hand toward his private office and watched her sway past him, her tight ass barely contained within the fabric of the skirt.

"What is it that we can do for you, Ms. McDowell?" Mr. Peterson asked with a degree of professionalism.

"I have a delicate matter to discuss with you, Mr. Peterson."

"Yes?"

"I am the office manager for Dr. Cipullo. We have offices in Fox Chapel and Oakland. We do business with your bank's branches in each of those locations."

The way she said "your bank" made Mr. Peterson feel that it was actually HIS bank—Hanna possessed that trait of making whoever was with her at any particular point in time feel important, if not special. This conduct misled many men over the years into believing that she actually found them to be important or special.

Mr. Peterson leaned forward, his body language posed as if to hear her more intently. "Those are very busy branch offices."

"That's precisely my point, Mr. Peterson…"

"Please, call me Frank, Ms. McDowell," he interrupted, hoping that she would now tell him her first name. She didn't.

"Thank you. That's precisely my point…Frank. I find the wait because of the crowds annoying, and because of the high volume, the tellers tend to be stressed and unfriendly. By chance, one day, I came here to your branch and found it refreshingly friendly—like the banks that we had back home." Hanna smiled at him. He smiled back.

"I'm glad that you found my branch to your liking."

"We need to open another account, and since I will probably be doing our banking here, I thought that I would just go ahead and open it here."

"We?"

"Yes, Dr. Cipullo and I will both have access to the account."

"Please do not misunderstand, Ms. McDowell, but isn't it a little unusual for a doctor and a staff member to have a joint account?"

"Your implication is?"

"I have no implication; it's just that as a banker, I want to be certain that there is no misunderstanding."

Hanna handed him the account number of the account that Tony had recently opened and given Hanna access to. "We already have a joint account with your bank. I am not merely a staff member; I am the doctor's office manager. If you have a problem, we can switch our banking to the bank across the street," Hanna said, as she looked him in the eye.

"There's no need for that. I'm sorry if my following policy offended you," Mr. Peterson said as he punched the account number into his computer. "Yes, you are correct; you and the doctor both have access to this account. May I ask the reason that you need to open another account?"

"The doctor is funny that way. He is very segmented. He finds it easier to keep his bookkeeping tasks organized with separate accounts. Again, if it's a problem for you…" Hanna got up to leave.

"No, please. It's no problem, really." Mr. Peterson opened his desk drawer and handed Hanna two signature cards. "I'll need both you and the doctor to sign these and return them to me before we can open the account."

"I understand. Thank you. I will return these tomorrow, Frank." Hanna took the signature cards as she smiled in his direction. She shook his hand and got up to leave.

Back at home, in the privacy of her bedroom, Hanna sat at her vanity. In the waste-can beside her were three discarded loose-leaf pages. Antonio *Cipullo, MD* was written repeatedly on each. In front of her, propped against her makeup mirror was a photocopy of Tony's signature card that he signed for the account that he opened for her to assist in her time of need. She referred to it as she started the fourth page of forged signatures. By the middle of the

140

fourth page, when she was satisfied with her reproduction, she took the signature card that she received from Mr. Peterson that day and transferred Tony's counterfeit signature onto it. She did this with no hesitation and with no guilt.

Charlie walked into the kitchen of his home in the Mt. Lebanon suburb of Pittsburgh. His wife was sitting at the kitchen table. One of Charlie's white cotton Oxford cloth shirts was on her lap. He thought nothing of it as he opened the refrigerator and looked for something to nibble on before dinner.

His wife got up and shoved the shirt in his face.

"What is this?" she said, referring to the lipstick stain on the collar.

Charlie looked at the shirt, then up at her. She then held the shirt up to her nose and took in the perfume scent.

"That is not my color of lipstick, nor have I ever worn that scent!" She threw the shirt at him and slapped his face hard.

"What's got into you, Beth?"

"What's got into me? That's not the question, Charlie. The question is: 'What have you been into?'"

Charlie backed away, reeling from the confrontation. His brain kicked into overdrive.

"Beth, why are you overreacting to an obvious 'mean-nothing' thank-you hug from a grateful client?"

"Thank-you hug? Grateful client? How stupid do you think that I am? You wore that shirt the day that you told me that you were meeting your brother for lunch at the Duquesne Club. You didn't even go into the office that day, you bastard!"

"You are mistaken, Beth. I have many white cotton shirts. You're confused."

Beth took her right hand and dragging her long fingernails across his neck, left three long scratch marks from his ear to his shirt collar. "I'm not confused about anything, you bastard. I called your office that day. Your secretary said that you weren't in all day!"

"I saw the client at the club. She thanked me for probating her father's will. That's all there is to it. Plain and simple!" Tony raised his hand to his bloody neck. "You're crazy, Beth!"

"No, I'm not crazy; I'm pissed off, Charlie!" She handed him a business card. It was Cathy's. On the reverse side was her home telephone number written in blue ink. "You left this in your wallet! You lied to me, Charlie! You said that your wandering days were over, that you'd be faithful to me! You bastard!"

Charlie looked at Cathy's card and then up to Beth. He didn't know what to say. He said nothing.

Cathy walked into the viewing room. Her father's mahogany casket that she had picked out earlier was flanked by two lamp stands. An American flag was neatly folded into a triangle and was propped up against the coffin's silk lining—a tribute to her father's service to his country. The suit that Cathy had chosen was neatly pressed. She was not accustomed to seeing her father look this neat and proper. He held a rosary in his left hand and Cathy mused how out of place it looked. His gray hair was combed back and slicked down with tonic. His skin was powdered, the flesh-toned makeup covering the blotchy areas created by alcohol abuse.

This is a caricature of the man that I called Dad, she thought, as she looked over the display that was once her father. She touched his cold hand. It was like touching a marble statue. She received as much warmth as she did from him in his redefined life.

Evelyn entered the viewing room with Tony. She held on to his upper arm as if clinging to a lifeline. She walked toward the casket with reserve and an almost cautious approach. She stood next to Cathy and, placing her arm around her daughter's waist, said how natural Frank looked. Cathy smiled at her mother, not commenting on how ridiculous her comment sounded to her.

Funeral viewings can be almost surreal. Fatigued family members, in a fog, greeting well-meaning visitors who have good intentions, but all say the same thing over and over again—shallow statements of how good the deceased looks or how good he was in life—as if they could fool the family into believing these lies. Visitors come out of the past and ask the same questions repeatedly—regarding the particulars of the death process and laced with an almost macabre curiosity.

Toward the end of the last evening of the viewing process, Cathy, unable to fight the fatigue and guilt any longer, broke down and began to cry inconsolably.

"Daddy, I knew that you were sick. I failed you miserably. I was ashamed of your sickness. I didn't do enough to help you. I let you down! I am so sorry! Can you hear me, Daddy?" She wept on his chest, pounding the coffin's silk lining with her fist as she did so.

Tony led her away into the next room as she pushed away from him and cried into her open palms. She asked to be left alone for a while. Tony complied and went outside for some fresh air. One of her aunts brought her a paper cup filled with water from the polar cooler.

When Tony returned, he saw Cathy standing next to the casket, flanked by her mother, talking to a gentleman who stood with his arm on Evelyn's shoulder and holding Cathy's hand. He took his hand off Evelyn's shoulder and began to rub the top of Cathy's hand, cupping it now between his open palms. His back was toward Tony, but Tony could tell from his head's position that he was looking right at Cathy as he spoke to her. Judging from the contact, this individual knew both Cathy and her mother well—a cousin from out of town, perhaps. There was something about this encounter that grabbed Tony's interest. His attention was drawn to them, although he didn't understand why. He watched them intently. After a brief moment, Tony saw him place his arms around Cathy's waist and embrace her with a hug that cousins usually do not engage in. He appeared to whisper into Cathy's ear. He saw Cathy nod in approval. Tony took a step forward.

Just then, Cathy's Uncle Mark grabbed Tony by the arm. He swung Tony towards him and away from Cathy's view. He entered into a long conversation with Tony about liver spots and benign nevi. When Tony could break away, and look back toward Cathy, she and Evelyn were standing alone. Tony surveyed the room. There was no sign of the gentleman.

The rain continued to fall as the funeral procession caravanned toward the cemetery. The weather suited the occasion. At the graveside, the priest stood with a large umbrella protecting him from the elements as he recited prayers intended to protect Frank from non-elemental forces. Tony stood there, holding his large umbrella over both Cathy and Evelyn. He looked out onto the group of mourners. In the background, behind raised umbrellas, Tony caught a glimpse of a familiar face. He hadn't seen him in over twenty-five years. He looked again to be certain. He stared in the direction of this person out of his and Cathy's past. It was Charlie Vantare. They made eye contact and Charlie looked away. Tony's heart sank as only a heart can sink when one encounters one's nemesis. Tony's mind raced. Suddenly, Tony felt a sinking in the very pit of his stomach. He felt the blood rush from his face. Could Charlie be the Hanna-equivalent in Cathy's life? The Tony that grew up in the tough ethnic neighborhood of Little Italy wanted to push his way through the crowd and first confront and then punch Charlie in the face—he owed him that much. The adult and professional Tony held those feelings in his heart but would never allow those juvenile urges to become manifested— especially at a time like this and in front of his children.

The priest finished and handed first to Evelyn and then to Cathy a small bottle of holy water for them to sprinkle onto the casket as a final good-bye. He took Tony by the arm and led him off to the side for some private words, as Tony handed the umbrella to Cathy. As the priest spoke to him, Tony looked past the cleric and in the direction of Cathy and Evelyn as they walked toward the waiting limousine. Charlie greeted them both with an embrace, Cathy's being punctuated with a kiss. Tony could not bring himself to be rude to the priest, who was now suggesting some counseling for Evelyn, knowing the devastation that can be wrought by unresolved guilt as only a priest can.

Tony thanked the priest for his concern and recommendation. They shook hands and Tony walked towards the waiting limousine, accepting the final good-byes of some of the straggling mourners as he did so, the rainwater running down his face. He saw no sight of Charlie now. The limousine's engine was running, presumably to run the heater and provide some sanctuary from the damp chill. The door was closed, the dark windows not allowing Tony to see inside the passenger compartment. An image formed by jealousy entered Tony's thought processes. Would Charlie be so brazen as to be sitting in the limo with Cathy and Evelyn? Each step towards the waiting car allowed an additional surge of adrenaline to course through Tony's veins, now causing his heart to race. He stopped for a brief moment as he reached the car door. The driver held his umbrella over Tony's rain-soaked head as he reached for the doorhandle.

"The three of them have been wondering where you were, sir."

The three of them? Tony took in a deep breath as the driver opened the car door.

Sitting facing each other knee to knee on the bench seats were Evelyn and Cathy. Angela was seated next to Evelyn, resting her head against her grandmother's arm. No Charlie. No confrontation. No problem.

"What took you so long, Tony?" Cathy said as she looked out of the window and away from Tony.

"Father McKenna wanted a word with me."

"Kathleen took the other children in the second limo. Angela wanted to ride with us. Mother's not feeling well."

Tony reached over and touched Angela's tiny knee. "It's good for you to comfort your grandmother, pumpkin. You've been a big help."

Tony said nothing to Cathy about seeing Charlie. How could he with Angela there? He looked out of his window as the driver pulled out onto the road and away from the graveside.

Chapter 12

After her father's funeral, Cathy stayed with her mother in Youngstown and helped her organize her affairs. Evelyn seemed so lost and helpless to Cathy. She pitied her.

On the Wednesday following the funeral, Tony drove to Youngstown to retrieve her. He finished office hours and called Claire to check on the children before getting on the Pennsylvania turnpike. The drive to Youngstown brought back memories of the many times that he made this trip to see Cathy during happier times—during their college years. As the mile markers of the turnpike rolled past, Tony's mind took him back to that time. The irony was that during those travels in the past to see Cathy, his mind invented images of her and Charlie together. He was more than his competition—he was his romantic nemesis. Images of her and Charlie together returned as he revisited those painful reflections.

The trip took less than an hour. It provided Tony the time to reflect on what he would say to Cathy about Charlie. It was a fifty-minute eternity.

Tony kissed Evelyn on the cheek. He told her to call if she thought of anything that he could do for her. He picked Cathy's suitcase up from the living room carpet, where she had set it next to the sofa, and walked to the car as Cathy said her good-byes to her weeping mother.

He waited by the passenger door until Cathy came down from the house. He opened it for her as a gentleman would and closed it with a loud slam—almost as punctuation to the silence between them.

Quiet can be a welcome friend at times. It can provide an environment for reflective thought and reverie. It can also be a cursed stillness before a storm. Such was the case as Tony started the drive back to Pittsburgh. His heart raced with anticipation, as he knew that confrontation was inevitable. After what seemed like endless moments, he broke the silence.

"How are you feeling?"

"I'm fine. Losing a parent is an inevitable part of life. I've accepted it." Her statement was devoid of any emotion. It reflected her lack of any emotional attachment to Tony at that point in time.

"Listen, I've got to talk to you about something." Tony's heart raced at an almost alarming rate at this point.

"Must you?"

"Yes, I'm afraid that I must, Cath. I know that you have been seeing Charlie."

Cathy now turned toward him. "You don't know anything. You don't know what you are talking about!" She turned her gaze back to the passenger-side window.

"I know that he came to the funeral home. I also saw him at the graveside as well."

"What you saw was an old family friend coming to pay his respects and offer his condolences."

"Cathy, you and I both know that he was more than an old family friend."

"Are we talking about what he was or what he is now? I'm confused."

"So you're saying that you haven't been seeing him?"

Cathy turned and looked at him once again. She wondered briefly if he knew more than what he had just confided to her. She had two options: admission or denial.

"I'm saying that an old family friend came to pay his respects—to both my mother and to me."

The tangled web was now spun.

Tony looked at the billboard to his left as he continued on their trek towards Pittsburgh. He distrusted Cathy's denial; however, he had no proof—only suspicions and an intense sense of burning jealousy. He drove on, feeling deceived and helpless to do anything about it. It was not a good feeling. It would be a long drive home.

"Can I ask one more thing?"

"Do I have a choice, Tony? I mean, the question is rhetorical, isn't it?"

"Is there any chance for us? I mean, can we ever get this back to where it once was?"

"Can any two people ever go back to where a relationship once was? Tony, look. Don't sit there all smug with your questions about Charlie. I know that you have been seeing another woman. I have suspected it for some time now." Cathy took Tony completely off guard. "Last week, I got a call from my cousin Lynn. She told me that she saw you with a very young and attractive woman over in Shadyside. You were getting into your car. Lynn knows your car, so don't insult me by denying it."

146

"Cathy, Lynn saw me with a staff person from my office. We had lunch, that's all."

"There have been signs, Tony. A woman knows. A woman always knows. The funny thing is that the news had almost a sense of relief for me. It's like I don't really care anymore." Cathy paused, but Tony had nothing to say. "You've slept with her, haven't you Tony?"

"Cathy! How could you ask that?"

"I see."

"Have you slept with Charlie?"

"You know that I slept with Charlie multiple times."

"I don't mean then. I mean have you slept with him recently?"

"Tony. How could you ask that?"

"I see."

"Tony, look. I think that I need some time to figure some things out. I need some distance. I think that a separation might be what we need right now."

The irony hit Tony as if someone had just kicked him in the head. He had wrestled with the proper way to confront Cathy with his decision to separate from her—one that would create the least amount of pain for each of them. Now, thanks to Charlie, Cathy opened the door to separation for him. The only problem was that instead of feeling palliation, he felt isolation. He came to a fuller understanding of what separation really is. It may ultimately lead to a deeper exploration of other relationships, but only after one travels through the mist of isolation first.

"All right—but we have to wait until after Angela's birthday. I want to create the least amount of pain for the children as possible."

Tony's failure to argue the separation spoke volumes to Cathy and revealed to her how much trouble there was in their marriage.

"All right. We can go through the motions until then. We've been going through them for quite some time now, anyway. At least, I have," Cathy said.

"Now that the decision has been made, I hope it defuses some of the tension and stress that has been in our relationship, and puts an end to the confrontations and arguments—for the sake of the children."

"By all means—for the sake of the children."

"I'll find a place tomorrow, and be ready to move in directly after the birthday, then."

"Fine."

Tony wasted little time. The next morning, he called a realtor who was a patient/acquaintance. The realtor didn't usually deal in rentals but as a favor to Tony found him an available two-bedroom in Oakmont Landing. The apartment complex was on the river, by the Oakmont Yacht Club. It had a swimming pool that Tony knew that he would never use. It was to be a roof over his head—a fire escape from a failing marriage—nothing more.

During his lunch break, he met the realtor at the apartment complex. It was a ten-minute drive from the Fox Chapel office, down old Route 28 and over the Hulton Bridge.

"Thanks for taking time out of your busy day, Frank. I really appreciate this!" Tony said as they walked to the vacant unit.

"No problem, Doc. I've been in these units. They are very nice."

Frank unlocked the door and followed Tony into the apartment. It had been freshly painted and the carpeting was newly installed. It smelled of paint thinner and carpet adhesive.

It had come to this—funny how life turns out. Tony thought of his humble beginnings—in the Little Italy section of Bloomfield. How after many years of struggling hard work he had moved into the large house in Fox Chapel, the type of home that doctors are supposed to live in. He was an unpretentious type and could be happy living anywhere—as long as there was a roof over his head—or so he had always thought. He now was introduced to the reality that creature comforts can become habit forming, and when removed, they can take away the self-serving solace that they provided. This fact became clear as he looked into the tiny kitchen. There was no island, no wrought iron pot rack, and no All-Clad cookware hanging within ready reach. There was no stainless steel Vulcan commercial-range top—no grill. No wine taster's table. Worse yet, the range had electric coils. *How can one be expected to cook creatively on those?* he thought.

Creating in the kitchen was one of his passions, and now his canvas had been reduced to a small piece of scrap paper.

He walked down the hall and looked into the second bedroom. It was an eight-by-ten foot cell. It could serve as his study—but could one produce original lecture presentations and become lost in creative thought in such a space?

In the living room, there was no log-burning fireplace to sit in front of with friends sipping port, eating truffles and debating adult issues after the children had gone to bed.

The contrast between his home and this place was brought to fullness with the realization of the intense quiet. How different a space could be without children's noises—no giggling, no cartoon sounds from the television, no teenage music, no doors slamming, no neighborhood-friend traffic. If this was a kind of freedom, he wondered if freedom was what he wanted.

148

Had he, as Sean had asked, counted the costs? Did he even realize what the costs were?

He rationalized that this was a temporary doorway that led to a new life—perhaps a new life with Hanna.

"I'll take it, Frank. It will do just fine," Tony said, as Frank removed the lease contract from his briefcase for Tony to sign. Tony signed it with a brief hesitation.

When he returned to the Fox Chapel office, the first thing that he did was to call Hanna at the Oakland office to tell her the news.

"I've taken the leap."

"Where did you jump to?"

"I jumped through a hoop and into a new life. I just rented an apartment."

"To have on the side?" Hanna asked, trying to get Tony to verbalize the separation.

"Are you trying to cheapen this? I'm talking about my separation from Cathy, and you know it." Tony's voice revealed the stress.

"I'm happy for you, if this is what you want—but I have a little guilt about the whole home-wrecker thing."

"We've been through this, Hanna—you are just a part of the equation," Tony said for Hanna's benefit—knowing full well that she was more a catalyst than a mere part of the equation. "A little emotional support right about now would be nice!" There was a pause, and then Tony added, "I want to make dinner for you in my new place. How's Saturday sound?"

"Let me check on what the children have going on. I'll let you know tomorrow, OK?"

"No problem. Hanna?"

"Yes?"

"I miss you!"

"I know."

The Friday night birthday party/sleepover for Angela finally arrived after much anticipation on her part. It seemed to her that it would never come. It was her ninth birthday. It was all that she talked about for the entire week.

Tony left the Oakland office early to run some pre-party errands and to pick up the ice cream cake and helium balloons before the children came home from school. He even intended to drive out to the Monroeville mall—a couple of dozen miles out of the way east to retrieve a couple of Mrs. Field's cookie cakes—Angela's favorite. Hanna kissed him and wished him well, knowing that his anticipation of the event and the events that were to follow regarding his physical separation from Cathy after the party were creating noticeable stress in his life.

"You'll be fine!" she said as she straightened the collar of his shirt. "Everything will work out." She brushed something from his shoulder. "I want you to eat something at the party. You're getting too thin!"

He embraced her as if to tap into her energy—to drain some from her for the strength that he would need to tell the children about his and Cathy's separation. He held her close to him as he filled his entire empty being with her scent.

Not only had Tony lost weight, he hadn't been sleeping well at all. As the birthday party approached, he became more and more agitated about the confrontation with the children regarding his revelation of his and Cathy's separation. He searched for and rehearsed dozens of scenarios to break the news to them in a painless manner—as if such a thing were possible. He came to the realization that there was no such thing as a painless presentation. To think that this could ever be done without pain and suffering was folly. He was overcome with guilt. Selfish-driven, self-serving guilt. It was more than he could bear, and it affected him emotionally as well as physically. Besides the lost weight and fatigued look around the eyes, he had developed a mild tick in his left eyelid, a result of the sleep deprivation and a manifestation of his anxious state. He was changing physically as sure as he was spiritually—an ugly metamorphosis.

As he left the office, he looked back at Hanna over his left shoulder, as if to gain one last charge of her energy. She had already turned back into the office. He continued toward his lot as well as the ice cream store.

Tony arrived at the house before the school bus. He carried in the ice cream cake and a bouquet of helium balloons. He held a bag from the party store containing favors, hats and such. He was wearing one of the party hats, held into place by an elastic band that ran under his chin. He looked intentionally silly, in case Angela had beaten him there—in order to give her a laugh before the bottom fell out of her world.

Claire laughed out loud, before covering her mouth with an open palm when she saw Tony enter the kitchen.

"The children have not yet arrived, Claire?"

"Non, Doctor. Quel dommage! This is a very funny sight!"

Tony set the packages on the island in the kitchen, as Claire put the cake in the freezer.

"Mrs. Cipullo called. She will be a little late. Marissa and Tookie will be coming home on the bus with Angela—Mrs. Cipullo's secretary called the school and arranged it," Claire said in reference to Angela's best friends from school. "The others will be dropped off by their parents, Doctor, sometime before five p.m."

"Thank you, Claire. Let's try and make it a wonderful party for Angela tonight."

"Oui, Doctor. But of course!"

As was always the case, Tony played the role of Master of Ceremonies for the birthday party. With Karaoke microphone in hand, he led each girl into singing their favorite song. He then played team *Family Feud*, nine-year-old *Jeopardy* and *"slime time live."* They ate pizza until it nearly came out of their ears and drank Pepsi until the bathroom was the most popular room in the house. After physical fatigue set in, they moved on to board games: *Chutes and Ladders, Life, Dream Date* and *Monopoly*.

Tony didn't remember becoming this weary this early when he played the same role at Kathleen's birthday parties—but he was ten years younger and unstressed by familial concerns back then.

Around midnight, Angela came to her father and thanked him for everything. She kissed him on the cheek, wrapped her little arms around his neck, and gave him a huge squeeze.

"You can go up to bed now, Daddy. We want to talk 'girl talk' now."

"I see. You don't have any plans of sneaking boys in here, do you, pumpkin?"

"Daddy! You are so silly!"

"I know, pumpkin. I know!" Tony held her tight. He held her as if to remember this moment forever—as if it was to be the last time that he would enjoy an end-of-the-birthday party hug. As if it was the last hug of the last child. Could he ever imagine her receiving his hugs as she now received this one? Could he ever look her in the eye as he now did, ever again? Could he ever look into the mirror ever again?

He walked up the stairs as a man on death row walks the last mile—reluctant and wishing things could be different—yet knowing that he deserves the fate that lies ahead of him. It was with informed knowledge and sufficient reflection that he made his decision—it was his choice. He must live with the consequences.

Tony tossed and turned on his study's sofa. He enjoyed little sleep. He had enjoyed little for the last several weeks. He and Cathy had not slept together since their conversation on the way back from Youngstown after her father's funeral. He rarely could sleep well without her beside him. It was even more difficult now, considering that their irreconcilable differences had been aired. It was a long night. He was about to throw in the towel on his marriage. He finally drifted into a shallow sleep. In the dream state that resulted, he saw Evan standing by the side of the road. He looked at Tony and spoke:

"Tony. Life is laced with irony. There is also no great shortage of tragedy. What I have learned is to always try and apply the best of yourself to any situation. Sometimes the best is to choose the lesser of two evils. Sometimes the best is extreme self-sacrifice. Sometimes the best is knowing when to throw in the towel. Always the best is to rest in the comfort of your decision...."

Tony awoke and found himself in a cold sweat. He was trembling and his heart was racing. He was without any degree of comfort. He did not sleep the remainder of the night. The children would be confronted with the news of the separation in the morning, after breakfast and after Angela's guests left for home. To delay it any longer would serve no useful purpose.

Charlie was waiting for Cathy in the lobby of her firm's building at the end of the day. It was nearly 7:00 p.m. and Cathy was not only dog-tired—she was late for Angela's birthday party as well. She had just closed a very important deal with a six-figure client, and her fatigue was tempered with elation that can only come from closing a hard-fought business arrangement. She saw Charlie and smiled. They embraced—she leaning into his body as much from a desire to be close to him as it was a statement of total release to his person.

"I did it, Charlie! I closed the Federated deal!"

"Was there ever any doubt?" he said as he held her at arm's length and smiled back at her.

She looked at her watch. "Damn, I'm so late!"

"I know. Let me walk you to your car."

The two walked to the parking garage, hand in hand, not unlike a schoolgirl with her beau.

"What's up with Tony?" Charlie asked with a self-serving tone.

"He's supposed to have a talk with the children tomorrow. I'm staying out of it, totally. It's his decision to leave me. I must maintain a posture of innocent victim in the children's eyes."

"Do you have time to have a drink with me?"

"I'm afraid not. I'm late as it is. I'd better get home. I hope that you understand."

"OK. We'll have plenty of time after tomorrow."

Cathy clicked the "unlock" button on her key chain as Charlie opened the door to her SL Mercedes. "Call me tomorrow after it's finalized."

"I will. It's almost like a weight being lifted. I'm so relieved!"

Cathy kissed him good-bye and drove off toward Angela's birthday party.

Tony saw the morning light through the window as the sun's glister descended on his study's wall. He hardly slept—lying awake as he did, reflecting on Evan's haunting words that came to him once again in his dream. He decided to go for a morning run—to clear the cobwebs before making breakfast for Angela's guests. He hoped to come back refreshed from his run, make some eggs, bacon and waffles and relive fond memories with the girls of last night's events, before they returned home and he was left with the dreaded task of facing his children with the news of his and Cathy's detachment.

It was a good run—a hard run. It was the kind of run that pushes you to your limit, and then some. His body welcomed the endorphin release. Still sweating and breathing hard, he entered the kitchen to find Cathy at the coffeemaker. He looked at the wall clock. It was nearly 9:00 a.m.

"Good morning, Cath."

She didn't respond, turning instead toward the refrigerator and retrieving the milk for her coffee.

Taking her lead, he returned her silence as he poured a cup of black coffee for himself. Walking into the laundry room, he picked up a towel from the laundry basket, wiped the sweat from his brow and draped it behind his neck. He walked up to take a shower. It then hit him like a blow from a heavyweight. Was this the last shower that he would take in his house? A chill ran up his spine. His hand quivered as he turned the porcelain shower knob. The finality of it all struck him hard.

The next three hours were an eternity. He stepped from the shower, dried himself with his still quivering hand, dressed, and went down to the kitchen. Angela and Marissa were sitting at the table dressing their Barbie dolls for a tea party. Cathy was pouring orange juice for the girls. Bacon was sizzling in the skillet. Waffles popped up from the toaster.

Cathy had started breakfast, taking this task from him—not in an effort to lend a helping hand so much as to get an upper hand on Tony. It was another slap in the face. A you're-not-needed-any-longer slap in the face. A hit-the-road-already-Jack slap in the face. Tony knew that if it were in her nature—if she had possessed the type of personality suited for it—she would have come down into the recreation room last night when she came home from the office. She would have stripped him of the microphone and relieved him of his role as Master of Ceremonies. Adults acting like children. Is there anything as sad?

153

The last parent came for the last child. It was 11:00 a.m. There was now a strange silence that comes when a half dozen or so nine-year-olds depart. Perhaps in different times and under different circumstances, it would have been welcome. This day, the energy drain added to the melancholy for Tony.

He called the children together in the kitchen.

"Not another family meeting! What did Troy do this time?" Dominick asked, upset by the disruption of his Saturday morning television show.

"Dominick, please. This is very important," Tony said as he began the most difficult monologue in his life. Angela came and climbed up onto Tony's lap as a tear rolled down his cheek.

"What's wrong, Dad?" Rob asked as he now put his book down onto the table.

"You all know how much your mother and I love you. You must know that nothing will EVER change that. You are also all old enough to know that your mother and I have been...well, different towards each other lately. We've been arguing more and we've brought this tension between us into the family circle—creating stress for you all. It has been totally unfair. Please believe me when I say that disruption in your lives was the last thing that we wanted to create."

"Dad, what are you saying?" Rob interrupted, impatient with the preface.

"I'm saying that your mother and I have discussed this and we feel that it might be best if we tried to avoid confrontation by separating from each other for a while. To regroup. To allow for more purity of thought—so that we might be able to figure things out better."

"You mean, like when you walk into a room, Mom leaves? You guys have been doing that already, Dad." Troy added.

"Well, that's the point, son. It's impossible to achieve separation while we are in the same house. It might be best if Daddy moved out for a little while—until we can solve this."

Angela looked up with the most puzzled look on her face as Tony's eyes glassed over.

"Dad. You're talking about leaving?" Rob asked, with a degree of disbelief, laced with a tone intended to bring embarrassment to Tony—as if he had been caught misbehaving.

"For a little while, at least. It's for the best."

"In whose eyes, Dad?" Rob now taking the posture of oldest son. "You always told us that it is never right to run away from a problem."

"I'm not running, son. I'm taking a retreated posture in order to see the problem more clearly," Tony said, finding himself on the defensive—not the position that he had intended.

154

"Sounds like semantics to me, Dad. Looks like running from where I'm sitting," Rob added.

Rob was right and Tony knew it. He was running. Both running from and running toward. Escape and presumed salvation—plain and simple.

"You're not going to live here anymore, Daddy?" Angela asked with the saddest of eyes.

"Daddy will always be here for you. Always! It's just that I will be staying somewhere else, pumpkin."

"I don't understand."

How could Tony expect her to understand?

"Sometimes things like this have to happen in order for things to improve. We all have to believe that the best will come from this." Tony looked at his children—trying to see them and not their pain. "Please remember this: Daddy's not leaving you. Daddy would NEVER leave you. I will always be just a phone call away."

"Bullshit! You're leaving. Don't pretend it to be something else! Bull-fuck'n-shit!" Rob shocked Tony with his vulgarity.

"Rob! Since when do you use such manner of speech?" Tony said in reference to Rob's language of pain.

"Which is worse, Dad? My language or your actions?"

A hush fell over the kitchen—five pairs of eyes fixed on Tony—who now fidgeted in his seat as he searched for what to say next. The words came only with great difficulty—his thoughts muddled as they were with emotional torment.

He sat there and talked to the children for what seemed to him to be an eternity—pleading his case as if a barrister before an already decided jury. In the end, he hadn't convinced himself, let alone the children, that leaving was the right and proper thing to do—yet leave is what he did.

He packed a small suitcase with essentials as if the excess baggage of guilt prevented him from carrying more, and left before more tears could be shed. He drove to Oakmont, needing to pull over twice on the way, to address his tears if not his pain and culpability.

Chapter 13

Tony brought the carciofi to the table and set them in front of Hanna. He poured her another glass of the Soave Bolla.

"Just half a glass, please. I've got to be driving home soon. I want to be able to see the road," Hanna said as she held her hand up and pointed to the middle of her glass.

"Must you be leaving so soon?" Tony asked as he poured himself another full glass.

"You make your stuffed artichokes a little different than my mother. I actually like yours better!" Hanna said in an effort to change the subject.

"It's only seven o'clock."

"How do you get them so tender?"

"Placing water in the roasting pan and basting." Tony looked at her, mildly annoyed at her obvious attempts. "The night is still young."

"I promised the sitter that I'd be home early—giving her such short notice as I did. She has plans to meet with her boyfriend later. She's doing me a huge favor."

"I thought that Bart took the kids tonight," Tony said in reference to Hanna's ex-husband.

"He called at the last minute. Something came up. He's so unreliable."

"Oh. I understand," Tony said as he peeled a leaf from the artichoke and immersed it into the pesto dipping sauce on the table between the two of them. "I'm having a difficult time adjusting to the electric stove in this apartment. It's more appropriate for heating up cans of soup than for creative cooking."

"I almost had to cancel tonight out, but I know how you were looking forward to it. I called Allison and asked her for this favor for you more than anything." Hanna looked up at him with those eyes—like ice on fire—that had opened doors for her all her life.

"You did it for me? Thank you. Actually, any time spent with you is better than no time." He dipped another leaf and held it out for her. She closed her lips around the offered leaf as he pulled it slowly through her clenched teeth—thus removing the tender artichoke flesh from the hard frond-like shell. She reached for his hand and, bringing it up to her lips, closed her mouth around his index finger. She pulled it through her closed lips, as if it were another leaf, as she removed the pesto from HIS flesh.

Gino walked to the window of his office on the forty-second floor of the U.S. Steel Building. He looked out onto the city that was sprawled out before him like a model-constructed movie set. Ant-people scurried along the sidewalks below. The energy of the city was distanced from him—insulated as he was standing behind the double-paned glass. He rubbed his tired eyes.

He was in the midst of doing a corporation's mid-fiscal audit. It was an important and long-standing client. Gino looked at his reflection in the glass of the window. He looked fatigued, because he was. His necktie—loosened long ago—hung in an open loop like a limp noodle.

He glanced at the time, walked over to his cluttered desk, and dialed Tony's cell phone.

"Tony, I thought that I'd catch you before you got to the office."

"What's up, little brother? How's God's gift to the CPA world and corporate America?"

"Fine. How's God's gift to the world of skin?"

"You know, when you say it like that, I feel like a producer of porn flicks."

Gino smiled as he initialed a profit-and-loss summary that his secretary slid in front of him as he spoke. "Tony, I'm supposed to see you at eleven this morning. No can do, big guy. Sorry."

"That's the second time that you canceled, Gino. You're not apprehensive about this lesion removal, are you?"

"I know that it must look like that, but really, I'm up to my neck here. I couldn't get away if I tried."

"I told you at Mama's last Sunday that it's probably an incipient basal cell," Tony said, referring to a skin lesion on Gino's upper right cheek that he showed Tony during casual conversation. "However, I want it off. It is unusual for someone with your dark complexion and as young as you to have a basal cell. The sooner that we get it off, the less chance there will be for scarring."

"I understand, Tony. It's just that this crusty pimple reared its ugly head in the middle of this corporate audit that I'm tied up with."

"Look, tomorrow's Saturday. How about if I meet you at the office and get this thing done?"

"You don't have Saturday office hours."

"I do for my little brother. You'll be in and out. I promise."

"No. I'm not going to screw up your day off. I'm not going to have you open your office just for me. No way!"

"I'll tell Mama. I'll tell her that you have skin cancer and that you won't let me treat it. She'll be on you like flies on shit!"

"Tony! You wouldn't do that!" Gino responded with an acknowledgment of the fear that persists in all Italian men of being scolded by their mothers. There was silence on the phone line. "Tony?"

"Yes, Gino?"

"What time on Saturday?"

"It's your call. I have nothing planned."

"How about late morning? The least that I can do is let you sleep in."

"How about eleven a.m.?"

"Fine. Are you sure that it's no problem?"

"I'm going to slap you!"

"Tony, it's not really skin cancer, is it?"

"I think that it's an atypical wart-like papilloma. At worst, it's an incipient basal cell lesion, but prudence dictates that we remove it and see. I don't question your accounting practices, do I, Gino? Why do you question MY recommendations?"

"You're right, Tony. You usually are. You have to let me buy you lunch."

"It's a deal! We'll do it at the Oakland office. We can then hop across to the South Side—to *Bruschetta's, Café Allegro* or maybe *Buca Di Beppo* for lunch."

Gino was waiting for Tony just outside the door to his Oakland office suite when Tony arrived.

"You haven't been waiting long, have you?" Tony said as he greeted his little brother with a hug.

"I just got here. I really appreciate this, Tony," Gino said as Tony unlocked the door.

"Don't be silly. I owe you big time, little brother. You save my ass every year at tax time. You're doing me a favor. Now I won't feel so much like a mooch!"

Tony pushed open the door. There was a pile of mail on the floor, having been deposited through the mail slot on the door.

"The mailman sure comes early on Saturday," Tony said as Gino stooped down and helped his brother pick the mail off the floor.

"Like you ever deal with the mail in your office!"

Tony shrugged his shoulders. "I'll put it on the desktop for Hanna to deal with on Monday."

Gino looked at Tony with a gaze that telegraphed his disapproval at the very mention of her name. Tony ignored the look, not wanting to discuss Hanna with Gino. They had been through it all before—dozens of times— and Tony did not wish to visit that place of disagreement with his brother.

"I'd better leave her a note, so she doesn't wonder how it got from the mail slot to her desk"

"Won't you be seeing her this weekend?" Gino asked with a tone that displayed some degree of delight.

"No. She has some activities planned with her children that will tie her up all weekend. I won't be seeing her until Monday evening."

"Too bad."

"I'll go get a treatment room set up, while you try to contain your jocularity."

Gino smiled as he reached past Tony and picked up a large envelope from the desk. "Your monthly Med-Shield reports came in today's mail. I'll go over them while you get set up."

"I didn't bring you in for you to do any work," Tony said as he tried to pull the envelope from his brother. "Hanna will send a synopsis to your office as usual."

"I'm here. It will make me feel a little better about disrupting your Saturday."

"Whatever makes you happy. Only an accountant would find joy in looking over column after column of figures."

"And only a dermatologist would get off on removing a piece of crusted skin!"

Tony went back to prepare a treatment room for Gino's procedure as Gino opened the envelope from Med-Shield and perused the figures displayed for him. As Tony set up a syringe of Lidocaine, a surgical blade, gauze and a small plastic jar of 40% Formalin, Gino went over the figures on the page.

In a moment, Gino asked a surprising question: "Tony, when did you get an associate in this office, and why didn't you inform your accountant of this?"

"What are you talking about, Gino? I don't have an associate. You know that!"

"I just assumed as much. Your production is up by nearly sixty percent!"

"What are you talking about, Gino?" Tony came out of the treatment room and walked toward his brother, who was standing at the front desk with the Med-Shield report in his hands

"Tony, I've been doing your books since I got my CPA. I know your numbers like I know my zip code. These figures are either inflated or there has been a mistake on some grand scale."

Gino had Tony's interest. He glanced over Gino's shoulder and onto the monthly report as if he knew what he was looking at.

"Look here, Tony. Your Med-Shield total disbursement for last month was $38,000. Your usual Med-shield deposit normally is around a quarter."

"A quarter?"

"Yes, $25,000, Tony. You are usually steady as a rock—give or take a thousand or two."

"How does that compare to last month? Was last month $25,000?"

"I believe that it was. Why do you ask?"

"It's just that we were swamped last month. I thought that we had the best production of the year."

"I'll check, Tony, as soon as I get back to the office. I don't want you to hold out a lot of hope, though. Your figures are pretty consistent."

"I'll ask Hanna what the problem could be, when I see her on Monday night."

"Tony—I don't want you to say a word to ANY member of your staff until I perform a complete audit."

"Are you implying that someone from my staff is involved in inappropriate activity, Gino?"

"All that I'm saying is that I found an alarming discrepancy involving only one of your insurance carriers. Embezzlement/fraud is a possibility. Prudence dictates appropriate action for your own protection, Tony. I'm going to take this monthly report with me as if it had never come in today's mail. We don't want to tip our hand to any of the possible perpetrators."

Gino's words hit Tony like a lead weight. Perpetrators. In HIS office? Nonsense! There must be some mistake!

Tony stepped out of the shower and reached for a towel. He was singing an Elton John tune as he dried himself. He thought that he sounded more like Elton with the water running and within the confines of the shower enclosure than he did standing as he did in front of the mirror in the open bathroom. Perspective—everything is perspective!

He took his watch from the sink top and hurried to get dressed. It was nearly 6:00 pm. Hanna would be there any minute. He had a busy day at the Fox Chapel office that day. He called Hanna at lunch, as usual, but followed Gino's advice and did not mention the Med-Shield incident. Her ex-husband was going to pick the children up from school to spend the night with him.

He had been out of town over the weekend and therefore had not had his weekly sleepover with the children. This gave Tony and Hanna an unusual weekday evening together. Tony looked forward to it like a child looks forward to a special event.

He walked into the kitchen and turned on the stove's front burner to heat the water for the pasta. His sauce was simmering and the delightful aroma filled the small apartment. He was opening a bottle of Chianti Classico, when the doorbell rang.

"It's open. Come on in!" Tony called out in the direction of the front door.

Hanna let herself in and walked into the kitchen. She was wearing a pair of tight-fitting black pants that looked to be spray-painted on. She had on black high-heeled boots, a taut white jersey top with sequins highlighting the scooped neckline and a sleeveless black vest. Forty-three going on thirty!

"Something smells delightful!"

"You expected me to greet you with a less-than-delightful smell?" Tony said as he put the bottle down and embraced her. "You look good enough to eat, and you smell even better!"

"I'll bet you say that to all the girls!"

"I don't actually smell ALL the girls, but if I did—"

"Stop it!"

Hanna was especially warm and friendly this evening. Tony noticed it right away. She had been the same way over the telephone.

"You seem to be in a good mood today! I'm not complaining, mind you."

"Why wouldn't I be in a good mood? I work for you. You cook for me. You stop traffic for me when we walk down the street..."

"Did you dress like that at the office today? If so, I bet the mailman was walking into walls after he left! Talk about stopping traffic!"

"I wanted to look good for you tonight," she said. She was an expert at telling people what they wanted to hear.

Tony poured and handed a glass of the wine to Hanna. She took a sip.

"Aren't you going to let it breathe a little?" Tony said, in reference to the Chianti.

"You seem to be breathing hard enough for both of you!" she said as she kissed him, setting the wineglass on the table—putting her hand on his chest and feeling his heart race as she did so. She looked at him with those eyes— framed with the makeup touch that had been perfected by years in the cosmetic industry.

Tony had wrestled with his guilt on a regular basis since that fateful morning when he left his home and family. It was moments like this, when

Hanna made him feel young and alive, that the guilt subsided. He was a schoolboy again with almost pubescent feelings. To say that he liked the way she made him feel was an understatement of immense proportions. It was more than that. She redefined him as a person—a person who needed an avenue for his passions to be vented—a person who realized that he was on the threshold of middle age. But these were selfish thoughts, and Tony was not by nature a selfish person. The result was that his guilt wasn't dismissed, just camouflaged for a short while, when he was in her presence and his ability for rational thought narcotized.

She had set a library book and her small hand purse on the table when she came in—nothing else.

"Didn't you pack an overnight bag?" Tony asked, afraid that he already knew the answer.

She ran her hand down his cheek as if to preface her statement with the defusing softness of her touch. "I can't stay. Something's come up."

Tony didn't say a word, waiting for her explanation.

"Tommy called me at the office today," she said, referring to her twelve-year-old son. "He completely forgot about a report that he has due on Wednesday. I went to the library to get a book that he needs. I have to drop it off at his father's tonight so that he can get started on it. I'm sorry, but his father would NEVER go out of his way for him. If I don't do this, it won't get done."

"I understand. It's no problem, really. We can drive over there after dinner and drop the book off. I presume that your overnight bag is in your car?" Tony said, relieved that the solution was so simple.

"No. Missy's sick. She has a temperature and she wants me to come and get her. She wants to sleep with me tonight, and not at her father's house," she said in reference to her six-year-old daughter. "You know how it is with kids. I told you from the very beginning that my kids are top priority."

"Of course they are. I understand. Do you want me to take a look at Missy?" Tony said with sincerity.

"No. That's all right. I'm sure that she's OK. It's probably a twenty-four-hour thing. Thanks for the offer, though." Hanna's tone was firm, her response quick and to the point. "I'm going to powder my nose before dinner," she said as she picked up her purse from the table and went to the small bathroom down the hall—her need to discharge discharging the conversation as well.

Tony set the table for dinner. He took the library book that Hanna had set on the table when she came in and placed it on top of the refrigerator, out of the way. When Hanna returned, Tony was tossing the spinach and feta cheese salad. The table was set and the wineglasses were full, next to each place setting.

"Everything looks wonderful," Hanna said with a smile, as Tony held out a chair for her.

"As do you!" Tony responded as he kissed the back of her slender neck, moving her long perfume-scented hair to one side as he did so.

Her freshly applied lip gloss glistened as she smiled. "You know—you are so nice to me! Come, sit down and eat." Hanna tapped the chair next to her with her right hand. "This salad looks too good!" she said as she glanced at her watch, then took a forkful of the salad.

Immediately after dinner, Hanna left. The apartment lost its temporary luster, like the moon losing its radiance as the sun hides behind the bulk of the earth. Tony cleared the table. Hanna had not even offered to help with the dishes. He could tell that she was anxious to go pick up Missy. He understood. A sick child can disrupt one's thought processes like nothing else. She seemed preoccupied during dinner—her mind and thoughts not anywhere near Oakmont, let alone in the apartment with Tony.

After loading the dishwasher and having another glass of the wine, Tony put the breadbasket from the table to its place on top of the refrigerator. He saw the library book that he had placed there earlier when setting the table for dinner. He felt responsible for Hanna forgetting it. He dialed her cell phone. It rang once, and then he heard her voice-mail message, indicating that she was on the phone with someone, or her phone was turned off. Knowing that she rarely checked her voice messages in a timely fashion, he left none.

He thumbed through the telephone book but couldn't find Hanna's ex-husband's name. Directory assistance confirmed the number to be unlisted. He dialed Hanna's house—no answer.

After a fifteen-minute wait, he dialed her cell phone again. This time it rang several times before the voice-mail message came on—indicating that the phone was on, but not answered.

"Why would she not answer her phone?" He wondered out loud. He rationalized that perhaps she had left it in the car when she went into her ex-husband's house to retrieve Missy. If that was the case, she would have realized that she had forgotten the library book by now, and would be calling Tony. Tony waited for the call. It didn't come. He was puzzled now. Again he dialed her cell phone, and again she did not answer it.

He was beginning to worry now that something had happened—something terrible. He grabbed his jacket and the keys to his car and hurried off to her house. On the way to her house he tried several more times to reach her. She still did not answer her phone. Had she been in an accident? Did she get into an argument with her ex-husband? Had he beaten her? Was Missy's fever more serious than she thought? Had she rushed her to the ER?

As he turned onto her cul-de-sac, he tried one more time to dial her cell phone.

"Hello?"

"Hanna? Thank God! I was beginning to worry!" Tony said as he breathed a sigh of relief.

"Did you try to call me?"

"Only about a dozen times! I thought that something terrible had happened to you!"

"There must be something wrong with my cell phone."

Just then, Tony reached the end of the cul-de-sac. Hanna's car was in her driveway. The lights were off in her house, and it was obvious that no one was home.

"Where are you now?" Tony asked, puzzled by her car's presence and the empty house.

"I'm on my way home. I have Missy here with me. I stopped off at my mother's house. She wanted to talk my ear off."

"You're driving home? Now?" Tony said, as he looked at her parked car in the driveway.

"No—I'm walking. Of course, I'm driving. What's wrong with you? You called me from your cell phone. Where are you?" Hanna said, seeing the number of his incoming call displayed on her phone.

"I'm on my way to Gino's house. He asked me to come over and take a look at Kit. She's not feeling well," Tony lied.

"There must be something going around. See—it's probably for the best the way that things turned out!"

Tony heard the start of the sound of a toilet flushing and giggling women's voices in the background before they were silenced as if a hand was quickly placed over the phone's receiver. It was obvious to him that she was speaking from a public bathroom somewhere—perhaps a bar or restaurant.

"Yes. I'm sure that it was for the best. Did you know that you left Tommy's book at my place?" Tony said as he looked down at the book next to him on the car seat and then up again at Hanna's car.

"I know, honey. Mommy's almost home!" Hanna said as if to reassure Missy. "Look, I've got to go now. Missy really isn't feeling well at all. I'll talk to you tomorrow. Tommy's report will have to wait until then. I'm kind of tired myself, and will turn in early—as soon as I get home."

"Good night." Tony hung up the phone. He went down the street and turned off his ignition. He waited there in the dark—hiding in the shadows and watching Hanna's house. He was upset with himself for behaving this way—like a jealous schoolboy—sunk to the depths of now spying on her to disprove his suspicions. Perhaps there was an explanation. Perhaps she had someone else's car and Missy really was with her, and she WAS nearly home. Perhaps he had imagined the flushing sound and the women in the background. Perhaps his imagination had run wild, and she was being honest and truthful with him. Perhaps she would be pulling into her driveway any moment now. Perhaps pigs can fly.

After an hour, Tony started his car and began the long drive back to his apartment. The depths of sadness and unrequited love now rearing their ugly heads in the pit of his being. He was being deceived—lied to by the person for whom he had begun the reorganization of his life. He touched his forehead. It felt cold and clammy. For the first time in his life, he knew what true depression was—and he was amazed at how it affected him physically. In an instant, it seemed, he had lost all purpose in his life. Life itself seemed to now have no meaning. He felt like an empty shell of a man—because he was.

Chapter 14

Several days had passed since the Monday of Hanna's deceit. Tony fought off the depression daily. He tried to maintain his normal relationship with her as if nothing had happened. It was one of the most difficult things that he had ever done. When he looked at her, there was a side of him that looked past the attractive facade and now saw a deceitful, lying and blemished persona. Having the relationship that he had with her, it was difficult for him to reconcile these different perceptions of the same person—like trying to envision graceful elegance and distorted squalor within the same package.

He had debated whether to confront her with her lie, but thought it better to play deceit with deceit. He despised game playing, yet felt his approach justified in this instance. The entire time there was a gnawing curiosity of what other lies had been told—what other threads of deception ran through their relationship.

When she spoke to him—when he was in her physical presence, when she could reach out and touch him, when he could inhale her scent—she possessed an ability to almost mask the dark side that Tony now suspected. When he fought to break through the masquerade, she could almost sense it, it seemed—and she could turn on the charm—allowing the attractive side to become so dominant as to nearly hide the dark side from view. But Tony was now in possession of the truth. The truth had set him free from the effects of this masking ability—or so he imagined.

Tony was in his private office filling out the charts for the morning treatments. Hanna knocked once and then entered.

"I have to talk to you about something." She had a serious look on her face. "I have a confession to make to you."

She had Tony's full attention. "Yes? What is it?" His heart raced.

"I have been feeling guilty about the way that I have been treating you. I know how much you looked forward to Monday night; and believe me, I would have rather been with you that night than anything else. You must believe me." She put her arms around his neck and kissed him. "You have been so wonderful to me. I have never felt like this before about anyone." A tear welled up in her eye and rolled down her cheek.

Tony was totally confused and disarmed at the same time. He looked at her and now only saw the beautiful side. Had he rash-judged her? Was there a rational explanation for what he assumed to be a lie on her part? His mind raced. His intellectual side cautioned him to the potential of this being a smoke screen. It cautioned him to the fact that she was just covering all of the bases in the event that he could have been at her house that evening—saw her car and the empty house—and suspected her deceit. His intellect encouraged him to look past the attractive facade and see the dark side. His emotional side fought the urge to listen to his intellect—choosing to believe that there was a plausible explanation and he really was the center of her universe, as he so much wanted to believe.

He decided to play the devil's advocate with her and confront her approach with cogent exchange, for the sake of seeking out the truth.

"You must understand my confusion, Hanna. I dialed your cell phone. It was on and you didn't answer it. It was my assumption that you saw that the call was from me and that you chose not to answer it."

"But why on earth would I do that?" Hanna asked with a straight face.

"Perhaps you were with someone else and decided that a conversation with me would be counterproductive to your efforts."

"That's ridiculous!"

"Then what is YOUR explanation?"

"I told you. My cell phone must not have been working properly."

"I am trained as a scientist. I utilize scientific methods and come to conclusions based on scientific thought processes. Please excuse my doubt, but in all the time that I have known you, your cell phone has not behaved in this manner. My first assumption is that your hypothesis is an unlikely one."

"Are you calling me a liar?"

"I am utilizing scientific thought processes."

"And what does that mean?"

"It means that given to natural chance, there is a possibility that your cell phone *could* become inoperable at a given point in time. The odds of it occurring at the particular point in time that we speak of to fit the needs of your argument and with the frequency that you imply, is highly unlikely. What's more, the manner in which the inoperable state occurred, displaying itself as a phone that was on but not answered, is highly improbable."

"I'm telling you the truth. I don't care what you believe. I came to you today because I felt badly regarding the way Monday turned out, and you're treating me this way!" Hanna pushed away from him and turned as if to leave.

His emotional side won out. Surely she was sincere about wanting to be with him. She did come to him and tell him as much. Why was he jumping to conclusions? It was *possible* that the cell phone malfunctioned. It wasn't as if he had proof. It wasn't as if he actually saw her with someone else. Why must he invent a dark side that may not exist? Why couldn't he enjoy the charming and beautiful side, which just now came to him and embraced him?

He reached out and grabbed her arm just above the elbow. "I'm sorry. You're right. I had no reason to behave like that. I had no reason to suggest that you were dishonest." His intellectual side flashed an image of her car in the driveway to his mind's eye and reminded him that he did indeed have reason to be suspect—but he repressed it.

"You hurt my feelings. That was the cruelest thing that you have ever said to me," she said with a pouting expression on her beautiful face.

Tony melted. "You're right. I am so sorry. Let me make it up to you."

"How?"

"You will have to wait and see."

It is sad when knights become pawns. It is immensely sad when they can't even see the metamorphosis

The following day, a deliveryman entered the Oakland office with three dozen long-stemmed roses—a dozen each of red, yellow and pink. Attached was a card that read,

> *I am sorry about our confrontation yesterday. Please accept this small token as a peace symbol.*

Attached to the card was a box from Bailey, Banks and Biddle jewelers. It contained a diamond tennis bracelet that she had admired when she and Tony strolled through the mall one day.

She put the bracelet on and smiled widely. It was a self-righteous smile. It was unfortunate that Tony was not there to see it—unfortunate for him, but a very good thing for her.

The phone rang early Saturday morning. Tony picked up the mobile phone in the kitchen. It was Gino.

"Tony, is this a good time?"

"It's always a good time for my little brother. What's up?"

"I have the results of your deposit audit that I ran. I'm afraid that it's a little alarming."

"Alarming?" Tony asked as he took another sip of his coffee.

"Yes. I crosschecked your deposits with the Med-Shield report that I took from your office last week. What I discovered was that your deposits were normal and consistent with average deposit history. They did not coincide with the Med-Shield report." Gino paused. "Tony, according to the Med-Shield statement, they issued you checks totaling $38,000 and change. Your deposit audit indicated that only $24,000 and change of Med-Shield's money was deposited. The question is: Where did the other $14,000 go?"

A cold chill ran down Tony's spine. "$14,000? There's a discrepancy of $14,000?"

"That's only for last month, and only one insurance carrier. Tony, we could have some big problems here. We have got to perform a complete internal audit of your practice."

"What are the possible causes?"

"I can only think of two possibilities: Either you or a member of your staff with access to your business office is engaging in fraudulent activity for personal gain. Knowing you as I do, that leaves me with only one explanation."

"There must be some mistake."

"Tony, open your eyes."

"What does that mean?"

"I suspect Hanna."

"Bullshit! You're saying that because you dislike her. You blame her for breaking up my marriage. Hanna is not a crook!"

"I do dislike her. I see her in a different light than you do, but *I'm* not accusing her. The facts are accusing her."

"I still think that this is some kind of fluke. Some mistake has been made somewhere."

"Listen. We must be intelligent about this. I'll go along with you. We will investigate this and give all parties the benefit of all doubt. However, we mustn't tip our hand. Hanna must not know that we suspect her. All right?"

"*We* don't suspect her. *You* suspect her."

"Believe me, Tony. I hope for your sake that I'm wrong. I copied the Med-Shield report that I took from your office last week and sent the original back to Hanna. I had a friend of mine who works at the post office secure for me a 'damaged by machine' sticker. I mangled the original envelope to make it look like it was torn by a post office machine and not opened by you or me. Unless she is very, very smart, she shouldn't suspect anything. When I receive her end-of-the month synopsis and she tells me that Med-Shield sent you $24,000 and she deposited $24,000, then we will have our proof. Fair enough?"

"Fair enough!"

During the next several weeks, Tony tried his best to carry on as normal a relationship with Hanna as possible, despite Gino's suspicions. In fact, he thought that she was especially warm and loving towards him. The more loving she became, the more distant the doubts placed by Gino in Tony's mind became.

They expanded their activities to include going to plays and high-profile restaurants together, Tony now not concerned with being seen with *the other woman* as he had once been before his separation. They also spent more time engaging in lovers' perks, like walking in the park and holding hands and kissing under oak trees in full view of anyone to see.

They shopped together in trendy shops in Shadyside, Sewickley and Mt. Lebanon—Tony deriving great pleasure in seeing in her the joy that these shopping safaris created. Tony was falling in love with her, and any troubles that may be on the horizon were far from his thought processes.

"Good morning, Dr. Cipullo's office. Hanna speaking. How may I help you?"

"Good morning, Hanna. This is Gino. How are you?"

"I'm fine, Gino. Your brother is not in this office today—he's in Fox Chapel." Hanna's tone was polite but abrupt. She was not very fond of Gino, knowing how he felt about her.

"I didn't call to speak with Tony. Actually, I wanted to speak with you. Mitch sent me the end-of-the-month third-party insurance synopsis for the Fox Chapel office three days ago. I was wondering when I might expect yours for the Oakland office." Gino's tone was firm, his statement rhetorical.

"I've been swamped here, Gino. I was thinking. It makes better sense to me to do the synopses on a quarterly basis. That gives me three months to juggle my various workloads."

"When you become the accountant for the practice, you can make those changes. Until then, and while I'm still doing the accounting work, let's just keep things the way they are."

Hanna could tell that playing hardball with Gino would get her nowhere. She turned on the charm, instead. "Gino, please don't misunderstand me. I meant in no way to undermine your authority. I think that you are a gifted accountant. The doctor loves and respects you very much. I wish that you and I could get to know each other a little better. When we talk, there seems to be tension between us."

Gino saw right through her—her coquettish approach being very transparent to him. "There's no misunderstanding on *my* part, Hanna. The misunderstanding seems to be all yours. Understand this: I need that synopsis!" Gino hesitated for a moment, thinking that his sudden and intense interest in last month's synopsis might tip his hand to Hanna and let her know that he suspected some impropriety on her part. He backpedaled. "I don't mean to place unreasonable demands on you regarding this—it's just that my practice has become quite busy. I have to organize my workload as well. It works better for me to have those reports on a monthly basis, that's all." Gino smiled, smug and pleased with his smoke screen.

"We'll have to come to some compromise, then. There's just no way that I can have that synopsis ready in the very near future. I'm sorry. Besides, I don't work for you. I work for the doctor. If he thinks that my not getting a stupid synopsis to you by a given date is grounds for dismissal, then he can give me my two-week notice!"

Gino was impressed with the way she maneuvered her way around the deadline issue. It was a chess match. Did she know that Gino suspected her? Did she piece together the facts—knowing that Tony had been to the office on that Saturday and placed the mail on her desk? Did she suspect that the Med-Shield monthly report was removed and scrutinized? Did she suspect that the arrival of the Med-Shield report in such a mutilated fashion was a cover-up? If such was the case, then his insistence in this matter would surely tip his hand. He had no choice but to give in to her on this point. He and Tony would have to come up with some other plan that would either convict her, as he suspected, or vindicate her, as Tony hoped. "I understand. I'm not trying to tell you how to do your job." He decided that he'd use method's familiar to her—the way that men usually allowed themselves to be manipulated by her. "I'll work around your schedule," he said, almost choking on the words.

Tony zippered his overnight bag closed. He put the slide carrousel in the especially designed briefcase that he had made to carry his slides when he traveled to give out-of-town lectures. He was old school. Many of his colleagues at the university had converted their 35mm slides over to computer-generated PowerPoint presentations. Instead of hauling cumbersome slide carrousels, they transported a small zip disk that could fit in their inside jacket pocket. Tony resisted change.

He had been invited to give a presentation in Columbus, Ohio, at the Ohio State University's Medical School. It was at the Chairman's guest lecture series hosted by the Department of Dermatology. These out-of-town lectures were a pleasant diversion for Tony. He enjoyed them very much, providing him, as they did, with a needed intellectual and academic exchange with colleagues of different backgrounds.

He had hoped that Hanna would join him on this trip. A weekend away together would be just what the doctor ordered. She had to decline. Her cousin Audrey was coming into town for the weekend. Audrey lived in Michigan, and Hanna rarely got to see her. It was just a case of poor timing, Tony thought. He had heard so much about Audrey—how she and Hanna were the same age—how they grew up together, more like sisters than cousins. He regretted not being able to meet her.

Audrey's flight was due into Pittsburgh at 7:00 p.m. Hanna was going to pick her up at the airport, so it was impossible for her to see Tony off. He intended to leave around 6:00 p.m. in order to get into Columbus, check in and get a good night's sleep before his 9:00 o'clock lecture on Saturday morning. They said their good-byes at the office.

Tony picked up his overnight bag as the telephone rang.

"Hello?"

"Hello. Is this Dr. Cipullo?"

"Speaking."

"Dr. Cipullo. I am so happy that I caught you. This is Mrs. Talitino, Dr. Kennedy's secretary. I'm afraid that I have some very tragic news." The chairman's secretary was noticeably upset.

"What is it, Mrs. Talitino?"

"Dr. Kennedy suffered a massive coronary this afternoon. They rushed him to our medical center here in Columbus, but..." She began to weep. "They did all that they could for him," she continued in between sobs.

"I am so sorry. Are you all right?"

"Yes, thank you. I meant to call you earlier, but I was in a state of shock. He was such a marvelous person, and a wonderful boss."

"Yes, I knew him well. It is such a tragic loss."

"I am happy that I was able to reach you before you left. Due to the tragedy, and under the circumstances, his guest lecture series has been canceled...." She broke down once more.

"I understand, totally. Is there anything that I can do?"

"No, thank you. You are so kind."

"Please let me know when the arrangements are finalized, will you?"

"Of course, Doctor. I will, and thank you again."

Tony was saddened by the news. He knew Tom Kennedy as an excellent educator and clinician. He walked into the kitchen and poured himself a drink—Jack Daniels on the rocks. He hadn't had a *hard* drink since the night of his separation. He called Jim Kerr, the chairman of his department at the University of Pittsburgh, and informed him of the news.

Tony looked up at the wall clock. It was nearly seven o'clock. Hanna would be picking up Audrey soon. He could meet them at Hanna's house and take them both out to dinner, he thought. He called directory assistance for the information number at the airport. He wanted to see if Audrey's flight was on time.

"Hello. Could you tell me if the seven p.m. flight from Detroit is on time? I'm afraid that I do not know the airline." Tony waited as the person on the other end of the line checked the incoming flights.

"Sir, I do not show any incoming flights from Detroit."

"Are you sure? Maybe it was 7:30 or 8:00."

"Sir, the only flight that I show came in at noon today."

"Did you check all the airlines?"

"Yes, sir, I did."

"Thank you." Tony hung up the phone. He was puzzled. He was certain that Hanna told him that Audrey lived in Grosse Point Woods—a suburb of Detroit. What other airport could she be flying in from? Hanna was with him at the office until three this afternoon, so she couldn't have picked her up at noon. He dialed her cell phone. He got her voice-mail. He dialed her home. No answer.

He picked up the keys to his car from the wall hook and left for Hanna's house.

Tony turned onto Hanna's cull-de-sac, following a black Porsche Boxster. It was half past seven. He was surprised when the Porsche pulled into her driveway. Her car was there. Tony pulled over, a safe distance away, and turned off his ignition.

The man in the Porsche looked around and then out each side window. He took something out of his jacket pocket and tapped it several times onto the back of his hand. He stooped down and brought his nose into contact with his hand, first one nostril, then, turning his head slightly, the other. He got out of the Porsche. He had wavy, long brown hair and appeared thirty-something. He walked up to the front door with a noticeable spring in his step and rang the doorbell.

Tony's heart raced and then sank as Hanna opened the door and her guest embraced her and kissed her full lips with what appeared from Tony's vantage point to be a long and passionate kiss. He slid his hand down and caressed her tight ass as he did so, pulling her close against him as if he were girding his loins.

After they entered the house, Tony sat and stared at the closed door for the longest time—a combination of disbelief and intense pain overcoming him. When the lights to Hanna's bedroom went on, he turned on the ignition to his car and headed home.

He parked in front of a bar on Allegheny Avenue within walking distance to his apartment. He went in and ordered a double Jack Daniels on the rocks. As he sat and sipped his drink, a young blonde woman in her apparent early thirties, who was quite attractive, but with a lot of mileage, came and sat next to him. Her speech was slurred. She said hello and asked if he would like to buy her a drink. He thanked her for the flattery but declined, saying that his life was complex enough for the moment.

He downed his drink and motioned for another. When the bartender brought him another double Jack Daniels on the rocks, Tony smiled at the simile. Like the Jack, now his life was also on the rocks.

Tony spent the remainder of the weekend in deep melancholy—the blues. At least that's what they used to call it. It was a cocktail of rainy days, missed opportunities and dreams of what might have been all rolled into one. His emotions ran the gamut, from the depths that only a crushed ego can feel to embarrassment to an intense sense of lack of worth. He had never experienced a sense of poor self-esteem before. He had also never felt this foolish or this jealous. He envied the man with the wavy brown hair. He envied him, when he should have pitied him—that's how distorted his thinking was.

He ate nothing. He couldn't eat. He did not sleep. He couldn't sleep. The pain wouldn't leave him, and by Sunday morning he thought that he would surely die. *Can one die from a broken heart?* he wondered. Surely death would be preferred to this constant pain and emotional anguish.

That is when he hit bottom. He walked into the bathroom, turned on the light and looked into the mirror. Whom or what he saw he did not recognize. It was some distorted caricature of who he once was. Could another person alter one so? It was there and then that the realization hit him: no one could do this to him unless he allowed it. It wasn't Hanna who did this to him. He did it to himself, by permitting it to happen. He had seen all the signs but refused to believe them. He saw it all coming, yet he chose not to act on it in a way that would have positively impacted his life and prevented this pain. It was about choice. When you come down to it—it's all about choice. He chose there and then to regain his life. He chose to not allow someone's dark side to change his light into darkness. In that moment in time, he saw Hanna as she really was—both the light side and the dark side in the same package—in a way so totally different than he had before. In this perspective, there could be no masking of the dark by any amount of charm brought to bear by the light side. It was a totally liberating experience for Tony—as if he had now finally come into possession of the truth, and *this* truth had surely set him free.

174

He knew that the storm of this weekend had cleared. He knew that he weathered it and survived. More than just survive it, he was now stronger because of it. He walked into his bedroom, reclined on the bed and fell into a deep and needed sleep.

Tony slept for a little over ten hours. He was awakened by his phone ringing. He looked at the caller ID. It was Hanna. The stronger Tony picked up the receiver.

"Hello?"

"Hey, big guy. It's me."

"Well, hello! How are you?"

"I'm fine. I was waiting for you to call. How was the conference?"

"It was fine. You know, if you've seen one conference, you've seen them all," Tony lied, thinking it best to allow her to believe that he actually was away for the weekend.

"How come you didn't call me when you got back? You did get back this afternoon, didn't you?"

"Very late this afternoon. I got a late start. I just took a small nap. Your call woke me up." Tony looked at the clock on his nightstand. It was 8:00 p.m. "How was your visit with your cousin Audrey?"

"It was the best! We had so much fun together. I just wish that you could have been here with us. I told her all about you. I took her back to the airport this afternoon."

"That's great! But you wouldn't have wanted me to be a third wheel in your plans this weekend!" Tony smiled at the thought of Hanna, the guy with the wavy brown hair and himself together. He knew, of course, that he was talking to the dark side and that her friendliness and charm were self-serving. He was surprised at how well he was doing with this, and now realized that he really had been healed. "How was her flight from... Where did you say that she was from?"

"Detroit. Her flight in from Detroit was right on time, Friday night."

Tony was having fun with her dark side now—watching her lie with regularity—as if she actually believed the lies to be the truth. When her dark side was exposed so clearly to him as it now was, it was easy for him to be comfortable in the loss of his relationship with her—that side making her so totally unattractive to him. "So, what did you two do?"

"Friday night, we went to my mother's right from the airport. We ate there and went back to my place around eleven or so. We stayed up late, just talking girl talk. On Saturday, I took her out to dinner at Café Sam's. I charged it to the office. That was OK, wasn't it?"

Tony picked up the pencil next to his phone and wrote on the scratch pad—*Change charge card numbers, first thing tomorrow!* "No problem!" He couldn't believe the nerve of this woman. Now she was taking her fuck friend out to dinner, and Tony was paying for it! "I'm happy that you had a wonderful time. Look, I'm a little tired. Do you mind if I turn in now?"

"Is everything all right? You sound a little different tonight. Didn't you miss me?"

"Oh, everything is just fine! In fact, I've never been better. I haven't felt this good in a very long time!" Tony said in all sincerity.

"OK, I'll let you go. Call me tomorrow when you get a chance. I missed you!"

"I know. Good-bye, Hanna."

Tony felt relief—relief like he had never known before—getting a monkey off one's back, relief. This newfound liberation energized him. He put his running clothes on, laced up his Nike Shox and went for a long run—down past Café Monaco on Adeline Brown Avenue to the park, past the ball field, and a mile around the cinder track, before heading up Hulton hill. The released endorphins were needed and welcomed. During his run, his thoughts turned to Hanna. His thoughts always turned toward her when he ran. This time, all he could see was the lying, self-serving, stab-a-friend-in-the-back, unattractive Hanna. Bringing her dark side into his consciousness was therapeutic. It was the best run of his life, because he needed it like he had never needed a run before.

Tony walked into the Fox Chapel office, prepared to take on the world. He wasn't prepared for what awaited him.

He didn't schedule his first patient until 11:00 a.m., thinking that he needed to unwind after the weekend conference. He saw the memo that Mitch left on his desk regarding Dr. Kennedy's funeral arrangements. He walked up to the front desk area.

"Good morning, Doctor. How was the conference?" Mitch asked.

"Just between you and I, Mitch, there was no conference. Dr. Kennedy died suddenly on Friday, and the conference was canceled. That's between you and me." Tony handed her the memo back. "Please have some flowers sent to this address with my condolences to the Kennedy family."

"Oh. I was wondering who Dr. Kennedy was. I'm sorry." Mitch looked up at her boss. "Are you all right? You look a little washed out."

"I'm fine. It's been an interesting weekend."

"You'd better take a look at this. It came registered mail, just a few minutes ago," Mitch said as she handed Tony an envelope.

He looked at the envelope as he walked back to his private office. It was registered mail from Med-Shield. He opened it immediately.

Dear Dr. Cipullo:

As you may know, we perform random computer audits of our participating doctors. The result of your recent audit revealed billing irregularities consistent with fraudulent behavior on the part of your practice. Our legal department has advised us to freeze all account activity, holding same in escrow until this issue is resolved. In the meantime, we have referred this issue to the State Department of Professional Licensure for investigation. We encourage you to cooperate with us for a quick resolution to this problem, and...

Tony fell into the chair behind him. His face, drained of blood, became pale—his skin covered with a cold sweat.

"Gino was so right! How could I have been so blind—so misled?" Tony asked himself. He looked down once again at the letter and then stared straight ahead, a puzzled and frightened blank expression on his face.

Tony thought of his reputation. Was he now to be grouped, in the eyes of the profession, with those sleazy docs who were involved with insurance fraud—the ones who always conjured up images of slicked-back hair and held the same degree of respect as dishonest used-car salesmen and snake-oil peddlers? He thought of his license to practice medicine. It could be revoked or suspended if he were found guilty. The shame of it all! After all he had worked for. How could Hanna have placed him in such jeopardy—and for what? Money? Was money more important than a man's life—than what a man worked for all his life—than that which defined him as a person? His reputation? Was her dark side THAT dark?

His first temptation was to call her and tell her to leave his office—immediately! His second was to hurt her—to get even in some way—but then that would bring him down to her level, wouldn't it? His third thought was that this was all punishment for him—as if this pain was to be a place that he had to go to wash away his sins.

He dismissed the later two temptations as ridiculous. The first was the most tempting. However, if he discharged her, how could he ever hope to vindicate himself in the eyes of the profession? In the eyes of the State Board of Licensure? In the eyes of the IRS?

This called for a level head to come up with an intelligent and well-planned course of action—not action coming from reflex, but from cunning and mother wit. He sat and thought as he rubbed the top of his head with the

177

fingers of his left hand. If there were such a thing as karma, then this would have to be resolved in his favor, and not hers, he rationalized.

After only moments, the solution came to him as if by heavenly inspiration. It was a perfect plan. A plan that would resolve all of his problems—a plan that would vindicate him as well as expose her for all that she was.

Chapter 15

The first thing that Tony did after receiving the registered letter from Med-Shield was to call his brother, Gino.

"Gino."

"Hey, Tony! What's up?"

"I wanted to call you and eat some crow in your presence."

"This doesn't sound good."

"I guess that you could say that."

"What happened?"

"You were so very, very right about Hanna. I feel so foolish."

"What happened?"

"She's everything that you always said that she was, and more."

"Will you frig'n tell me what happened!"

Tony told his brother all about the Med-Shield audit. He told Gino that his suspicions regarding Hanna were correct. He told him about the deceit and the lies. He told him about the dark side of her. Besides the news of the audit, he didn't tell Gino anything that he did not already know.

"Tony, I am so sorry for you. I can't tell you. I was hoping that we could correct this with our own internal audit and resolve it from our end before Med-Shield suspected any wrongdoing. Their awareness changes things. It changes things big time! Now we are implicated. Now we look like the perpetrators. Now we look like the crooks! Damn it!"

Gino used the plural pronoun 'we.' Tony recognized it as a statement of solidarity—that Tony was not in this alone, even though it was his practice and not Gino's. Tony appreciated his brother's support and his love.

"Thanks for being here for me, Gino."

"Where else would I be?" Gino paused. "I'm impressed with Med-Shield's ability to pick up on this discrepancy. Their computers must be programmed to kick out any provider's display that sways from their normal profile. When the computer 'noticed' the sixty-percent increase in your claim submissions, it set off an alarm and thus their audit. I'm impressed with their programmers!" Gino spoke as only an accountant would. "I should have known that. I should have demanded a more aggressive approach from us! Damn it!"

"How could you have known, Gino? You didn't know because you don't think like an embezzler!"

"I had my proof when I called Hanna about the end-of-month synopsis—the way she stalled. She knew that the figures would implicate her. She's shrewd. I didn't give her enough credit. Damn it!"

"I always knew that she was a smart cookie. But I have a plan, Gino."

"I hope so. You need one, big brother! Tell me."

"Not on the phone. Meet me for dinner tonight at *Michael A's*. I'll tell you all about it."

"I can't wait. Give me a hint."

"Do you remember Brother Jerome's chess club when we were at Central Catholic?"

"Of course I do. High school wasn't THAT long ago. So, what… You're going to challenge her to a chess match?"

"Not quite, but I am going to use the principles that Brother Jerome taught us."

"Which were?"

"Use an opponent's strengths against them, for your advantage. Lull your opponent into a sense of false security. Hide YOUR strengths behind a cloak of weakness. Make intentional small mistakes to lead the opponent into making larger ones. Let them believe that they are in control while giving them enough rope to hang themselves."

"So what are her strengths?"

"She is very strong in the arena of greed. She also has an incredible ability to endear people to her cause."

"What about the false security?"

"I intend to allow her to think that she is in control of a situation that, in fact, I will be creating and manipulating."

"What about your hidden strength?"

"My strength will be that I am now in possession of the truth about her. I will hide it behind the cloak of allowing her to think that her charm continues to disarm me and hide her dark side from me."

"I can't wait to hear the particulars of this plan."

"Tonight, Gino, at dinner."

"You always were the smart one, Tony. Now I know why Mama loves you best."

"If I were so smart, I would have never allowed myself to be in this position, Gino. Regarding who Mama loves best: You are the one who does her will and embraces the traditions that she holds dear. You never turned your back on your family, or the Church, or your vows."

"Regarding 'the position that you are in': That's only because you did your thinking with the wrong head. If you had used the one on top of your shoulders, none of this would have happened. When you say 'vows,' why do you use the plural?"

Tony hesitated for a moment, as if in deep and reflective thought. "Gino, I only made two sacred vows in my life: My Hippocratic oath and my marriage vows. In the end, when push came to shove, when the wheat was separated from the chaff, I wasn't strong enough to keep either one. I am ashamed, and by my accounts—by all accounts, I am a failure."

"Ridiculous! You are not a failure by ANY accounts. You are what I strive to be. You have always been what I have strived to be!"

"I'll see you tonight, Gino."

The success of Tony's plan rested in his employing Brother Jerome's imparted wisdom regarding the strategy of the game of chess. He often told the boys at Central Catholic High School during the *chalk talk* sessions in the chess club that lessons learned in the small knotty pine-paneled room adjacent to the cafeteria, if extrapolated and applied, could benefit them in the game of life.

"If you are here to simply learn how to play a game—to learn how to move little figures on a checkered board—then you are missing out on a valuable lesson. The reason that Central boys do well in life is because we expect you to grasp the esoteric concepts. When combined with six letters of the alphabet, these principles form the foundation of what I'm speaking about." Brother Jerome turned his back on the group, as he was accustomed to doing when he called upon a student to answer a question—feeling that eye-contact intimidation by a figure of authority stymied creative thought. "Perhaps you can enlighten us, Mr. Cipullo, as to what letters of the alphabet I refer to."

"I would imagine that you are referring to the precepts of the character of a Central Catholic graduate, Brother."

"I am. Would you care to enlighten us as to what they are, Mr. Cipullo? We wait in excited anticipation."

"They are the three R's and the three D's: Respect, reverence, responsibility and desire, discipline and dedication, sir."

"Precisely. Apply what I will teach you regarding the game of chess with these precepts, and you will have an advantage in the game of life."

Tony reflected back on Brother Jerome's mentoring wisdom. He had always tried to apply Central Catholic's precepts in his life. Success usually followed when the precepts led the way. Failure often resulted when they did not.

His failed marriage was an illustrated case in point.

Tony knew what he had to do. He just needed to find the right time—knowing as he did that timing was everything in life. The next day, in the Oakland office, Hanna provided the right timing for him.

Tony walked out of treatment room #2. He was washing his hands in the central scrub area when Hanna approached him from his left.

"Your last lesion removal before lunch just canceled. You're done for the morning," Hanna said, with no small degree of pleasure, knowing that she now also had an opportunity for an extended lunchtime.

"Is that so?" Tony said, looking at his wristwatch. "It's only 11:30. Our next patient isn't due until 1:00. Sounds like lunch to me."

Hanna smiled at him, not being one to turn down a lunch date with anyone.

"Are you asking me to go to lunch with you?"

Tony hesitated for a brief moment. "I'm asking you to go to lunch with me. Give me a minute to change out of my scrubs."

After they ordered, Tony leaned forward, as if to tell Hanna something that he wanted no one else to hear. "I have to let you in on a secret. It's something that is very exciting to me!" She looked at him with little change of expression on her face. "A colleague of mine at the university has perfected a technique, so revolutionary—so innovative—that it will transform the fields of dermatology and perhaps all of medicine. Dr. Anook Sidiqui has developed an isolation agent that when injected under an invasive lesion, like a malignant melanoma, can elicit tissue separation."

Hanna looked up from her iced tea. "What are you saying?"

"I am saying that if this technique is employed early enough, not only can it isolate a potentially dangerous lesion—it can prevent hemangiogenisis. It can also physically lift the tumor away from the underlying tissues, separating it from the underlying fascia, and deny the lesion access into the lymphatic system and refuse it access for metastasis."

"Which means?"

"Which means that it renders the lesion harmless—reduces it to an isolated group of nothing more than once potentially dangerous and life-threatening killer cancer cells. It turns them into the immunological equivalent of a glorified splinter, which elicits only a localized area of inflammation and nothing more."

Hanna squeezed some lemon into her iced tea, with a rather uninterested look on her face. "Would you pass me the saccharin, please?"

Tony decided that it was time to bring the conversation into an arena of more personalized interest for her. "Needless to say, the third-party medical insurance carriers see the potential of this new treatment modality to greatly minimize the extremely expensive costs involved in the management and treatment of malignant melanoma. They stand to save huge benefit payments for extended cancer victim therapies."

Tony handed her the saccharin, knowing that he now had her attention. "Money talks in health care, Hanna—especially where the insurance industry is involved. Therefore, Anook has been approached by the Med-Shield insurance group. They have set up a select group of clinicians to act as a pilot study in clinical trials to evaluate this new treatment modality. I have been asked to be one of the participating clinicians in the trials."

Tony's story had holes in it from a standpoint of medical ethics and protocol. He was betting that ethics was not one of Hanna's strong suits, and that she would center in on the third-party disbursement aspect of his scenario. He was correct, of course, but her next question, involving protocol, surprised and impressed him.

"What about FDA approval—I mean human testing and all?"

"That's an excellent question!" Tony said, having learned long ago to never underestimate her. He was prepared for any dialogue regarding his entrapment scheme. "That's part of the beauty of it all. Since Anook's formula involves individual components that have already been approved by the FDA for other treatments, and Anook only combined those already approved components in a different and unique combination, he is able to circumvent years of laboratory studies and apply it presently for patient care."

Tony could tell that she was buying his story. It was time to *close the deal*. "Med-Shield has agreed to provide access for the participating clinicians a special insurance code. When submitted, the code provides for remuneration of $10,000 per case." Tony had her full attention now. "We clinicians involved in the treatment have entered into a non-committal agreement to *donate* 80% of the remuneration back into Anook's study, thereby underwriting his research. It's a win-win-win-win scenario. We who are involved in health care win by having access to an innovative treatment modality. The third-party carriers save huge amounts of disbursement payouts, thereby increasing profits tremendously. Anook's research gets funded without the hand-tying and time-consuming grant proposal bullshit. Most importantly, the suffering patients benefit by having their potentially life-threatening cancer abated."

"You treated several cases of melanoma last month."

Tony could see Hanna's mind working, as if she could see another *win* in the scenario. *Greed can be such a predictable foe,* he thought.

Tony stopped off at his apartment to take a quick shower before meeting Gino for dinner. He thought that his lunch date with Hanna went well and that she bought into his plan—hook, line and sinker. To *sink her* was exactly what he intended to do.

At the restaurant, Gino leaned toward his brother across the small table and over a dish of *Michael A's* la trippa.

"So tell me, Tony. What's your plan? I've been on the edge of my seat since yesterday!"

"Before I tell you about my conversation with Hanna this afternoon, I want you to read this. I wrote it last night."

Tony retrieved a letter from his inside jacket pocket and slid it across the table to his younger brother. It read,

Mr. N.J. Moraitis
Director of Audit Investigation
Med-Shield Health Group

Dear Mr. Moraitis,

As per our telephone conversation regarding the investigation into possible fraudulent insurance submissions from my practice, I suspect that a staff member, unbeknownst to me, has been filling fraudulent claims for personal financial gain. In an attempt to prove my innocence in this matter and maintain my good standing in the medical community, I have devised a sting *operation.*

Insurance claims will be submitted under my Med-Shield ID number, with a contrived submission code, prefaced with the letter "Z." These claims are for nonexistent treatment and designed to be markers *to monitor procedures performed as opposed to claims processed by you for my practice, for this particular nonexistent treatment. I suspect that the totals will not be equal.*

If I prorate past fraudulent performance by this staff member, then

I expect that for every ten marked procedures presumably performed in any given month, there will be 11.4 processed. This will indicate that 1.4 procedures will be submitted for payment where no treatment was rendered, thus implicating this staff member.

I ask that you consider my unblemished past record and my stature in the medical community as reason to consider my innocence in this alleged unprofessional behavior.

As per our conversation, I am sending a copy of this letter to Dr. Fay of the State Board of Professional Licensure.

I intend to cooperate with your office fully for a quick and just resolution of this unfortunate development, and I thank you in advance for this opportunity to vindicate myself...

Gino looked up at his brother, as Tony told him about his conversation with Hanna and the particulars of his whole sting operation. As Tony finished, Gino held up his glass of wine.

"Salute!"

The remainder of the month was stress filled for Tony. He was comfortable in the fact that he had done the best that he could do in setting up Hanna's entrapment. His vindication was now in God's hands. Still, brewing in the back of his mind was the constant gnawing fear that his plan would somehow fail, and he would lose everything that he had worked for professionally. He reflected often on how, due to poor judgment, he had thrown away his marriage and home life—already having lost everything that he had worked for in his personal life. His injured ego occasionally crept back into the picture, although he suppressed those urges to dwell on it as best he could under the circumstances.

He was drinking more than he was accustomed to during this time, in order to help him get some sleep—only to wake in the middle of the night, tossing, turning, missing Cathy and the children, and regretting his decision to leave them more than ever. The stress was beginning to show. He had to recapture part of his pre-Hanna life.

That's when he decided to swallow his pride and call Sean. He had not seen his old friend since the separation—his time being dedicated to, if not monopolized by, his developing relationship with Hanna. Prior to the separation, for months, Sean had tried to convince Tony that he was making a huge mistake with Hanna. These dialogues reached a climax when Sean and Tony went to Manhattan on a three-day weekend together. It was the closest thing to a heated argument that the two friends ever had, with Hanna being the accelerant. In truth, after that, Tony had avoided his friend, not wanting to be lectured to regarding Hanna any longer.

In hindsight, Tony now saw Sean's wisdom. How was it that everyone close to him could see Hanna for what she was, yet Tony could only see what she wanted him to see?

"Hello?"

"Hello, Sean."

"Tony! Well, this is a surprise! How are you?"

"Is that a sincere question?"

"Of course it is! I thought that the earth swallowed you up. We played phone tag there for a while, and then... Well, it's good to hear from you!"

"I have a lot of ground to cover with you, Sean. Are you free this Friday night?"

"If you want to know the truth—no, but for you I will make myself free. This sounds important."

"I don't want to impose. If you already have plans..."

"I'll decide if you are an imposition. I want to see you."

"How about if we meet at *the fish bowl* at seven thirty?"

"*Palomino's* at half past seven, this Friday. No problem!" Sean paused, and then he broke the silence. Tony?"

"Yes, Sean?"

"Are you all right?"

"Never been worse. Never been better. See you at *Palomino's* on Friday, old friend."

At *Palomino's* restaurant, Sean and Tony finished the grilled calamari and sipped the Pinot Grigio before their entrée arrived.

"OK, I told you I have the time. Now tell me your *long story*, Tony," Sean said in reference to the letter that Tony showed him regarding his Med-Shield audit and insurance fraud accusation.

Tony told his old friend everything that had happened to him since the day that Hanna entered his office and his life. He told Sean how he had been absolutely right about her. He told him about the plan to vindicate himself regarding the fraud issue and to implicate her as the perpetrator. He apologized for ignoring his good counsel. He thanked him for being such a good and loyal friend. This was all done within a shroud of embarrassment for Tony.

In the ensuing weeks, Tony's plan unfolded as karma dictated. A leopard does not change its spots, and Hanna's greed-driven actions were consistent with her past performances. It all played out as Tony assumed and hoped that it would. In the end, Med-Shield's audit director was as convinced of Tony's innocence as he was of Hanna's guilt.

When Tony received the notification of his reinstatement of participator's status from Mr. Moraitis, he breathed a sigh of relief. He got down on his knees and repented for his poor judgment. He also thanked God for his exoneration.

Tony walked into the front desk area of his Oakland office as Hanna opened the registered letter addressed to her from Mr. Joseph Krenn, State Attorney General's Office, Department of Insurance. She read it with a somber look on her face. When she was finished, she turned to Tony.

"Are you going to testify against me, Tony?" It hit him like a brick. She referred to him by name. It was the first time in his memory. He knew in his heart that he couldn't testify against her, despite what she had done. He would leave her fate in the hands of karma.

He looked into her eyes for what he knew would be the last time, but he couldn't speak. That is how he left her.

Encounters like this that reach back and touch the spiritual side of a relationship—where neither dark nor light predominate nor cloud the interpretation in the physical realm—are more meaningful than those on any other level. Tony would carry that image as well as this lesson with him for all time.

Chapter 16

Tony got the call at twenty after nine in the evening. It was Claire. He knew immediately that something terrible had happened. Claire was audibly shaken. She was breathing rapidly and had trouble finding words in English.

Tony grabbed his sports jacket and the keys to his car and raced out of his apartment. He pieced together enough of Claire's disjointed conversation to know that Cathy had been involved in a car accident. She had been taken by ambulance to Presbyterian University Hospital's trauma center. The children were not with her at the time of the accident. Tony was thankful for that. They were home safe with Claire. Tony punched a programmed button on his cell phone as he raced to the hospital.

"Gino? It's me, Tony. Listen, I need a favor. I need you to go get Mama and take her to the house. Cathy's been in an accident, and the kids are home with Claire. They need to be with family right now."

"Is everything all right?"

"I really don't know. I hope so. I'll call you when I know more."

Tony thanked his little brother and hit the programmed button for his home.

"Claire, it's me. I'm on my way to the hospital now. I need you to try and remain calm. You mustn't alarm the children."

"Oui, Doctor. I understand. I feel better now that I got in contact with you. I have said nothing to the children. They know nothing, Doctor."

"Fine. My brother is on his way there. I will call you when I know more. Let me talk to Rob."

Claire set the phone down and went to retrieve Tony's oldest son.

"Dad?"

"Hi, Rob. Listen, I need to tell you something. I'm certain that everything is going to be just fine, but Mom's been in an accident. It may just be some minor injury. I don't know. I'm on my way to the hospital now. No reason for alarm at this point. Uncle Gino and Nana are on their way over to be with you. As the oldest one there, I'm counting on you to help keep the younger children calm."

"I understand, Dad. I hope Mom's all right. Should I call Kathleen at school?"

"No. There's no need to right now. I'll call her when I know more. I knew that you could handle this, son."

"I'll do whatever you need me to do, Dad."

"Rob..."

"Yes, Dad?"

"I love you, son."

"I love you too, Dad."

Tony raced into the ambulance entrance of the busy ER. As one of the premier trauma centers in the western part of the state, it was usually a hub of activity. On any given night, medical emergencies could present from gunshot wounds to stabbings, from industrial mishaps to car accidents—not to mention patients being life-flighted in from surrounding lesser-equipped hospitals.

Tony approached the woman at the desk. "I'm Dr. Cipullo. My wife was brought in by ambulance this evening."

Emergency room personnel become callused out of necessity. Very little rattles their cage. In fact, the more agitated and animated visitors become, the slower they move, it seems. Tony was familiar with this behavior—he just never understood it.

Dermatology is considered an elective field of medicine. It is as foreign to emergency room personnel as physiatrics is. The woman did not know Dr. Cipullo. For all she knew, he could have been a professor of English literature or a podiatrist. She would cut him no slack. She glanced casually down at her computer monitor. "Your wife is being tended to. You will have to take a seat and wait for one of the doctors to come out and speak with you. I will tell them that you are here."

Tony turned and took a seat next to a black woman who was crying into her open hand. Tony reached into his back pocket and handed her his clean handkerchief. She accepted it gratefully. There was a young boy, perhaps ten years old, who was bleeding through his torn blue jeans just above his knee. His mother was dabbing the area with a blood-soaked dishrag. He looked up at the woman behind the desk. She seemed oblivious to the people in the waiting area. Over the years, she had learned to block them out to the point where they now were invisible non-entities.

Tony went to the rest room and returned with a handful of paper towels.

189

He handed them to the boy's mother and told her to elevate the leg and compress the wound area—not to dab it.

He went back to the woman behind the desk. "Pardon me, but you said that you would inform the treatment area that I was here."

"They are very busy, sir. Please have a seat. Someone will be with you shortly." Her tone was matter-of-fact and monotone. It would have served the same purpose if she had played a recorded message to him.

"Could you please tell me who the attendings are who are on tonight?"

She looked up at Tony, surprised by his request. "Are you on staff here, Doctor?"

"No, I'm not. I'm a dermatologist. I'm not involved with inpatient care. I am on the faculty here at the medical school and see patients at the outpatient clinic at Falk. I therefore have consultation status here at Presby. Now could you please tell me who the attendings are in the ER tonight?"

"Doctors Evans and Kirkly are in house. Dr. Shah is on call."

Tony did not know any of them. "What residents are on tonight?"

"Doctors Perrine, Ghormani and Vento."

"Dr. Asfar Ghormani?"

"Yes. Do you know him?"

"Yes. He was in my PBL group in medical school. Could you tell him that I would like to speak with him please?"

"I'm not permitted to ask a resident to come out and speak to family, Doctor. Only a staff doctor can do that."

"Oh for crying out load!" Tony walked down the corridor and picked up a house phone. "This is Dr. Cipullo. Could you please page Dr. Ghormani for me, stat!"

In less than two minutes, Dr. Ghormani came on the line.

"This is Dr. Ghormani."

"Asfar. It's Dr. Cipullo. I'm sorry about the stat page, but I need to have some news on my wife's status."

"Dr. Cipullo. Is Catherine Cipullo your wife, then? I wondered if she was related. Where are you?"

"I'm in the waiting area here in the ER."

"I'll be right out."

Tony's former student came out and greeted him with a warm handshake. The two men walked past the woman behind the desk and past the jealous stares of the people who had been waiting for hours in the reception area. They entered the ER through the automatic double doors, and walked down the corridor and into the nurses' area.

"Dr. Perrine saw Catherine, Dr. Cipullo. He's in with a possible MI right now. We're waiting on the enzymes to come back. As soon as he's finished, I'll have him come and speak with you."

"Where's Cathy now?" Tony's voice cracked at the end of the question.

"She's in surgery."

"Surgery? Who was the staff surgeon on call?"

"Dr. Zubrow."

"Thank God!" Tony said, in reference to the fact that Tony not only knew Harold Zubrow, but he knew him to be a technically excellent surgeon as well.

"Yes, she lucked out on that one! Also, her passenger was not seriously injured."

"Passenger?"

"Yes, there was a passenger. Actually, the car was registered in his name." The resident turned and thumbed through the files on the desk in the nurses' station and handed Tony a copy of the police report. "He sustained a compound femoral fracture, nothing else of note."

"Fecundity intact, I presume?" Tony said as he read the police report and saw that the car was registered to a Mr. Charles Vantare.

"Oh, I'm sorry, Dr. Cipullo. I assumed he was a family friend or a relative."

Tony paced back and forth in the nurses' station, still holding the police report and waiting for Dr. Perrine to come and give him the details of Cathy's status. Two floors above where he paced and twenty-two years before, Cathy came back into his life—in the cafeteria on the morning after Danny's death. He couldn't bear to think that she may be leaving him now. He rubbed his eyes and prayed for her recovery—regardless of what the future held for their relationship.

Cathy looked at her watch—the Rolex that Charlie gave her for Christmas, 1978. She ran her finger around the crystal and traveled back, for a moment, to that point in time. She had been expecting an engagement ring. The Rolex was a nice second prize. Charlie knew how to hedge his bets.

Charlie was twenty minutes late. They were supposed to meet for a drink at the Duquesne Club before going out to dinner. She lied to Claire and asked her to tell Tony that she had a late business meeting if he called home.

She called the waiter over and asked if Mr. Vantare had left a message for her. He shook his head. "Not that I know of. I'll check with the receptionist, though. Would you like another lime and tonic water in the meantime?"

She nodded a yes in his direction.

A moment later, she saw Charlie enter the bar area. His tie was loosened and it was obvious to her that he had been drinking. She rose as he approached her.

"Charlie, I was beginning to worry."

He kissed her on the cheek and ran his hand down and across her ass. "I stopped and had a drink or two with Frank before I got here."

"I just saw Frank not more than ten minutes ago. He left with Harry. He was sitting right over there." Cathy said, pointing in the direction of the bar.

"Not Frank Proctor, another Frank—Frank Nesbit. We went to law school together. I ran into him on my way over here. I was so anxious to see you! You look great, Cath!"

"I don't know any Frank Nesbit. Why would you assume that your calling him Frank would identify him to me? Besides, I have my cell phone on me. Why couldn't you call and let me know that you were running late?"

"I don't want to call you on your cell phone if I don't have to. I was just trying to be discrete."

"You've called me plenty of times on my cell phone. What makes this time any different?"

"Cath, why are you making such a big deal out of this? We're together now. That's all that matters, isn't it?" He put his arms around her waist and drew her close against him. "You smell great. What is that scent? I could smell you all night."

Charlie could defuse her anger better than anyone that she had ever met. When he held her, she melted like hot butter.

"Perhaps I overreacted, Charlie. I'm sorry. It's just that I got a little nervous waiting, and add to that the guilt of having to lie to Tony.... I'm sorry."

"Fuck Tony!" Charlie motioned to the waiter. "Let's forget about it and just pick it up from here. Double CC. And water."

They sat and talked as Charlie downed his drink and ordered another. He held and kissed her soft hand and told her what she wanted to hear.

"I didn't have time for any lunch today, Charlie. Let's go to dinner. I'm getting very hungry."

"Have a real drink first. That tonic water's not going to relax you, Cathy."

"No, I'm fine. Come on, let's go to dinner. Where did you make reservations anyway?"

"I booked a room at the Wyndham Gardens in Oakland. We can do room service," Charlie said without skipping a beat, as if he could change the plans for the evening from dinner to a liaison without involving input from her.

"You're serious."

"I thought that we could have some real privacy and have a nice relaxing meal with some real meaningful conversation if we did this instead. Also, there's less chance of us being seen together than if we were in a crowded restaurant."

"Hold on, cowboy. You think that we would be exercising more discretion if we checked into a hotel room together than if we were seen dining in a public place?"

"We don't have to be seen doing anything. You can have a drink at the bar and I'll call your cell phone with the room number once I've checked in."

"So now it's all right to call my cell phone number—so long as I'm in the bar at the hotel waiting for you to get your fuck room ready. I suppose that there are more demeaning ways for me to feel cheap. I just can't think of any at the moment."

"Cathy, why are you so melodramatic about this?"

"You're talking about adultery here, Charlie. You want me to be casual about it?"

"No one is saying that you have to sew a scarlet letter onto your Donna Karan jacket, Cathy. It's the new millennium!"

"How much have you had to drink?"

"I just want to drink you in with my eyes, Cathy. If you don't want to make love, we don't have to. The ball will be in your court the entire time."

"I don't know, Charlie. I mean, to place myself in a situation that might spiral out of control…"

"Come on, Cathy, admit it. It would be nice for us to just hold each other again and visit a happier time and place, wouldn't it?"

Cathy looked into Charlie's eyes as he spoke to her. She was weak when she was in his presence. She always was. He was rock and she was paper. Somewhere deep down inside of her, she liked the fact that he was in control and he knew it. He always did.

"All right. But remember, if I say no, I mean no!"

"Of course, Cathy. Of course!"

"You'd better let me drive."

"Fine. We'll take my car, it's right out front," Charlie said as he handed her the keys to his BMW.

Cathy was nervous as she turned the ignition key; a mild tremor visible in her hands as she gripped the steering wheel. She eased into the traffic flow and headed toward Oakland and the event that would change the direction of her life forever.

Dr. Perrine entered the nurses' station and extended his hand towards a very somber Tony. "Jim Perrine."

"Tony Cipullo. Thanks for taking the time to speak with me," Tony said as the two medics shook hands.

"No problem. I'd say that your wife was very fortunate. It could have been a lot worse."

Tony breathed a sigh of relief at the hint of good news. "Thank God!"

"She's not out of the woods just yet. You know that she's in surgery. She lost an awful lot of blood. Her vitals were almost nonexistent when she came in. She presented with a severe laceration. There was massive internal hemorrhage. Someone ran a red light and struck the driver's side of your wife's car broadside. The impact sent the armrest into her left flank, causing a fracture of at least her tenth and eleventh ribs. The ribs lacerated her spleen and kidney on the involved side. Judging from the amount of hemorrhage, the fractured rib probably nicked the splenic artery as well. Fortunately for her, the accident occurred only a few blocks from the hospital. The paramedics were on the scene within minutes, containing the hemorrhage and wasting no time getting her here."

Tony was visibly shaken.

"You'd better sit down. I don't need any more patients tonight."

"I've got to give some blood. Cathy and I have been typed and cross-matched before—during her last C-section. We're compatible. I need to give her some of my blood."

"It's the best thing that you can do for her right now."

Giving his blood gave Tony some sense of contribution into Cathy's care. It also was a productive way to pass the time until Harold Zubrow came out of surgery and could give Tony an assessment of her prognosis. The wait was the longest three hours of his life.

Tony walked up to the operating room's dressing suit. It was the same room where he changed his scrubs after Danny's death and before being reunited with Cathy. He sat down and waited for Harold Zubrow to come out of surgery. He looked at his watch. It was almost midnight. He took his cell phone out and called home. Philamena answered the phone.

"Mama. You're still awake?"

"Antonio. How could I sleep? I have been praying all night. How is Cathy?"

"I don't know yet, Mama. She's still in surgery. It's in God's hands."

"Antonio. Everything is in God's hands. Everything has always been in God's hands."

"You should know, Mama. You have a direct pipeline to Him."

194

"He answers my prayers because He reads my heart. He hears me because I talk to Him every day. He wants to know when you are going to talk to Him," Philamena said in reference to Tony's falling away from his faith. He hadn't been to Mass in over a year—a fact that affected Philamena in no small way.

"Is Gino still there, Mama?" Tony said to change the subject.

"He just left. He asked me to call him when I know something."

"How are the children?"

"All sleeping. We told them very little—only that Cathy will be just fine, because that is what we believe, Antonio."

"Thank you, Mama. I love you, Mama."

"I love you too, Antonio."

Tony clicked off his cell phone and got down on his knees. He had the first conversation that he had had with God in a very long time.

Harold Zubrow was a large man with a wide girth and oversized hands. He looked more like a football coach than a gifted surgeon. He was in Tony's class in medical school and Tony respected him very much—both as a person and as a skilled surgeon.

He entered the dressing suit. Perspiration dampened the underarm areas of his scrub top as well as the front below the neckline. He was more than a little surprised to see Tony sitting there as he entered the room.

"Tony. What the hell!"

Tony got up and gave his old friend a long hug. Med school flashbacks to anatomy lab and studying together for National Boards came to Harold as they embraced—Italian/Jewish mishpacha.

"Harold, that was my wife, Cathy, in the OR."

"The trauma case was your wife? I had no idea." Trauma surgeons on call, never having met the patient before, rarely get bogged down with inquiries as to surnames. He did ask the scrub nurse for Cathy's first name, using it to speak to her unconscious state with the hopes of subliminal benefit with encouragement such as "Come on, Cathy, we can get through this together" and such.

"How is she, Harold?"

Harold took his friend by the hand and looked into his bloodshot eyes. "I think that she's going to make it, Tony. I really do. Once we controlled the hemorrhage and restored her blood volume, her vitals began to stabilize. It was a little scary there for a while, though." Harold paused for a moment, and then continued. "I had to do a splenectomy and a nephro-ureterectomy."

"You had to remove both the spleen AND the kidney?"

195

"I had no choice, Tony. The fractured rib did an awful lot of damage in there. The kidney was nearly severed in two, with a major tear in the renal artery. I tied it off but still could not achieve hemostasis due to a major tear in the splenic artery close to the anastomosis with the aorta. Even after I tied off all visible tears, the splenic ooze from the wound in the body proper told me that it had to be sacrificed. As far as the kidney was concerned, it came down to a decision to save her life or to try and salvage a terribly damaged organ. I am sorry, Tony. I did the best that I could under the circumstances. I am comfortable in my decision."

Tony reached out and embraced his friend once more, tapping him on the back as he did so.

"I know that you did the best job that anyone could have done. I wouldn't have wanted any other surgeon in there but you, Harold. I am deeply indebted to you, my friend. Thank you."

"She'll be in recovery for another couple of hours before we move her down to ICU. Why don't you go home and get some rest?"

"I want to see her, Harold."

Tony followed Harold into the recovery room. It was surprising how comfortable Cathy looked. She was still under the effects of the anesthetic and in a deep sleep. Tony touched her cold forehead. He leaned over and whispered something into her ear that Harold could not hear. It sounded as if Tony was softly singing something in her ear. When he finished, Tony kissed her and turned and left the room, a tear rolling down each cheek as he did so.

Cathy remained in ICU for two days. When she was transferred to a private room, she was able to sit up in bed and even had a return of her appetite. Tony visited her every day but was received coldly. Her approach was civil, but still cold. Every evening Tony brought the children in to see their mother. It was the best medicine for her. After three days out of intensive care, she began to feel fatigued. She assumed that it was because of a lack of activity. She didn't report it to her PCP.

Charlie called her every day. She found herself looking forward to his calls with a schoolgirl anticipation. He was recuperating at home from his fractured femur.

"Cathy, I feel so guilty about the accident. I don't know what to say."

"You don't have to say anything, Charlie. I should be getting discharged in a few days or so. I can't wait to see you."

"I can't wait to see you either. Listen, I have some news for you. Beth and I are getting separated."

"Charlie. What are you saying?"

"I'm saying that I am leaving my wife. She agreed to a separation. I'll continue to live here at the house for a while, until I can find a place."

"You are getting a separation, but will continue to live there? Isn't that a contradiction?"

"Only for a little while."

"Tony moved out the very next day after we agreed on a separation."

"I have to find a place."

"Tony found a place the very next day."

"I hear someone coming. I have to go. I'll call you tomorrow. I love you."

"But, Charlie, if..." There was silence on the other end.

Cathy felt a little dizzy as she hung up the phone. The nurse came in with Cathy's medications and began to take her blood pressure. A mildly surprised look came on the nurse's face. She walked over to the other side of the bed and began to take Cathy's pressure in her other arm.

"Is there something wrong, nurse?"

"Of course not. Just relax. I think that there's a problem with this cuff." The nurse wrote something down on Cathy's vitals page. "How are you feeling?"

"Fine. I feel just fine."

Just then, Tony walked into her room. He was carrying a single long-stem red rose bud. He removed yesterday's rose, now opened, from the bud vase and replaced it with today's offering. Cathy smiled in his direction but said nothing. He bent down and gave her a kiss. He hesitated briefly, pausing with his cheek next to hers. A concerned look came to his face.

"Did you have fish for lunch, Cath?"

"No. I wasn't hungry. I just had a bite of my hamburger."

"No fish?"

"No, why do you ask?"

"How are you feeling?"

"Fine, why."

"You don't have any symptoms that are new to you—I mean besides the lost appetite?"

"Well, I have been feeling a little fatigued, lately. If you had to lie here in bed all day, you'd feel fatigued as well."

"Anything else?"

"I've been a little itchy today. I think that they put too much starch in the sheets at the laundry."

Tony lifted her eyelid with his thumb, and then he pulled back her sheet and looked at her ankles.

"Tony, what are you doing?"

"I'm just checking my wife to see if she's all right. Is there any law against that?"

"We're separated, Tony."

"You are still my wife."

"You're a dermatologist."

"I'm a doctor first."

As soon as he heard the words come out of his mouth, he reflected on his meeting with Sean at *Palomino's* a few weeks before. Sean said the exact same thing to him.

Tony continued with his visit, not wishing to alarm Cathy with his suspicions.

Tony walked to the nurses' station. An RN was completing some chart entries.

"Excuse me, nurse. Could you check and see if John Shue, my wife's PCP, is still in house?"

"I don't have to check, he's in 7324 with a patient."

"Thank you, I'll wait for him."

Tony walked down to 7324 and met Dr. Shue as he was leaving the room.

"John, I'm glad that I caught you."

"Hi, Tony, what's up?"

"Any change in Cathy's status?"

"I saw her this morning. She's coming along fine. I noted an increase in her BP, but I asked the nurse to monitor it for me."

"John, I'm not trying to tell you how to do your job, but is there any chance that we can get a nephrology consult? I suspect uremia."

"Why do you ask?"

"I just came from her room. There's a marked fishy uremic fetor to her breath, and she complained of fatigue to me. She has a mild anorexia and she's beginning to develop some pitting-edema in her ankles. Can we check that BP?"

"I think that we had better."

Tony followed John to Cathy's room.

"Cathy, look who I just bumped into down the hall."

"Hello again, John. When can I go home?"

John wrapped the BP cuff around Cathy's arm. As he pumped the bulb, he made small talk. "When people see me, it's never 'How are you, John?' or 'You look good, John'—it's always 'When can I go home, John?'"

John pulled back her sheet and examined her ankles.

"We've been through this." Cathy looked at Tony. "What did you tell him?"

"All I said was that my wife had the best-looking legs on the floor, is all, Cath."

"Cathy, I'm going to order some additional blood studies. I just want to make certain that you are as good as you look."

"I'm married to a doctor; I know that you guys are up to something. What's wrong?"

"Actually, we're separated," Tony said in order to get a smile out of Cathy.

"Nothing's wrong, Cathy. We are just making sure that you receive the best of care."

"You're fine, Cath. John wants to make sure that a change in medication is not in order. The sooner you are stabilized, the sooner you can go home."

He bent down and kissed her on the forehead.

"I've kissed you more in the last few days than I did in the last three months."

"Meaning?"

"Meaning that I didn't realize how much I missed kissing you."

"Tony..."

"Yes, Cath?"

"Am I all right?"

"Listen to me! You are where you need to be right now, Cath—and what is needed to be done is being done. You have my word on that!"

"Tony..."

"My word! I would never let anything ever happen to you. Ever!"

He kissed her once again, this time on the opposite cheek.

He caught up to John at the nurses' station.

"Good eye, Tony! You are right. A nephrologist needs to be brought in. I'm ordering a CBC and differential to rule out infection, but that's just chasing our tail and covering our ass, as they taught us in medical school. People with an infection do not feel cold and clammy. I'm also ordering a BUN and a serum creatinine for the nephrologist. You were correct in your fears, Tony. It sure looks like end-stage renal failure."

"How about a CAT scan of her remaining kidney, to see what's going on over there?"

"Way ahead of you, Tony." John showed the order to Tony as they spoke. "You know, Tony, you would have made a very good *real* doctor. How is it that you ended up in dermatology?"

"It's a long story, John. A very long story!"

"Anyhow, I'm a little embarrassed. You had to do my job for me."

"You have many patients in house. I have one. You would have come to the same conclusions yourself regarding Cathy's care. All I did was assist you."

"Thank you, Tony. You are a class act."

Tony was on pins and needles until he spoke with the nephrologist. His name was Dr. Samer Gumpta. He came highly recommended by John Shue. Tony didn't know him. He trained in Boston at Massachusetts General.

"Dr. Cipullo. I must say that my suspicions parallel yours. Your wife is in end-stage renal failure. The CAT scan shows a large mass on the remaining kidney, rendering it near useless with only five percent efficiency in kidney function, verified with blood studies. Of course, the trauma surgeon had no way of knowing this at the time that he removed her other kidney. I am sure that he operated with her best interest in mind. With neither you nor I being there, it would be inappropriate to venture a second-guess opinion as to his actions."

"Dr. Gumpta. There is no need for colleague protection here. If I had to do it all over again, I would want Harold Zubrow in the OR with my wife."

"Fine, then we understand each other. I'm going to set up a renal team to be assigned to your wife. The sooner that we begin dialysis, the better."

Tony cupped his hand over his eyes and began to weep.

"Dr. Cipullo. It's her best option right now. It's her only option for the short term."

"I understand that, Dr. Gumpta. It's just that you do not know Cathy. Dialysis. Shit! You just don't know Cathy. It will turn her into an invalid compared to the active lifestyle that she led. Power meetings—on the go constantly. Her whole life will have to change. She will have a tough time dealing with this on the psychological level."

"That's why we have renal 'teams,' Doctor. We have a mental health professional on the team. We prepare the patient for the physical as well as the psychological demands of dialysis."

"You don't know Cathy. This will kill her. I know that for certain, it will kill her!"

"You are not speaking like a professional, Doctor."

"You can say that because it's not your wife. I just wish that this would have happened to me instead of her. I could handle it. I know that she can't."

"There's no other short-term option. She will have to adapt."

"I want to be tissue matched. She and I cross match for blood, let's cross match for tissue, to see if I can be her donor. I don't think that she will survive the two-year wait for a cadaver kidney!"

"I want you to know that without you being a genetic relative, the odds are—"

"Fuck the odds! I've been bucking the odds all my life! We are talking about the most important person in my life right now!"

"You are willing to give one of your kidneys for her?"

"I would give both of my kidneys to her, Dr. Gumpta."

Cathy dialed Charlie's cell phone. She needed to speak to someone to whom she had emotional ties and who was not even remotely connected to the medical profession or to a hospital.

"Hello?"

"Charlie?"

"Cathy. I didn't expect you to call. I was just dozing off."

"I need to talk to you, Charlie. I'm a little worried about my condition. Tony's been acting strangely and so has my PCP. They were—"

Charlie interrupted her in mid sentence. "I've got to go now. I'll call you in a little bit."

Cathy could not believe that Charlie cut her off the way that he did. Couldn't he tell that she was reaching out to him? Couldn't he tell that she was emotionally strained? Was his cell phone battery low?

It's almost funny how love ties can alter the way that normally intelligent people behave and think—how they can become blinded by the truth as well as to it. Out of some kind of difficult-to-explain desperation, she dialed his home phone number.

"Hello?" It was Beth Vantare.

"Hello. May I speak with Charlie, please?"

"Charlie is resting. May I take a message?"

"I need to speak with him. I just now spoke with him on his cell phone. It must have gone dead. It's important."

"Who is this?"

"Tell him that it's Cathy Cipullo."

"You have some nerve, calling here—you slut!"

Beth's words cut deep. They cut deeper than the surgeon's knife did the other day in the OR.

"I'm sorry. I know that you must be upset about the separation. I don't mean for you to be stressed any more than you—"

"What separation? What the hell are you talking about?" Beth said as she interrupted Cathy in mid sentence.

"I'm talking about your marriage separation."

"Separation? Separation? What the hell are you talking about? Charlie and I are not separated. What the hell is going on?"

Cathy was caught so off guard that she didn't know what to say. Cathy was rarely at a loss for words. This conversation was an exception to the norm.

"I am so sorry to have bothered you, Mrs. Vantare. It was obviously my error. I will never call there again. Please tell Charlie that I called and that I said that he can go fuck himself. Oh, and by the way, I feel sorry for you. Good-bye."

Cathy hung up the phone and cried into her pillow. It was the second time that Charlie broke her heart. She scolded herself for not learning from the first time.

"Fool me once, shame on you. Fool me twice, shame on me!" Cathy said as she remembered wisdom lent to her from a dear friend who lurked in the past but now invaded her present.

She cried herself to near-sleep, thoughts of her children and thoughts of Tony accompanying her into near-slumber. Just before the fatigue that demands slumber set it, she had an unquenchable desire to call Tony and speak with him. She fought the temptation to resist—the demands dictated by the love bond between them trumping any other force.

She picked up the receiver of the telephone. Before she could dial any numbers, she fell into a deep, medication-induced sleep.

Tony lay on the bed in his *near home*. Others would call it an apartment. Those who had a leaning for the weaker side of the male libido would call it a *bachelor's pad*. Tony called it his *prison*. It held him in bondage to the events that kept him from Cathy and the children, as sure as if there were steel bars on the windows.

He was as unhappy as he had ever been in his life. He tried to intellectually decipher the events that led to his imprisonment. Intellect alone could not solve this puzzle for him. The predicament was created by emotional and spiritual forces. It could not be understood at the intellectual level alone.

During his reflection, the telephone rang. It was Michele Melvin. She was the transplant coordinator.

"Dr. Cipullo. This is Michele with the transplant team."

"Yes, Michele, what can I do for you?" Tony's heart was sprinting—sprinting as it had never sprinted before.

"Dr. Gumpta asked me to call you. I have some news for you."

"Yes?" The suspense was about to cause Tony to burst.

"He told me to tell you that, overcoming all odds, you are a perfect tissue match for your wife. The transplant is good to go on your call."

Tony didn't know what to do first: shout for joy, or cry. He did neither. What he did was to fall on his knees in a thankful posture and remain silent—remain silent in the presence of the One who makes all things possible.

Tony called Dr. Gumpta after the effects of the news settled in. He thanked him for his professional care. He had one request.

"What is it, Dr. Cipullo?"

"My only request is that Cathy never know where the kidney came from. It must remain within the protection of doctor-patient confidentiality."

"You want me to remove a vital organ from your body and give it to your wife and never let her know that it was you who gave it to her?"

"Precisely."

"I don't understand the romanticism of the western world. I never will. I refuse to try!

"Understand this: She would refuse it if she knew that it came from me. Telling her would jeopardize her treatment outcome."

"Treatment refusal, I understand. I will honor your wishes. Your secret will remain safe with me."

Tony went about the necessary actions of putting his house in order. He named Gino executor of his estate. He placed all insurance polices as well as his last will and testament in an envelope and placed them in his desk drawer for Gino to find, if the unthinkable were to happen. The last thing that he did was to write four letters.

One was to his mother. In it, he told her how much he loved her. How much he appreciated all that she did for him in his life. How much he appreciated all of her prayers. How he hoped to see her in heaven one day.

The second was to Gino. In it, he expressed that if in the entire world he were to choose the definitive brother, it would have to be him. How much he respected him and admired the talents that God gave him in the realm of accounting. He entrusted his children into his care as guardian, not only of his estate, but as guardian of their welfare in all regards.

The third was to his children. Each was named by name within the letter proper. This letter was tear stained. The contents of this letter shall remain private between Tony and each of the children, and not revealed to anyone, including the readers of this story.

The fourth was addressed to the love of his life: to Cathy. In it, he attempted to convey all that had been building up within him since that fateful day that he saw her walking toward the grandstand in the early 1970s.

How life had no meaning without her, and if the prospect presented that she may leave him forever, then he would surely and gladly give his life that she may continue to live.

He repented having been led by temptation down the wrong path and asked her forgiveness. He tried to explain that his actions were wrapped within the shroud of human frailty, and he hoped that she would understand, although he understood if she did not.

He tried to explain how he knew from the very first time that he touched her flesh—at their first encounter at the sorority house—that they shared more than a normal intimacy. When their tissues matched, science confirmed what he knew all along in his heart—they were more than just kindred spirits. The two were as one.

This letter was tear stained as well.

He sealed each letter and placed them in his desk drawer for Gino to find and disperse if he did not return.

When these tasks were accomplished, Tony left his apartment and drove to the hospital. He was ready for anything that life dealt him.

The transplant surgeon met with Tony in the pre-op suit. He handed Tony an advised consent form for Tony to read. In it was listed all the possible complications of the procedure. Tony initialed the form where indicated. The nurse came in and handed Tony a surgical gown.

"Please remove all of your clothing and put this on. It ties in the back," she said, as if Tony wouldn't know how to put on a patient gown. Tony laughed out loud as he envisioned a foolish patient, putting the gown on backwards and walking down the hall with his family jewels hanging out and swaying back and forth, to the amusement if not the amazement of the nursing staff.

It was good therapy for Tony to find some humor in this situation. He had to for the sake of his own sanity. If he stopped to think about what he was about to do and deal with it only on the intellectual level, he feared that he would return to his senses and go running out of the hospital and to the sanctuary of his self-serving needs and wants. This act required more from him. It was Herculean and it required Herculean strength that taps into strengths on levels far beyond the mere intellectual level. It required spiritual strengths—strengths found in the soul as well.

If only he could see Cathy as he did on that fateful day at the anti-war rally. He would move heaven and earth as well as fight demons both seen and unseen—slay dragons—to possess her. Giving a kidney would be a simple task in comparison. It was no simple task at this point. He had reservations.

She was no longer his. He knew that. This was not an act to win her back. It was an act to pay her back—reparation for all that she had given to him over the years. It was the least that he could do to repay her. A kidney was a small price to pay.

Tony sat on the edge of the hospital table, his feet dangling from the side. He felt silly, because he looked silly in the hospital gown. It was another sacrifice that he made. Another small price to pay.

A woman entered with a clipboard in her hand.

"Mr. Cipullo?"

"Dr. Cipullo."

"Oh, you're a doctor. A doctor of what?"

"Of medicine."

"You're a physician?"

"If that is what a doctor of medicine is, then yes, I am a physician."

"I've never had an MD as a patient before."

"Don't be nervous, we don't bite. Besides, I'm sure that I am more nervous than you are. As a matter of fact, I guarantee it!"

"I need you to sign the anesthesia informed consent form."

She handed him the clipboard. He perused it, familiar with the informed consent mumbo jumbo.

"It says here that I may suffer an allergic reaction to the anesthetic. It says that I could lapse into a coma or die."

"Yes, sir, that's right."

"Then tell me, would you sign the form, knowing that?"

"No, I wouldn't. In fact, I would not be sitting here placing myself into that position."

"Thank you. That's what I wanted to hear."

Tony took the form and signed it. He handed the clipboard back to the young lady and smiled.

"Thank you. Ann will be coming in to prep you now."

She turned and left the room.

Tony was now alone. He felt alone. He wondered how Cathy was doing. He wondered how she had reacted when Dr. Gumpta told her that she had end stage renal failure. Tony knew that she had no idea of the consequences of that horrible fate. How she would have to face dialysis. How she would need to have a shunt placed in an artery in her arm. How she would have to sit, tied to the dreaded machine for up to three hours, three times a week, as the machine took her blood and *scrubbed* it clean of wastes. How she would have to deal with the side effects of weakness and nausea and lost libido. She had never seen patients go through the process as Tony had. Many managed to accept the treatment as their new life. Cathy was not the normal patient. She was the high-powered executive who pushed herself through stress-filled sixty-hour workweeks, rarely taking a lunch break. Tony knew that Cathy could never accept it. He would do all that was in his power to have her avoid it.

The point was moot, because Tony was now providing her with a potential escape from this fate. He wondered what her reaction was when Dr. Gumpta told her that they found a donor for her. He wondered if she realized how rare it was to have a donor before she even experienced her first dialysis.

A woman came into Tony's room. She introduced herself as Ann. She was there to prep him for the surgery. She carried a tray with a syringe, a razor and a small can of shaving lather on it.

"Interesting combination, Ann."

"I thought so. I mixed it myself. Now, behave, or I'll have to hurt you."

He liked her and her approach.

She had Tony lie on his stomach. She peeled back his gown and exposed his back to her.

"Relax. I know that you must be tense, but I'm not going to hurt you. I was just kidding before."

Her humor defused the situation and relaxed Tony.

She dispensed some of the shaving lather onto her hand and rubbed it into Tony's back, from the top of his buttock to the middle of his back and around his rib cage. She did this with a slow and rhythmic motion. If the circumstances were different, Tony would have found it sensual.

"Do you come here very often?"

Her humor was not only what was needed—her timing was perfect. What a perfect personality to have in this position when people needed to be relaxed.

She took the safety razor and prepped the surgical area with gentle care and deftness.

"You're not very hairy down here."

"Is that good or bad?"

"I guess that it's good. Most women do not like hairy backs. I don't because I have to shave them!"

"I'm glad that you have a kind of follicular fondness for me."

"Follicular fondness. I like that. An alliteration joke. We don't get many of those down here. You must promise to come back!"

"Once is enough!"

"If you are trying to quote Ian Fleming, I think that it's: 'Once is never enough'!"

"Touché!"

"I already did."

Jane took an alcohol swab and rubbed Tony's buttock. She removed the sheath from the syringe with clenched teeth and injected the pre-op sedative.

"Ouch!"

"That's as good as it's going to get!"

"I'll take it any day of the week."

Tony started to feel groggy. He turned over onto his back. Ann took his BP.

"My—aren't we getting glassy-eyed?"

"Don't tell anyone. I told them that I could drink you under the table."

"In your dreams, big guy!"

Ann turned and left the room. Tony lay there. The room wasn't spinning, but it was close to it.

The door opened once again. It was Sean. At least it looked like Sean.

"Are you Sean?"

"No. I'm the rabbit from *Alice in wonderland*! Don't tell me. You are the Cheshire Cat! I'd know that grin anywhere."

"If Ann had injected into your butt what she just gave me, you'd be smiling too, Sean. It's better than Jack Daniels!"

"I guess so. Let's talk. Do you know what the fuck you are doing, Sir Lancelot?"

"And all the time, I thought that I was Galahad."

"No. Galahad found the Holy Grail. Lancelot was found in bed with Guinevere, remember?"

"You are right, as usual, Sean! This is a love story, I forgot. We are not seeking higher callings—not seeking the Cup of Kings. We are trying to justify love's calling. The problem is I'm not in bed with Guinevere, or anyone else. I'm in bed with a shaved back!"

"Seriously, Tony. Do you know what you are doing? Do you know the ramifications and the risks?" Sean looked at him with a caring concern.

"You keep forgetting, I'm a physician too, Sean. I understand exactly what I am doing." Tony paused. "I have to ask you something as a friend, not a psychiatrist, Sean."

"What is it?"

"Do you believe in premonition?"

"Why do you ask?"

"Ever since I found out about the go-ahead for the transplant, I've had a very strong premonition that I'm not going to survive this."

"Premonition is just a manifestation of your fears, Tony—nothing more. It's natural to be fearful."

"You're probably right."

"I'm glad that I came."

"Me too. How the hell did you find me anyway?"

"John Shue called me. He did not breach professional ethics, he just thought that you were behaving as loony as a shit house rat and that to cover all the bases we should get a psychiatric consult. That's all."

"Excuse me. We are crossing the line of professionalism here. You are my best friend. You must recuse yourself from this consultation! How could you possibly provide counsel when you are emotionally involved with the patient?"

"That is exactly the point, Tony. I am emotionally involved with the patient. How can I sit idly by and let you throw away a vital organ and not be certain that you are cogent in your decision process?"

"Look. Sean, I love you like a brother. You know that. Please hear me. The person whom I love more than life itself needs something that I have. Without it, in my opinion, she will wither and die. How can I sit idly by and do nothing? How could I live with myself? It is a choice made from rational thought, not improvisation. I understand the risks."

"You have no reservations, then…even in light of your premonition?"

"Sean, listen! Until Cathy's accident, I didn't realize fully how much I loved her and how much I regretted throwing what we had together away as I did. Coming that close to losing her forever opened my eyes to the light. Now I look at her and I can see clearly that everything I wanted was everything I had. I touch her lips and I tremble, and I ask myself, 'Would you die for the one that you love?' My only answer is 'Gladly.' My regret is that if I only have the one life, I can only die for her the one time. It is a realization of the fact that Cathy is truly my soul mate. Logic demands that I share my flesh with her, because she truly is 'flesh of my flesh and bone of my bone'!"

Sean wrote something into the notepad that he held in his hand. He closed it and looked up at his friend. "You have the soul of a poet, Tony. I always knew that. I just never knew it to the degree that I know it now."

He got up and embraced his friend—catching Tony a little off guard. "I love you, Tony. I always have. I always will!"

For the first time in his life, Tony was speechless. It's not that he didn't want to speak to Sean; it's just that he didn't know how. He watched his friend turn and leave the room. The air in the room now reeked of a lost opportunity. Tony was not one to miss an opportunity. He missed one now, and he regretted it as he now felt the effects of the sedative and drifted off into slumber.

The head of the transplant team asked the anesthesiologist as to the status of the patients.

"Vital signs are stable. Anesthesia is profound."

Tony and Cathy lay side by side in the OR, the anesthesia state creating not only a deep sleep, but a paralyzed presentation as well. The surgical team began the process: skilled and well-trained hands preparing the receptor site as the harvest was initiated. Incisions into the tissue that moments before belonged to persons with an identity but were now only flesh to be cut into to achieve a common goal. Excision and insertion—that's what it came down to if you reduced the event into its basic elements.

Before long, the transfer was complete. The procedure was ready to be billed and the participants were ready to be wheeled into recovery.

The nurse anesthetist sitting at the head of Tony's table stood up with an alarmed look on her face that was not hidden by her surgical mask.

Tony ceased breathing.

"We have a code red here. Get the anesthesiologist in here! STAT!"

She placed the positive-pressure ventilator onto the endotracheal tube and forced oxygen into Tony's lungs. The anesthesiologist came running to Tony's side.

"What's his BP?"

"80 over 40 and falling!"

"Anaphylaxis! Get epinephrine and solu-cortef into his line stat!"

The drugs were administered with efficiency and quickness.

Tony's blood pressure continued to fall. He flat-lined.

"Get me a crash cart in here. Now!"

The anesthesiologist prepared a cardiac needle with epinephrine. He injected it into the ventricular cavity of Tony's heart and began cardiac compression. The nurse anesthetist continued positive-pressure ventilation.

The anesthesiologist looked at the monitor. "He's in ventricular fibrillation. Prepare the paddles!"

The scrub nurse squirted contact gel onto the defibrillator paddles and handed them to the anesthesiologist. He placed the paddles on Tony's chest.

"Clear!" He pressed the buttons on the side of the paddles. Tony's body jumped off the table and returned with a thud. The doctor looked again at the monitor. "Clear!"

Tony found himself at the opening of a dark tunnel. The walls of the tunnel were spinning, creating a moving frame around the internal darkness of the tunnel. He was disoriented. He looked around and saw no one and nothing. He peered into the tunnel. Through the darkness and at the very end of the tunnel he saw a bright light. He looked behind him and saw only darkness. To his left and to his right he looked, again only darkness and a quiet, almost sub-audible moaning. He stepped into the tunnel and began to walk toward the light. Once inside the tunnel, he felt a cold chill. The walls of the tunnel were now spinning around him as he continued toward the light.

As he approached the light, it became larger and brighter. He was drawn to it like steel to a magnet—like a moth to a flame. As he got close to the end of the tunnel and closer to the light, he began to hear melodic voices—angelic melodic voices. Something between a chant and a hum.

He then heard a whisper in his ear.

"Welcome all who are welcome. Enter into the light. Depart from here all who are not deserving. Return to the darkness. If you can proceed then proceed."

Tony continued toward the light. Once through the tunnel, he found himself in an open field. It was thick with fog. Stepping out of the fog and toward Tony was a man dressed in a long white robe. Walking beside him was Tony's father. The man spoke as Tony's father watched with a look of extreme pride on his face.

"Tony. I was sent to tell you that you learned Evan's secret. The secret was this: There is no shortage of tragedy in life. What is required is for one to always apply the best of oneself in any situation. For you, the best was extreme self-sacrifice. You may now rest in the comfort of your decision. This is your redemption."

As suddenly as they had appeared, the man and Tony's father vanished. Tony looked toward the light. Out of the fog and walking toward Tony was another figure. It was Danny. It was a young and healthy Danny. He was smiling and waving to Tony. He reached out his hand toward him as Tony took a step in his direction. As soon as they touched, they were immediately transported onto the commons at Bucknell. They were in the middle of the anti-war rally. Tony turned and saw Cathy walking toward them. She walked in slow motion and Tony took her in with each slow and bouncing step. She was more beautiful than Tony remembered.

"We're back in the past, Danny."

"Tony. The past never left us. We are now outside of space and time. Time has no meaning here. The past is now and now is the past."

Cathy smiled at him as she approached.

The nurse adjusted Cathy's IV drip rate and entered some notes in her progress page. As she left the room, Sean walked in.

"Hi, Cathy. How are you feeling?"

"Like a truck hit me—but I feel much stronger than I did yesterday. The surgeon said that I am doing very well for three days post-op. My plumbing is working fine and there's no sign of rejection."

"That's great!"

"Sean. Why has Tony abandoned me? He has not been in to see me. Not even once. He hasn't even called. You've been here every day. What happened? He was here every day before the surgery."

Sean looked at her, as he held back tears. "Cathy—"

"He's run off with that woman, hasn't he, Sean? I can't believe that he would do this to me now. Not now. It's so unlike him."

Mama Cipullo walked into the kitchen of Tony's house. She had been staying there since the accident when Tony called and asked Gino to take her there for the sake of the children. It had been nine days. This being the ninth day she kept her novena commitment and knelt down—on arthritic knees—at the kitchen table as if it were an alter. She bowed her head in reverence. Her prayers were silent—between her and the Almighty. She made the sign of the cross and clutched a rosary in her right hand, moving the beads one by one between her thumb tip and the fold in her index finger. All other gestures and sounds remained between her and her God.

Gino entered the room. He spent the night on Mrs. Cipullo's request. He saw his mother in her reverent posture and knew better than to interrupt her. Respect and reverence are instilled in all Italian boys from an early age.

When she finished she strained to get up, arthritis not allowing the skeletal system to do what the mind dictated.

"Gino! Buon giorno!"

"Buon giorno, Mama! I see that you were praying for Tony and Cathy. Sta bene!"

"Gino, I must tell you something. God sometimes works in strange ways. Nine days ago, He spoke to my heart. He told me that it was Tony and not Cathy that I needed to pray for."

"Mama, that doesn't make sense. Cathy was the one who was involved in the accident. Tony was fine!"

"In your eyes he was fine, but God sees things that you cannot see, Gino. Faith tells you to do some things that may not make sense at the time. Hope gives you the strength. Love allows it to be brought to completion."

"So this was the ninth day. You made a novena, then?"

"Si, figlio mio."

Gino cupped his hands on either side of his sainted mother's cheeks and kissed her on the forehead. He saw the pained look on her face and the anguish in her eyes since she first saw her elder son lying there in his comatose state in the ICU. *Is there a stronger force on earth than a mother's prayers?* Gino wondered.

Sean pressed the up button for the elevator. He had spent a sleepless night wrestling with the decision on whether or not to tell Cathy about Tony. It was the ninth day since her fateful accident. She had been through so much physically; need he allow her to now suffer the emotional trauma of knowing that Tony was now lying in a coma resulting from his surgery?

The doors opened and he pressed the button for the seventh floor. It struck him that if Tony were to die and Cathy was denied a last chance to see him—to speak to him for a final time-when he was just a few floors below her—it could haunt her for the rest of her life. He concluded that he must tell her. He must tell her today.

He entered Cathy's room and found her sitting up in bed—a very good sign. She looked like she had been crying. How many tears can a person have? They don't teach you such things in medical school. They teach you so very little about so many things.

"Hi, Cathy. How are you feeling?"

She looked up at Sean and then looked away, as if to convey a message of disapproval—as if he were responsible in some way for Tony's no-show. "Hello. I'm fine, thank you. Thank you for asking."

"I'm glad that you are fine, Cathy, but there are degrees of fine. I would venture a guess that your *fine* is not the kind of *fine* that the rest of us desire."

Cathy looked up at Sean—knowing that his posture was that of a friend and his statement was designed to convey not only that message to her, but to inform her of the non- propriety of her actions as well. "I'm a little upset with you, Sean. I don't mean to be rude."

"Cathy, we've known each other for a lot of years. We go back. Don't discount that fact. Don't you dare treat me as you would someone who has no history with you—has no love for you—don't you dare!"

Cathy looked at him with tears running down her cheeks. "It's just that I can't believe that Tony would leave me at a time like this, Sean. If you were my friend, you would not let him do this to me!"

Sean took her hand. There were tears now running down his cheek as well. "Tony did not leave you, Cathy. He is here with you now."

"Don't give me that shit, Sean. Don't tell me that he is with me here in spirit."

"That's not what I mean, Cathy. I mean that Tony is here with you right now. He is here inside of you."

Cathy could see that Sean was speaking from a deep part of his being. This was not a casual statement. There was depth and poetic meaning in his words. She just didn't know what it all meant. "Inside of me? What do you mean, inside of me, Sean?"

Sean took a deep breath—his mind racing to find the proper presentation—the proper phraseology. "Cathy…I need to preface this with a few comments. I have known Tony for over a quarter of a century. He has always been the most stable of persons—both in character and behavior. I also have not ever encountered anyone who has ever loved another human—either living or deceased—as I have known Tony to have loved you. I was with him during your relationship's rediscovery back in our residencies. I know the depth of his being that it touched. I was with you both, as best man at your wedding. I know the joy that your union brought to him.

"I was also with him, in both an emotional and supportive way, during the stress-filled times of late. I have to tell you that as a loving observer, I am witness to the fact that the schism in your relationship affected him as only the tearing of one's own flesh can. It altered him. For a period of time, that person we both love looked like Tony, but his actions and motivations were driven by someone I did not know. During this squalid masquerade, he yielded to temptations that I know Tony would never have yielded to in the past. In the end, when he finally confronted his own self-deceptions, when he came back to his senses, if you will, he found that his love for you was what defined him as a person. Without it, he became that other person who tried to recapture what he had with you with someone else. What he found was that with you he had white lace and promises. With her it was black leather and deceit."

He had Cathy's interest. Her focus was on him and all the intensity that he brought to the conversation. "All right, Sean. I know all about our histories. What exactly does all of this have to do with Tony's absence in my life right now?"

Sean took in a deep breath. He had rehearsed repeatedly what he would say to her, but now his mind drew a blank. "I don't know how to tell you this, Cathy—all that I do know is that I have to tell you. It is too cruel to allow you to continue to believe that Tony left you for that other woman. It also is too cruel for you to not know the truth."

"Where's Tony?"

"I told you. Tony is here with you now."

"You mean that he is here with me in spirit."

"More than that. I mean that he is here with you. Your blood is coursing through him as we speak. Tony was your donor. It is Tony's kidney that you received."

213

Cathy squeezed Sean's hand. He felt her tremble and he saw the look of lost innocence come to her face. He embraced her as she began to weep uncontrollably. Inconsolably she wept. He held her for the longest time, neither saying a word.

Cathy finally broke the silence. "Something's wrong. Why hasn't he called me?"

"Cathy, I need you to be strong right now." Sean looked into her eyes. "There was an anesthesia incident in the OR. Tony had an acute allergic reaction. His heart stopped. He was clinically dead for minutes. They did revive him, but he has been in a coma ever since. I just came from seeing him. He's still unresponsive."

"I need to see him, Sean."

"Are you up to it?"

"If I were moments away from my last breath, I would need to see him."

The nurse wheeled Cathy into the ICU as Sean followed closely behind them. Tony lay motionless save for the rising and falling of his chest as the ventilator filled and then emptied his lungs with air. He looked pale. It frightened Cathy to see him this way. She leaned forward, as if to get up out of the wheelchair—the nurse's forward progress not getting her to Tony soon enough—but the nurse placed a hand on her shoulder.

"You can't get up, Mrs. Cipullo. I'll position the chair next to your husband's bed."

Tony looked at Danny and smiled. He turned back to Cathy. She was now only a few feet away from them—the noise of the anti-war rally now made silent by his vision of her. Her long brown hair was gently flowing in the tender breeze. She was close enough now for him to see her soft and youthful features. She reached out her hand to Tony, as he took a step in her direction.

Cathy reached her hand through the side safety bars on Tony's bed. She touched the back of his hand. It felt cold—so unlike Tony's normally warm flesh. She slid her hand under his and cupped her trembling fingers around Tony's motionless hand. She ran her other hand across his forehead, brushing back his hair. She leaned forward and sang Lennon and McCartney softly into his ear:

Who knows how long I've loved you? You know I love you still.
Will I wait a lonely lifetime, if you want me to, I will!

She felt Tony's hand come to life and return her squeeze. He opened his eyes and turned towards her. He tried to speak, but the ventilator prevented him— he smiled at her with his eyes instead. She got up out of the wheel chair and embraced the love of her life, on the ninth day.

Epilogue

Some may come to call this work a kind of Gen-X love story, laced with the passions and urgings that brought it to fruition and the struggles and dark forces that sought to destroy it. Some may see it as the unyielding testament of a mother's love and the power of intercessory prayer—the kind of force that can move mountains. Still others may come to see it as an affirmation that one's circle of family and confidants and the love and counsel that they provide are as necessary as the air that one breathes.

As a "boomer" myself, I see it as all of these things within the framework of my generation's perspective. We, like all generations that precede and follow, were molded by events that shaped and defined us. We who learned how to mourn and briefly lose hope with the Kennedy and King assassinations, who learned fear and mistrust with the war in South-East Asia, the Cold War and Watergate—with the backdrop of immense prosperity—had events presented for those with pondering minds to consider.

As Evan taught us, there is no great shortage of tragedy in life. What we must learn is to always apply the very best of ourselves to any situation—both on the grand as well as the inter-personal scale.

The characters in this book are fictitious, and any resemblances to any persons living or deceased are strictly coincidental. Many of the actual places presented in the book do exist, but the events reside only in the writer's imagination. It is my hope that these figments came to life for you within the presented schema.

Regarding the novel's title and prayer—I write from the posture of my experience in the Catholic/Christian perspective. A novena is simply a prayer commitment for each of nine consecutive days—from the Latin, novem (nine). However, all faith traditions rely on the power of prayer—reliance on intervention by a loving God—only the format differs. In fact, one of my first exposures to intercessory prayer comes from the Jewish Pentateuch, in Exodus, when Moses raised his hands as the Israelites waged battle with

216

Amelek. Prayer must be necessary and important, for God said to Moses: "Write this down in a document as something to be remembered..."

I can testify to the fact that prayer has moved mountains in my life—to not incorporate it in an event as important to me as my first novel would be unthinkable.

*

Printed in the United States
46825LVS00006B/1-135